Inked
Birth of a Sorceress

Inked
Birth of a Sorceress

BOOK ONE

JV DELANEY

Inked: Birth of a Sorceress by JV Delaney
Published by JV Delaney

1st Edition 2020, paperback.

ISBN: 978-1-925999-43-3 (print)
        978-1-925999-44-0 (epub)
        978-1-925999-45-7 (mobi)

Publishing services by: PublishMyBook.Online

For James, who left this world too early.

Acknowledgements

My love and thanks to Tara, for her support, encouragement and love. Your eagerness for the next chapter kept pushing me forward.

Equally I thank Darlene, whose continual encouragement for me to pursue my dreams was invaluable.

Also to my loving parents, your guidance through life has always been encouraging. You are my world!

Lastly, thank you to Australian eBook Publisher for making the editing, design and publishing process a joy.

CHAPTER ONE

'DO IT AGAIN, Attor, but make the flame bigger this time!'

'*If it's bigger, it's hotter. I will singe all the hair on your head,*' says Attor telepathically. '*Your grandfather will scale me if I return you burnt and bald.*'

'You're his best friend and he trusts you more than any other dragon. Plus, you give the best rides and you throw the biggest flame.'

'*Is that why I take you flying every time you visit?*'

'Yep.'

'*Gee, lucky me.*'

'Admit it, Attor, you love me.' I giggle and lean down with open arms, cuddling what I can of a full-grown dragon.

Without warning, grey clouds appear and start to swirl, darkening the once clear blue sky. I blink several times before being transported to an out-of-body vision.

I'm inside Nogard Hollow, the home of the dragons, with my cousin Sky sitting beside me. Attor, in human form, and my grandfather are in a heated conversation. There's a gargoyle slumped on the ground, the blue glow from its eyes gone.

My skin lifts, flooding my body with goosebumps. For some reason, I know what is about to happen. I've seen it before. Grandfather is about to die at the hand of his best friend. I open my mouth to warn him of Attor's intentions but nothing comes out. I try again but my voice is silent and my body unable to move.

I watch helplessly as my grandfather's heart is ripped from his chest, giving its last beat in Attor's clawed hand.

Attor's eyes rise from his bloodied claw to lock with mine. 'You're next, baby girl.'

With shock and fear mixing in my veins, I try with all my might to run but my feet stay firmly cemented to the ground. He glides across the room and, in a blink, is towering over me. My body trembles as his clawed hand reaches for my chest. The tip of it pierces my skin. My mouth shoots open and releases a bellowing scream.

'Wake up, Jasmine! Wake up. It's only a dream. You're safe.'

My eyes shoot open to my mother's calm face. Her warm eyes soothe my beating heart and clear my head. I've had this dream many times before.

'I could have saved him. I should've yelled louder but my voice…'

'It's a nightmare, Jasmine. You had nothing to do with your grandfather's death. You know that, don't you?'

My hand shoots to my throat in search of my stone pendant. 'Your necklace fell off. The clasp is broken. I'll get you a new chain but for now, let's get this back on you so you can sleep in peace.'

She knots the chain and slips it over my head. This magical stone is my calm, my peace, my sanity.

MY HEART BEATS double-time to help circulate the adrenaline spiking my veins. The anxiety of leaving my parents and the safety of my home has hit me square in the face. But a part of me, deep inside, is being drawn away from here and pointing me in an unknown direction towards the Outback.

I feel claustrophobic here even though our ten-acre farm backs onto a forest and the only noise I can hear is the creatures that roam through it. Our property is isolated, due to the corrugated dirt road which turns lost drivers away. But our overpopulated town centre is a short ten-minute drive away. I feel trapped, unable to breathe, unable to see my future. Getting away from untrustworthy people is one of the things that keeps me focused and moving forward.

I lead my faithful horse, Blue Boy, up the ramp and into the back of the float. With several firm nuzzles in my back, he tells me he is eager to get moving; a naughty habit I've become accustomed to.

My mother tries to control her emotions but the sniffing on the other side of the float is a dead giveaway. My father coos her, trying to calm her hiccupping breaths. I take a deep breath before walking back out of the float to face my mother's tear-stained face.

'Stop with the tears, Mum. I'll call you whenever I have reception.' I walk towards her with my arms open wide, trying to hold back my tears.

'I know you're a sensible girl, it's just that I will miss my baby.'

'You have raised me well. I'm an extremely sensible girl who will miss you both.'

'I'm afraid your life will change and I won't be there to see it.'

'I hope it changes. I want to see new and exciting things. I want to see the Outback.'

'I know but—.'

'But nothing, Mum. Be happy because I'm happy.' Over the last three months, she has been nagging for me to stay. She uses the same excuses, over and over—that she needs to be close to me in case I can't control my nightmares or if I get ill.

She wraps her firm arms around me and we rock back and forth, waltzing in a loving embrace. My father encases us with his large comforting arms and continues our dance.

Blue Boy's becoming agitated, stomping his hooves and giving a few short sharp kicks, telling me to get the truck moving. His impatience makes us loosen our tight embrace and as I draw back, I take in the loving faces of my parents. I will miss them both but I have a wild and free spirit which is being smothered living here in suburban Melbourne.

'I better get a move on or Blue might kick a hole in the tailgate,' I snigger, trying to lighten the mood.

'You be careful riding out in the middle of nowhere. If you fall off, I won't be there to pick you up.' She blinks away her tears, looking at my father for support.

'She'll be fine, love. Jasmine has a solid connection with Blue and I can guarantee he's happier with her on top than letting her fall off.' He puts his arm around her and pulls her in tightly.

'No doubt I will have my guardian angel flying with me.' I smile.

Most weekends, to escape my humdrum life, I pack up my horse and head out, riding until we are both tired and sore. Without fail, while on my trails, a wedge-tailed eagle visits me. The first sign I have that the eagle has joined us is a shadow that consumes my entire truck. The first time it happened I thought a small plane was flying above me, sheltering the sun. But, to my amazement, it was a massive eagle gliding above me. Its wingspan is the largest I've ever seen on a bird; even its legs are the same size as mine.

At first, I considered it a threat, fearing it may attack us. Its razor-sharp beak could easily shred the flesh from our bones, not to mention his claws. But while riding, I'd find it perched on a naked tree branch, observing me and Blue Boy. It'd flick its head side to side, with its keen black eye always on guard. It gave me the impression it was keeping a lookout for any danger and for that reason I call it my guardian angel.

I found telling the eagle my problems helped me get through the long boring weeks. And, as if listening to every word I said, it patiently waits until I've finished my story before flying away.

I sometimes wonder if I am normal, as I'm happier spending my time talking to animals rather than people. At least they don't lie and they never talk back. I once told my friends about the continual visits I got from this large eagle but they laughed at me, so I kept its visits quiet, avoiding further humiliation.

My parents would just nod and smile without comment. I presume they were humouring me or wondering if their daughter had truly lost the plot!

'We best let them go or Jasmine will hit the traffic heading out of town,' says Dad.

In a quick move, I kiss them both, holding back the flood of tears that threaten to appear. 'I will phone or email you when I can. And stop worrying about me, Mum. I will be fine.'

'It's my job to worry about you.' Fresh tears roll down her face. 'Go, before I change my mind and pry the truck keys from your hand.'

'I love you both.' I take a deep breath and force a smile on my lips so their last memory of me is one of happiness.

I jump into the driver's seat and turn on the ignition. As my truck gurgles to life, Blue gives out a loud whinny of approval. His anxiousness makes the float and my truck rock side to side. A surge of adrenaline shoots through my veins when I release the hand brake and press the accelerator. I'm doing this!

I'm leaving behind my nightmares, ready to put the death of my grandfather and my missing cousin Sky at peace. And the negativity of an ex-boyfriend of two years, who was, in secret, having an affair with Kelly, my ex-best friend of ten years. She was everything I am not—blonde wavy hair, whereas I have long straight brunette hair. Her eyes were brown; mine are large and aqua blue. She was short with the size and shape of a pretzel where I am of medium height with sensual curves. I share my father's tanned olive complexion, where her skin was porcelain. She was beautiful.

'I'll never ever forgive you! Our ten-year friendship was a lie.' Those were the last words I said to her before she drove off a cliff to her death. My unforgiving, hateful words pushed her to the edge; guilt I live with every day.

At twenty-five years of age, my heart has been shattered more times than any girl my age.

So I've worked hard every day and night, saving every cent, working for an arrogant pig of a man, so I can pack up Blue Boy and together we can travel anywhere we want within Australia. We can stop to explore the countryside together, galloping over endless hills, camping anywhere we want.

My nostrils flare as I inhale a deep cleansing breath. I blow out hard, blowing away my negative past. Goodbye to my ex-boyfriend and goodbye to my nightmares. I take a moment to lock away in my heart the last memory of my parents' faces while keeping my eyes fixed on the path ahead.

My free hand shoots to my throat, clasping my fingers around my calm, my peace—my magical stone. Wearing it balances my mind and settles my emotions. I found it in my grandfather's room not long after he died and claimed it as my own.

Feeling exhausted, I pull the truck over and reach for the satellite phone.

'It's three days since I left home. How can that be possible? I can only remember stopping and sleeping by the creek for one night.' I slap my cheeks, trying to wake myself up. 'Anything is possible. I'm now talking to myself.'

I drop the phone onto the closed maps beside me. I remember

closing the maps, turning off the main highway and heading towards the setting sun. I don't know, care or fear where I am or which direction is home. This is what I dreamt of.

There are uninterrupted views of rolling hills and large mountains. The surrounding land is fence-free so I presume it's crown land or an Outback station that is too large to fence. I search the horizon for any signs of civilisation, but there's nothing as far as my eyes can see. There are no car tread marks or flattened grass where a motorbike or tractor has been, nothing.

I turn off a thin, near non-existent road, and head towards the base of the largest mountain. It sits amongst several others but I'm drawn to it as though a magnetic force is pulling me. It has a smouldering blue haze that sits ghostly around the top. I admire its enormity but it's the mystery of what it may hold that makes it an easy decision for this to be home for the next week.

I bump and hit holes and wonder if I'm the first person to drive over this uncultivated land. Blue Boy is thumping around in the back of the float, displeased with my choice of route.

It takes a good hour of rocking and rolling over the land before I come to a small running river. I jump out and inspect our new home. It is magical! I couldn't have stopped at a better spot. There are plenty of tall trees running along the creek's edge so I can set up the corral for Blue Boy and use the trees' canopy to shade him and my tent. The fresh water from the river is a bonus. I can use it for cooking, watering Blue Boy and re-filling my drinking water.

I race to the back of the float and undo the tailgate. Blue Boy is jogging on the spot, impatient to see his new surroundings. I'm quick to untie him and watch as he waddles out backwards. He gives a few loud snorts then drops his head to eat the lush grass. He's not as impressed as I am but the rumble in his stomach tells me he's happy to have fresh grass in his mouth. I unclip his lead, leaving his halter on so he can graze while I unpack the truck.

With the enthusiasm of a snail, I open the truck and wonder where to start. I look past the boxes piled in the back of my truck through the front windscreen to the glorious mountains. A sign flashing in neon lights blinks before my eyes, telling me to investigate these mountains now and to hell with unpacking!

The excitement and adrenaline are quick to build up in my stomach. With a quick flick, I shut the door and return to the float, grabbing my saddle and bridle. I should let Blue Boy rest and stretch his legs but I'm sure a short ride won't hurt him.

He doesn't lift his head from the lush grass when I throw the saddle onto his back. He only complains when I slide the bit between his teeth, removing any unswallowed grass he has in his mouth. I slip my foot into the stirrup and pull myself up, throwing my leg over his rump, sitting comfortably in the saddle. I gather the reins and click him towards the river to let him drink the cool refreshing water before we start our journey.

His ears prick as his hooves slip and slide over the few river rocks that lie under the crystal-clear water. He slurps it down while keeping his ears pricked and alert. His keen eyes are surveying the forest on the opposite side of the river.

I close my eyes and listen to the sounds that surround me. There are no cars passing by, no aeroplanes flying above, no voices to hear, only the rustling of the trees as a soft warm breeze blows through them. The birds living amongst them sing loudly, as though telling the other creatures we have arrived. The slow current ripples over and around the exposed rocks, adding to nature's orchestra. My tense shoulders drop.

Blue Boy lifts his head after filling his belly and walks across the creek with confidence, heading towards the base of the mountain. I chuckle; he's heading in the direction I wanted to explore first.

With a loose rein, my hips roll back and forth in time with Blue Boy's relaxed walk. My head is on a swivel, trying to take in every tree, leaf, bush and critter we pass. Under a group of large trees, I spot cow manure but there's no sign of cows. I now know I'm trespassing on a grazier's property and pray they are obliging in letting me stay for a while.

I twist in the saddle, checking to see if I can see a homestead or smoke from a chimney or fire. There is nothing—only Blue Boy, me and nature. Just the way I want it.

Confident I'm alone, I again relax into the saddle and let Blue Boy take control of our direction. He continues to amble along the base of the mountain, heading towards a thick forest. As we come to the edge of the trees, his head lifts and his ears prick.

Suddenly, a dark shadow casts over us, interrupting the sun's rays. When I lift my head to look at the sky, the sun reappears, blinding me momentarily. I blink, trying to see what large bird is flying above us. Maybe it's my guardian angel? I hear the sound of air whooshing and the wings of a bird flapping. It must be the wedge-tailed eagle following me.

Blue Boy's back tenses and he draws backwards, away from the thick canopy of trees. This is out of character for him. He's never shied from another creature, especially not the eagle.

From out of nowhere, a bellowing roar echoes from behind me, vibrating my eardrums. I spin to witness a large flying creature heading for us. Its dangling legs miss us by a short metre. Its movement is so quick I don't have time to focus on what breed of eagle it is.

Its large wing clips Blue Boy on the rump and hit me in the back, forcing me forward onto the horse's neck. Blue Boy panics and jumps sideways. I become dislodged from the saddle and fall to the soft grassy ground. I lie on the ground, dumbfounded by what has just occurred.

Blue Boy has bolted and is heading back in the direction from which we came. I slowly move each arm and leg, careful to acknowledge any broken bones. I'm pleased when every part moves as it should. I shake my head in disbelief, chuckling because now I have to walk the long distance back to the truck.

My chuckle is short-lived as another shadow blocks out the sunlight. I glance up to see an enormous bird. It looks like a swan with a long tail. I shake my head before feeling for any lumps or bumps on it. I must have hit it when I fell because that large ugly-looking swan could only be a figment of my imagination.

I stand up, dusting away a few clumps of dirt that are stuck to my jeans. I look towards where my trusted steed has galloped and see him cantering back towards our camp. Taking a deep breath, I head off in the same direction as I doubt there's a taxi roaming around out here.

After a few short steps, I hear a large rustling noise in the bush and a low whimpering sound, like a dog in pain. It stops me in my tracks. I stand still, listening and looking towards the distressing sound. I scan the masses of trees searching for any sign of life. The large eagle must be wounded and needs help.

I walk under the canopy of trees. It's unusually quiet except for the noise my feet are making as I crunch the dried leaves and twigs. I tread softly, trying to place my foot on soil instead of twigs, but it only makes it worse. The further I go, the denser the trees, the darker it gets.

'Hello? Is anyone there?' I whisper, hearing a slight quiver. I shake my head at my stupidity. 'Of course no one's there. I'm in the middle of nowhere. You are an idiot, Jazz.'

Out the corner of my eye, I see a black object move behind

the base of a large tree trunk. I turn to face it. It's wider than the tree—at least a metre either side.

I move with a slow steady walk so as not to scare it. 'Take it easy, fella. I will not hurt you.'

With every step, I continue to crunch the fallen debris which makes my presence well known. The creature tries to shrink behind the tree trunk. Moving cautiously, I round the side of the tree to see its true form.

'Wow!' I gasp, lowering my stance so I can get a good look at its face. 'You're no eagle.'

It's sitting but its large form is still taller than me when I'm standing upright. I look into the black creature's glowing eyes and see the most amazing blue colour. People constantly comment on the bright blue of my eyes but compared with the set staring at me, mine are dull.

Our eyes lock and it instantly reminds me of a dream. Is this a dream about to turn into a nightmare? I reach for my necklace and calm when my fingers feel the stone's smooth surface.

The creature's eyes follow my hand before returning to my eyes. The blue glow of its eyes calm me as my mother's do.

Eager to see more of what breed of animal it is, I move closer. It has wrapped its bat-looking wings around itself, only allowing its eyes to be visible. There's blood dripping from a large tear on one of its wings.

If it was going to attack me it would have done it by now so, in slow motion, I move so I am less than three metres away. It pulls its wings in tightly and lets out a low intimidating growl as if to warn me to stay away.

'Shh, big fella. I won't hurt you. Let me help you.' I keep my tone soft and low. The creature pulls its wings even tighter and whimpers as it does. 'Don't move, you silly creature.'

It replies with another growl.

'Oh, stop being grumpy and let me look at your wing.'

I swallow hard and lift my hand to reach over to touch it. My movements are slow and cautious and I'm ready to flee if it lashes out at me. 'Now don't growl at me as it scares the poop out of me.' Shuffling closer, I touch its wing. It flinches away. 'Shh, please sit still. I don't want to hurt you.'

It gives a heavy sigh before relaxing its rigid hold, allowing my fingers to glide gently over its damaged wing. Its wing is smooth and cool to touch but seems paper-thin.

My curiosity makes me test it further. With a soft touch, I push my finger into the wing—it's as tough as elephant hide. I get a feeling that I've felt this before.

I pull out a handkerchief from my jean pocket and try to wipe the blood away from the wound. The creature relaxes further and loosens its wing-hold, allowing me to see what it's concealing. I fall backward, landing square on my bottom.

'What on Earth are you?' It has the body and shape of a bodybuilder, but it's not human. Its hands and feet are identical to eagle claws but longer. Its frowning face is hard-looking, with razor-sharp teeth protruding from its grey lips.

My eyes run up and down its enormous size, trying to take in what is before me. He doesn't move and I'm too frightened to. I don't want to startle him and make him attack me.

His head flips up as if hearing something. I place my feet flat on the ground so I can push myself up and take off out of the bush.

Before I can move, it opens its mouth. 'Leave now,' he says in a low rumbling tone.

'Did you speak?' I ask, gasping in shock.

'Trouble is coming. Leave now.'

'What about you? You're hurt.'

'Go,' he snarls, rolling back his lips, showing me his pointed and sharp teeth.

'Okay! I'm going.' I scamper to my feet and run out of the bush. My heart is pounding. I've seen a creature like that in my dreams but not in reality.

As I reach the outskirts of the trees, I see a tall man leading Blue Boy towards me. He's wearing a pair of jeans. His chest is bare, as are his feet, making me wonder how he can walk on the harsh ground. He has a tattoo on his left pectoral muscle, over his heart, and one strapping his rounding bicep.

'Hello, I believe this may be your horse,' he says with a wide smile.

'Yes, thank you. I fell off him when he spooked at something.' I force a smile then scan the area behind him, wondering where this man has come from.

With a cool arrogant demeanour, he walks towards me and hands me the reins. My hand brushes against his, making me inhale a short sharp gasp. The heat radiating from his skin is as if I've walked past an oven or fire. It throws me for a split second. 'Oh, um, thank you. My name is Jasmine. Do you own this land?'

'No, I live on a neighbouring parcel of land.'

He stands in my personal space, making me uncomfortable. Why so close? I take a step back. There's plenty of open land out here for everyone to have their own spot.

Intrigued by his tattoo, I drop my eyes to his chest but am quick to return to his gaze. Being caught staring at his naked torso may give him the wrong idea. But he catches me and the corner of his lip curves up into a smile. So smug!

'Well, thanks for returning my horse. I should get back to my campsite before it gets too dark.' I want him to leave so I can go back and help the poor injured creature.

'Your heart is beating fast. It's trying to control the burst of adrenaline you received, Jasmine,' he says, full of confidence.

'My heart! How do you know how my heart is beating?' I

throw the reins over Blue Boy's head and climb up into the saddle.

'There's a lot I can tell about you. Where did he go?' He stands in front of Blue Boy, holding onto the reins so I can't move.

'I don't know what you mean. You're the first person I've seen in days.' My reply is nervous.

'Ah, now that's not true. Your heart is ricocheting around in your chest cavity.' He spreads a wide grin over his lips; one I believe the devil should own.

'I don't lie! I have not set eyes on another person in days. Now if you'll excuse me, I need to head back to camp so please let go of my horse's reins.' I try to express a frustrated tone but fear I may have failed.

'Oh, I believe you do lie, Jasmine. You know what and who I mean and if you want to stay in one healthy piece, you better tell me what you know.' He moves so he is next to my leg. The warmth I felt before returns, heating my body.

Staring defiantly into his eyes, I notice they are a stunning lime green colour. But what strikes me as unusual are the fact that his pupils are not round—they're slit like a cat.

Lifting my hand to my head, I rub the circumference in search of any bumps. When falling off Blue Boy, I must have hit my head, as the past hour has been surreal.

Taking a deep breath, I try to calm my racing heart and tell him what he wants. 'There was a big ugly bird that crashed into the trees over there.' I point in the opposite direction to where the actual creature is.

'Thank you, Jazz.'

'My name is Jasmine. Only my friends call me Jazz and you're definitely not one of them!' I wrench the reins from his hands, making Blue Boy jump. 'If you'll excuse me, I have better things to do than be accused of lying.' I turn Blue Boy and squeeze my heels into his sides, making him jump into a canter, heading back towards our campsite.

We canter at a slow lope for a good few minutes then pull back to a walk. I twist in my saddle to see if I'm being followed. There is no sign of the half-naked guy or the creature.

I stop and turn Blue Boy around and, with slow meticulous eyes, scan the vacant land. Satisfied that no one is following me, I head back to camp and gather my first aid kit before returning to help the creature. I click Blue Boy on and we are soon back at the truck.

When I open the back of the truck, several boxes and bags have been opened and moved. The green-eyed guy must have gone through my gear.

I gather Blue Boy's first aid kit, which is filled with bandages and antiseptic, placing it in my backpack together with food and water, before strapping it and my swag to the back of the saddle. I lock my car before leaving and place the key on top of the front wheel, in case I lose it while riding.

My heart is pounding in my chest as I step up into the saddle and throw my leg over Blue Boy's back. It reminds me of the conversation I had with the green-eyed guy. How on Earth could he have known my heart was racing? Maybe he saw me running out of the trees and was playing mind games with me. Any person running would be the same.

But what type of person mentions someone's heartbeat? And why was his hand so hot? I've never known or felt anyone that temperature. Maybe he was ill? But his face had shown no sign of being sick.

I walk Blue Boy back to the forest and dismount before reaching the creature. I don't want to spook either Blue Boy or the creature as I've had enough excitement for one day.

As I approach the large tree that sheltered it, I notice it has changed colour and is now a light grey. My heart thuds hard as I expect the worst—that the creature has died.

Together with Blue Boy, I move closer, watching Blue's ears and reaction. If he pricks his ears or shies away, I will know the creature is alive. But he walks towards it with a confident and relaxed demeanour.

I round the tree and have to blink my eyes several times to work out what I am seeing. The creature is no longer flesh and blood but is now concrete. I move close enough to touch him. It resembles and feels identical to the concrete statues in plant nurseries.

I swear, black and blue, that this large blob of concrete had been living and breathing. It even spoke! I pinch my arm hard to see if I'm dreaming but the instant pain tells me I am well and awake.

I run my hands over the smooth sculpture that sits before me. He's stone cold; different from the warm green-eyed guy. I trace the outline of its injured wing. It matches the other wing with no evidence of it being torn. Its head is facing the ground, its eyes closed.

I continue to trace over its face with both my hands, letting my fingers dip into its muscle outline. I run my hands over its strong-looking arms and across its broad bold chest. Its fingers and toes are long claws that could rip through the skin of a cow or the trunk of a tree with ease.

I circle around the creature several times, stopping to see its back. It's bound with muscles and its large bat wings are pulled in tightly to the side.

Who brings a concrete statue into a forest? I haven't seen a homestead for days and it's not as if the creature got here by itself. Concrete statues don't just fall out of the sky!

I realise how much smaller I am, even as it sits. But I'm not afraid or intimidated by it, even though many movie producers label wild creatures to be dangerous monsters who could, with one finger, kill and eat me!

I unsaddle Blue Boy to let him roam around and eat what little grass is growing under the trees. I roll out my swag and grab a bottle of water and food. I gather twigs to light a fire but stop, remembering the green-eyed guy and his interest in this creature. I snuggle into my swag, using my elbow to hold up my head so I can admire its features.

Then it hits me like a freight train—he is a gargoyle! Why didn't I recognise this sooner? These mystical creatures flood my dreams every night. If I don't see a dragon or gargoyle flying around, I usually can't sleep.

I look around behind me to see if I can spot any structural ruins or more concrete gargoyles. Maybe there's a castle nearby and he's here to protect it. There's nothing but I notice it's getting dark and the animal noises are increasing in volume. I whistle for Blue Boy and he returns to my side with a mouthful of grass.

'Stay close, Blue. And goodnight to you, my gargoyle friend.' I snuggle deep into my swag and flip the canvas hood over my head, trying to keep the small amount of heat I have enclosed. I wish the green-eyed guy was passing by, as I'd get him to warm my swag for me. I get the giggles but it's not long before my lead-weight eyelids close and I drift off to sleep.

CHAPTER TWO

'GRANDFATHER! ATTOR SAID *he will take me for a ride and Sky too if she wants.'*

'*Is he back from feeding?' asks my grandfather.*

'*Yep! His belly is full and apparently I smell like rotten fish,' I answer, looking up at the man I idolise.*

'*I'm glad you smell like rotten fish to him. Attor has one sharp set of teeth.'*

'*He'd never eat me. I'm full of bones and he said he hates bony humans. They get stuck in his big large teeth.'*

'*Attor is one of my oldest friends. He'd never hurt you. Go for your ride but make it short. We need to head back home. It's been three weeks since we left home and your parents will be missing you.'*

'*Wahoo! Can you lift me up onto his back?'*

'*Sure thing, kiddo. Where is your cousin, Sky?'*

'*She is already waiting for you. She knew your answer would be yes.' I giggle.*

I skip outside then stop in my tracks, remembering I must walk slowly towards Attor. He swings his long neck around and blinks at me, snorting a puff of smoke from his nostrils. I love how dragons can do that. So cool!

Sky is standing still beside Attor's large front leg and I move to join her. Grandfather lifts his hands and, with a look on his face that tells me he is concentrating, we are both elevated into the air and lifted onto the dragon's back. We squeal with excitement and run our fingers over his scaly leather skin.

'*Girls! No squealing or yelling or jigging on his back. Attor is a dragon, not a horse,' grandfather scolds, but I can see he has a small curve to his mouth. He loves seeing us play with dragons and the other creatures.*

'We will,' both Sky and I say in unison.

With a downward thrust of Attor's outstretched wings, we lift off the ground. Sky, who is sitting behind me, wraps her arms around my waist, pulling us together. I love being with her and my grandfather, visiting all our magical friends.

Attor flies over the castle and the forest that sits at the foothills. When I feel the wind against my body, I close my eyes and pretend that I am a dragon flying free amongst the clouds.

We wave to Grandfather and the other dragons that are in human form.

'Stop waving and hold on tightly,' says Grandfather telepathically. It makes me laugh when he uses his telepathic powers to scold us.

I wake from my recurring dream to the echo of singing birds. Without fail, my right hand is lightly clasped around my pendant which I swear gives me the childish dreams of mythical creatures. It always involves my grandfather and my cousin, Sky.

I flip the hood of my swag off my head and stretch my arms to relieve the stiffness in my back. I glance over to my concrete friend who is still staring down at the ground motionless.

'Well, good morning, handsome. I see your still here,' I say with a smile on my face. 'What surprise do you have in store for me today?'

I pull myself out of my swag and whistle for Blue Boy. I hear the crunching of branches before I see him coming from the depth of the trees. 'Hey, fella! You've gone the wrong direction if you want lush grass. It's the other way.' He sniffs me before doing the same to the concrete statue. He stands relaxed in front of it and licks its head. 'Taste good, Blue? Or do you think it needs a wash?' I laugh at his antics.

After eating a can of fruit, I saddle Blue Boy, as I'm interested in riding further through the trees in the same direction that he came from this morning. Leaving my swag and backpack with the statue, I swing up into the saddle. 'I'll see you later, big fella. Now, don't you go running off anywhere.' I smile, looking at its solid rock features.

We walk for an hour under the cover of the trees, eventually coming out at a creek. I presume it's the same creek where I've parked my truck. While Blue Boy has a good drink, I take the time to absorb the majestic landscape that surrounds me. I close my eyes and let my ears be my sight. I hear the water trickling along the creek, happy birds chirping and a bellow from a cow. A cow? I flick my eyes open and search the other side of the creek to find, at a guess, at least one hundred cows grazing the luxuriant grass.

'That's where you guys have been hiding,' I say out loud, patting the neck of my thirsty horse.

'Who are you?' I hear a voice smaller than a whisper.

Out the corner of my eye, I catch a quick glimpse of a small fly-sized light. When I spin my head to get a better look, it's gone.

'Hello! Is someone there?' I gather my reins, ready to take off back to camp. There's no answer. I sit as still as I can for several long minutes, then get the giggles when I hear nothing further. First, I dreamt I heard a voice, then I started to talk to myself and now I'm hearing things.

Without warning, Blue Boy jumps and spins around to face the other direction. I sit deep in the saddle and am lucky to stay on board.

'Whoa boy, it's all right.' I calm him by softly rubbing his neck. I search for why he took fright and stop when my eyes land on a handsome sight. The green-eyed guy has returned.

'Morning, Jasmine! That was a nice save.' His white toothy smile is warming.

He is sitting on top of a lovely quarter horse, tacked up with a western saddle and bridle. It's quite an impressive steed.

'Practice makes perfect. I have a sore rear from falling off yesterday so I suppose I've learnt my lesson.' I return a polite smile. 'He's stunning.' I point to his horse to make sure he understands who I was complimenting.

'Yes, he is.'

'Are you following me?' I tease.

'Don't flatter yourself, Jasmine. What are you doing in these parts?' His smile drops, as does his tone.

'I'm exploring. You said this wasn't your land and I couldn't find a homestead nearby to ask if I could ride here. Do you know the owners? I'm happy to ask for their permission.'

'You could say I know them.' He sniggers.

'What's so funny?'

'Why are you here, Jasmine?'

'I packed up my horse and left home so I can travel around riding wherever I want. I want to get in touch with nature without being hassled by untrustworthy and inquisitive people.'

'Ouch, sounds as though someone's been burnt.'

'Excuse me? You're the only thing burning around here,' I murmur, remembering the heat he radiated when I first met him.

He chuckles. 'I should let you know, Jazz, that I have extraordinarily good hearing.'

In a blink, my cheeks glow red from embarrassment.

'Why don't you ride with me for a while? I have to take some of these cows back along the river to my land. Unless you're still looking for that large ugly bird.' He raises an eyebrow as if to question me.

'That thing? Nah, I gave up on it last night. I suspect it flew away.' I flip my hand as if to brush the comment away.

'I see.' He stares straight through me. I get the impression he knows I'm lying. 'Well, the day is young, mysterious, and the sun is shining, so come along and ride with me.'

'Sure, why not? I need to pick up more food from my truck and I presume this creek is the same one running past where I left it.' I gather my reins and cross the shallow creek. He nods, smiling a grin that is warm but also a little on the smug side.

We walk side by side, herding at least twenty of the cows, which dawdle along the creek edge.

'So where do you live? And what's your name? I never asked.'

'My name is Lazarus. I live on the next parcel of land.' He rocks back and forth in his saddle to his horse's relaxed gait.

I look into his eyes but can't quite see his pupils. I'm curious to see if they are slits as I remember them to be from our meeting yesterday. Or was I seeing things? He turns his head to concentrate on the whereabouts of the cattle, which gives me time to take in his features.

He is a handsome man with black hair and light stubble outlining his jawline. His tall frame bursts with muscles, making his t-shirt look two sizes too small, as do his jeans, which fit firmly on his long legs. He must be at least six foot two or three.

And even though his words are meant to intimidate me, I'm not the slightest bit afraid of him. I lift my eyes back up to his face to see him staring at me with a huge grin stretching across his lips.

'Have you finished assessing me?' His tone is sexy.

'Oh, um, I was admiring your saddle,' I spit out, hoping I had covered my butt.

'Really, Jazz, you need to learn how to lie better.' He chuckles.

I blush and change the subject. 'So do you live out here with your family?'

'You could say that.'

'Gee, Lazarus, don't give too much away now.' I roll my eyes at him.

'Yes, I live here with my two brothers.'

'And your parents?'

'Probably in the same place as your parents—at home.'

'Oh, so this isn't your home?' I'm becoming confused.

'Yes, I call here my home but my parents prefer to live in England.'

'Oh, I see. You must miss them. Do you visit them or vice versa?'

'You ask a lot of questions, Jazz. Why did you leave home?' He turns the tables so I am now in the line of questioning.

'I told you. I need to escape my boring humdrum life.'

'You told me you were burnt by people.' He pulls on his horse's reins, making him move over closer to mine.

'No, you said I got burnt.' I glance up and he is staring at me. I stare back, targeting my gaze at his eyes and when he blinks I notice his pupils are as I first thought. Slit like a cat. 'Has anyone told you that your eyes are—?'

'We are not all the same.'

'Oh, I didn't mean to offend you.'

'You didn't. Are my eyes a good thing or a bad thing, Jasmine?' He stops his horse and keeps his eyes locked with mine.

'I think they are intriguing. I've never seen someone with lime green eyes and pupils so narrow.' I drop my head to keep from staring. 'Except…' I bite my tongue. If I reveal my dreams to Lazarus, he will think me mad, like everyone back home does.

'Except what, Jazz?' I shake my head and turn to face away from him. 'I find your eyes extraordinary. You don't find too many brunette women with eyes bluer than the sky. One might say they have a mystical tone to them. Where are you from, exactly?'

'Everyone says my eyes are the colour of the ocean. But I believe the t-shirt I'm wearing is closer to that colour.'

'I wouldn't know if your top is blue or if it's not. I am colour-blind but oddly enough, I recognise the colour in eyes.'

'Oh, I'm sorry,' I say in a soft tone.

'Why? Because I can't see colours? My other senses are highly receptive.' He chuckles.

'Like yesterday when you thought my heart was racing?' I say.

'Exactly. Now answer my question, where are you from?'

'I live on a small property in an outer suburb of Melbourne.'

'You are a long distance from home.'

'I don't even know where I am and which direction I'm heading. I turned off the main highway and headed in the direction I felt had a positive energy. I thought I was alone in the middle of nowhere but here you are.'

'I see. You were drawn here by your senses.'

'It just felt right.'

'We need to cross the creek here. I need you to cross first and I'll push the cattle from behind. They should follow you across.' He canters off behind the herd and heads them back towards me.

He is a skilful rider and the cattle scatter away from his horse's clapping hooves. With a nudge of my heels, I encourage Blue Boy across the river and watch in amazement as the cattle follow behind me, splashing as they jump into the water, some slowing to sip it. Lazarus follows the last cow, cantering up the bank of the creek.

I notice that my truck is a short distance away when he rides up beside me. He turns so our horses are facing nose to tail and we are face to face less than a metre away.

I feel the same warmth from him I had the first day I met him. I can't rule out that my body isn't reacting to a handsome man being so close.

He leans forward in his saddle so our faces are close. The heat radiating from him intensifies and I lock my eyes with his catlike ones.

'Your truck is there,' he says, with a flick of his head.

'Yes, I see that,' I murmur, hypnotised by his gaze.

'This is where we will say goodbye, Jasmine.' He smiles.

'I'm more than happy to help you drive the cattle to your property if you want company.'

'My brothers will be around somewhere. I can guarantee they will help take the cattle off my hands.' He smirks.

He leans forward and I'm stunned when he places his lips on mine. They're hot but nowhere as hot as his hand.

'Don't kiss her,' says a whispering voice from behind me. I pull back and spin in my saddle, trying to spot the tiny tone. Lazarus lets out a hearty laugh.

'Did you hear that?' I ask.

'What did you hear?'

'A small voice saying… just saying something.'

'Sometimes the creek talks to you. I swear it's alive. Or it could be an annoying little fairy that needs to mind her own business before she gets her wings clipped.' He keeps a large smile on his face.

'Fairies, huh!'

He backs his horse away, 'It was nice to meet you, Jasmine, from the suburbs of Melbourne. But you need to leave this area. The landowners around here won't be as polite to you as I have been.'

'Hang on, you kiss me then tell me nick off!'

'I am politely warning you to leave.' He heads away from me towards the cattle.

'Sheesh, men! Why do I even try to understand them? They're all untrustworthy,' I whisper under my breath.

He stops his horse and turns to face my direction. He smiles and taps his ear with his index finger.

'Oh, that's right, he has extraordinarily good hearing— my blue bum he does,' I whisper as quietly as I can, knowing he is too far away to read my lips. He chuckles and canters off, making the cattle stampede ahead of him.

I walk Blue Boy over to the truck and find the keys are sitting on the front tyre where I had left them. I open the truck and again notice that someone has been going through my gear and this time they have gone through my clothes. How odd!

I grab fresh clothes and food and chaff for Blue. I throw it into a pack then attach it to the back of my saddle. Within fifteen minutes I'm ready to return to my concrete friend. I want to make sure the gargoyle is safe and that Lazarus didn't find him before he met up with me.

I scan the land for Lazarus and the cattle but all I see is open pasture. I mount and am on my way back towards the forest, letting Blue walk at a relaxed pace.

When we approach the large tree sheltering the creature, I slide off and let Blue graze the grass he missed yesterday. I throw my pack to the ground in front of the same sad face I left this morning.

'Hello, my concrete friend. How was your day?' I run my eye over his stone features, looking for any sign of life. I tap my knuckles on his head, expecting a hollow sound, but instead, it resonates solidly as a rock.

Clearing a safe area in front of the gargoyle, I gather twigs and small bushes to start a fire. I grab a lighter from my pack and a handful of dry leaves to get it going. Within minutes it's humming along and expelling warmth into my chilled body. After feeding Blue his chaff I sit in front of the fire and eat my dinner before the sun sets.

'Well, my silent friend, it looks like it's dinner for two and since you aren't in a talkative mood, I may as well tell you about my day. Blue and I rode to the other side of the forest and I met the guy who was looking for you yesterday. I know what you're thinking—did I tell him where you were? Well, to answer your question, no I didn't. I felt compelled to protect you, probably because you're such a great talker.' I chuckle then laugh out loud. If anyone was listening, they would think I've gone mad. Maybe I have.

'Anyhow,' I continue, calming my giggling fit, 'I rode with him to help herd his cattle back to his property.' I turn behind me to grab a few more twigs to throw on the fire.

'His cattle!' shouts a deep voice, making me jump to my feet in fear.

Spinning back around I'm faced with a tall muscle-bound man standing in front of me.

'Who are you?' In slow motion I back away from him. 'Please don't hurt me.'

'Hurt you? Why on Earth would I hurt you?' says the figure standing before me, moving in my direction. I keep moving backward and he keeps moving forward. 'Stop, Jasmine. I won't hurt you. You can trust me.'

'Trust you! I don't know you.' My chest is rising and falling at a massive speed. 'If you stand still, I'll stop moving.'

He holds both his hands up and squats down low but keeps his remarkable blue eyes on me.

'What do you want? How do you know my name?'

'I want nothing from you, Jasmine.'

'Why are you here? I'll put the fire out and leave first thing in the morning if that's what you want.' My tone has a definite quiver which makes me panic even more. I squat down, keeping the fire between us.

'You're not safe staying here, especially if Lazarus has your scent,' he says, sitting cross-legged on the ground in front of me. His eyes are glowing blue, lighting up the ground in front of me.

'Who are you?'

'I'm Drake.'

'Where did you come from, Drake?' I look behind him to see if the concrete creature is still sitting beside the large tree trunk. It's disappeared. 'What did you do to my concrete statue?'

I shoot up so I can see over the top of him. There's broken concrete scattered on the ground. 'You smashed it! Why? It was an innocent creature!' I lift my hand to my gaping mouth.

'It's not concrete. It's stone.'

'Who cares what it's made out of?'

'For one, I care and two, I smashed nothing,' he says, standing upright.

'Are all the guys out here weird? There's got to be something in the water you drink!'

I hear the crunching of twigs and pray that Blue Boy is walking up behind Drake. My heart pumps at a frantic beat until I see Blue Boy walking towards us. He nudges Drake on the arm.

'Hello, Blue Boy, get your fill of grass?' Drake asks.

'Blue, come here.' I'm glad he obeys.

As the horse walks by, Drake runs his hand along his neck, back and rump. 'He's a fine horse, Jasmine.'

'He's not for sale if that's your next question. And how do you know his name? Are you spying on me?'

'Yes, I suppose I was. You are trespassing on my family's land.' He puts his hands on his hips.

I hide behind Blue, patting his lovely white coat. I sneak my eye around the corner to take a longer look at Drake. His eyes are still giving off a fluorescent blue, with his hair a similar colour to mine. He has thicker stubble than Lazarus and his body ripples with larger muscles.

'I tried to find a farmhouse so I could ask if I could camp and ride the land around here. I didn't mean to trespass and I apologise if I have upset anyone in your family.'

'I think it's best you move on as landowners around here won't be as polite to you as I have been.' He moves towards Blue Boy, giving him another pat.

'Wow, you guys must drink the same water,' I shake my head in disbelief.

'What do you mean?'

'Lazarus said the same thing before he disappeared.'

'Did he now? What else did my dear neighbour have to say?' His tone drips with sarcasm.

'Not much. He was tight-lipped. But he said he believes in fairies. I think it's a bit odd for a full-grown man to believe in fairies.' I snigger.

'Well, don't we all?'

'No, I don't. I did when I was a child and for years I never wanted to say they weren't real because I didn't want one to die but as an adult, I can say it without fear of hurting a little make-believe creature. They don't exist!'

'Make believe—I love it!' He claps his hands in amusement.

'Okay. Um, I promise I will leave first thing in the morning and please apologise to your family.' I hope he will leave.

'They don't know you're here yet but it won't take long for them to spot you. If you promise to leave in the morning, they won't prosecute you for trespassing.'

'Prosecute me! I have done nothing wrong. At least I didn't smash an innocent statue to pieces.'

'I told you I smashed nothing. Anyhow, why are you so protective of it? What does it mean to you if it's broken?' He moves to the same side of Blue Boy that I'm on.

'It had a torn wing and… and… I'm fond of concrete statues. That's all.' I move to the rump of my horse, keeping a good arm's length between Drake and me. I didn't want to explain that I saw it living and breathing. Plus, the last time I told anyone I had a wedge-tailed eagle as a friend they thought I was crazy.

'I believe you imagined it injured, Jasmine. You also mentioned it was made of stone.' He glides his hand all the way down Blue's back to where my hand rests on his rump. His fingers graze past mine. His touch is cool, not like Lazarus' heated touch. Why do these men need to touch me?

'I said concrete!'

'As you wish.' He smirks and moves away from me and my horse. 'Keep your promise and leave my land first thing, Jasmine.' He turns his back and disappears as quickly as he had arrived.

'I will!' I yell at his back, then whisper, 'Nice talking to you Drake, not!'

'It was nice talking to you, Jasmine,' he says from the dark.

He heard me? That is it! I am, without fail, boiling the creek water before I drink it. I look at Blue. 'If you start to talk or dance I know it's the creek water because you can't get enough of that fresh stream.'

I throw a few larger branches onto the fire and snuggle into my swag. I flip the hood over my head, feeling safe and tucked away from the world. I lie still, listening to any sounds that may be feet coming in my direction. In the end, I'm scared of the sound of my own breath. I must have laid there for hours, eventually exhausting myself asleep.

I wake to the smell and sound of cooking. I flip off the

hood of my swag to see Lazarus squatting next to my fire with a frypan in his hand.

'Good morning, Jazz. I wanted to apologise for rudely telling you to leave yesterday. My family would like to extend a warm invitation for you to visit us.' His tone is sweet.

'Ah… good morning and thanks for the offer but I've been told to leave this parcel of land. I promised to do so first thing this morning.' I quickly and inelegantly scramble out of my swag.

'Here, I have cooked you breakfast.' Lazarus tilts the pan, showing me it's filled with food.

I move closer to him, rubbing my tired eyes. 'It looks delicious but who eats steak for breakfast?'

'We love our meat and eat steak with every meal.'

'It looks great, thanks.' I smile, not wanting to offend him. 'Let me clean my teeth first.' I walk over to my pack to where the rubble of concrete lies. I stop momentarily to glance at it.

'Are you all right, Jazz?'

'Yes, I won't be a minute.' I wonder if he noticed the rubble beside the tree trunk. I quickly grab my toothbrush and paste and brush my teeth.

'There's a fresh bottle of water I brought up from the creek.'

I nearly choke on my toothbrush, shaking my head no. I grab my boiled bottled water and continue to wash my mouth out. 'No thanks, that water definitely has something running through it.'

'What makes you say that?'

'I met a guy last night that repeated the same warning you did—to leave the forest.' He passes me a plate full of steak, mushrooms and eggs. The meat is only just cooked and the piece he has taken is bloody and raw.

'What was his name?'

'Drake was his first name. He didn't hang around long

enough to give me his surname. He was adamant his family own this land.'

I cut into my steak and place it in my mouth. Lazarus watches my hand move towards my mouth and smiles the devil's grin when I close my lips around my fork, pulling the meat from it. I chew it and it's divine. 'Mm, this meat is so tasty.'

'It must be the way I cooked it.' He chuckles.

'Or maybe it's the lack of cooking. I guarantee your piece is still mooing.' I giggle.

'Oh, I hope it is.' He laughs. 'So will you take up my family's offer? You will be on our land which you're welcome to roam around if you and your steed wish.'

Wow, that's a different version from yesterday's conversation. I love it here and exploring the mountains excites me. I suppose it couldn't hurt to visit his family.

'Sure, why not? As long as I'm not imposing.'

After we finish eating, Lazarus cleans the plates and dowses the fire while I saddle up Blue Boy. We walk back with me on Blue and Lazarus jumping up behind me, sitting just behind the saddle. He rests one hand on my waist and it radiates the same heat I'd felt when I'd first touched him. His body does the same, which my chilled body is glad to accept.

When he speaks, he leans in close to my ear; I can feel the heat from his breath on the back on my neck and cheek, as it's the same temperature as his gripping hand. He's one hot-blooded guy.

Lazarus quizzes me regarding my family—curious about our history. He chooses his words carefully when I ask him what he does here, apart from farming his cattle. He answers my questions with a short non-descriptive sentence, then turns it around so I am the one answering questions.

We arrive back at the truck and Lazarus helps me load Blue Boy into the float. I open the back to find an absolute mess. Someone has again gone through my gear.

'What the hell? Someone keeps going through my clothes.'

'It's probably those little fairies I was mentioning.' He looks towards the creek.

'I've gotta tell you, hearing a grown man talk about fairies is peculiar.'

'Depends if you believe in them or not.'

'As I said to Drake last night—I don't!'

Lazarus lets out a boisterous laugh. 'Come on, let's get going. My impatient family is waiting to meet you.'

We drive with minimal conversation but I notice Lazarus constantly inhaling deep and long breaths through his nose. Each time he does it, it puts a smile on his face.

I wonder why his family has an immediate interest in meeting me. I presume it gets lonely out here so someone new to talk to would be refreshing.

As we approach an old but solid house, I see the cattle we drove yesterday. The two-storey house is made of stone and mud-brick and backs onto a huge mountain with a rocky formation.

I pull the truck up and move to let Blue Boy out of the float. When I reach the tailgate I'm met by a smiling young man—shirtless and barefooted! I stop and watch him unhitch the tailgate, letting Blue Boy waddle out backwards.

'Hello, Jasmine. I'm Corbin.' His smile is bright and before I can move, he leans over to kiss my cheek, inhaling through his nose, similar to what Lazarus did on our drive over here. He resembles Lazarus, with his black hair and tattoos with the added bonus of a dimpled cheeky smile. Plus, he can wear the hell out of a pair of jeans. Corbin is the perfect fit for a model on the front cover of a male muscle magazine.

'Hello.' Is all I can say as I'm still in shock that a stranger just kissed my cheek.

'I'll take Blue Boy over to the fenced paddock where our horses are if you wish?' he offers.

'I can do that,' I say.

'You're our guest, Jasmine,' a voice from behind me says. 'Welcome to Nogard Hollow. My name is Falcon.'

My eyes run up and down Falcon's naked chest which displays the same tattoo as his brothers. The local tattoo shop must have had a deal—three for the price of one! He stands tall and muscular in only a pair of black jeans, his feet bare. His eyes are the same lime green colour as Lazarus, his black hair an inch longer.

He moves towards me and places a long soft kiss on my cheek. I immediately step back, remembering that Lazarus had mentioned that neither of his parents lived here; that it was only he and his two brothers. Oh boy, what have I got myself into? My heart thuds in my chest as panic floods my veins. Coming here with Lazarus may have been an idiotic, dangerous and wrong decision.

'You're nervous, Jasmine. What worries you?' asks Falcon.

'No, I'm not nervous, I don't want to put you out, that's all. Maybe I'll stay for a quick cuppa and be on my way.' I feel the heat grow in my cheeks, reddening as my anxiety rises.

Corbin returns from the paddock, giving me the opportunity to search his eyes. They are identical to his brothers'. Apart from that, although the three of them have similarities, I'd never pick them as brothers.

'You're not in danger here, Jasmine,' says Corbin.

'I didn't think I was.' I swallow hard, forcing my fear away.

'Jazz, you have to stop lying,' says Lazarus. 'Come inside and relax. You need to slow that heartbeat.' He smirks at me then holds his hand out, gesturing for me to take hold of it. In slow motion, I place my hand into his heated palm. He guides me towards the house with the other two men following behind us. I turn my head slightly to see them both staring straight back at me.

'A quick cuppa will be nice but then I must head out to see to my horse.' I feel the fear still flooding my veins. Lazarus gives my hand a quick squeeze and when I look up at him he is smiling at me.

The house is old but superbly kept. There is no garden but there's a vegetable garden at the far end of the house. A veranda runs along the front, broken in the middle by several oversized stairs. As I get closer, the bigger the house's features become. The windows, stairs and doors are fit for a giant. Two elephants could walk side-by-side through the king-sized entry.

Lazarus opens the front door and tugs me inside. The furniture looks dated but in good condition, as if rarely used. The full-length windows let the sunlight fill the room, giving the house a warm feel. The room we are standing in is large enough for multiple elephants to move around in, with enough height for a giraffe. There are large lounge chairs scattered around a huge golden-coloured rug with a stunning red dragon embroidered onto it.

'Your rug is spectacular,' I say.

'Thank you, it has been in our family for generations,' says Falcon in a proud tone.

'You have a stunning home,' I say after a long pause.

'Please make yourself at home, Jazz,' Lazarus says.

'Thank you but I must head off on before dark.' I sit in one of the scattered chairs.

Within seconds Lazarus is by my side, making me jump when his hot hand rests on my shoulder. 'You've only just arrived and we have so much we want to show you.'

'Lazarus tells me you protected Drake two nights ago in the woods,' says Falcon.

'Wow, get straight to the point, bro,' says Lazarus.

'I protected no one. I found a concrete statue but it's broken now.'

Lazarus laughs. 'Concrete. I bet they'd love to hear that.'

'Broken or released?' asks Corbin, ignoring his brother's laughter.

'Drake smashed it into little pieces.' I scan the room and notice a large statue similar to the one that kept me company. 'It looked like that one over there.' I point towards a gargoyle statue made of concrete and move to run my hand over its wings and across its face. 'It's beautiful.'

'Yes, she is,' says Falcon, moving towards me.

'She has a very sad face.' I trace her lips and her sharp-looking teeth with my index finger.

'So why did you lie to Lazarus when he asked you if you had found Drake?' snaps Falcon, grabbing hold of my hand and flicking it away from the statue's face.

'I didn't find Drake. I found a creature and I was scared Lazarus would kill it so I wanted to protect it. I did what any kind person would do.' I bend forward so my face is level with the statue. 'What does this statue resemble? Or is it just art?'

'It's a gargoyle in stone sleep,' replies Falcon.

'So the concrete creature I was protecting was a gargoyle? Is that what you want me to believe?' I laugh, then realise none of them are laughing. 'Do you seriously want me to believe the gargoyle I was caring for turned into a statue? Like this lump of concrete here?' I shake my head and move away from Falcon and closer to the front door.

'Yes, that is exactly what we want you to believe, Jasmine,' says Falcon in a low stern tone.

'Okay, I believe it. Oh, look at the time. I really have to be going or I'll be driving in the dark.' I lift my wrist and pretend to glance down at my non-existent watch. I fake a smile and head to the door. Corbin moves like lightning towards the door then leans up against it. 'Am I a prisoner here?'

'No, Jasmine, you're not but you haven't had a tour of the house yet,' says Lazarus. 'Have the tour then you can leave.'

'I suppose another few minutes won't hurt,' I say with fear seeping through my words. I silently kick myself for getting into a position of being in a strange house with three peculiar men. I felt so comfortable with Lazarus yesterday. I can hear my mother tutting me for not being more cautious when it comes to strangers.

'Relax. Your heart is pounding so loud it's deafening,' growls Lazarus. He holds his hand out and guides me through several large rooms towards the biggest pair of timber doors I have ever seen. 'I bet you're keen to know what is behind these large doors.'

'Not particularly.'

'Breathe, Jazz. I promise nothing will hurt you.' He slips his warm arm around my waist and draws me forward. The doors open, releasing a gush of cool air. It's dark and it takes several minutes to focus on the ground in front of me.

'You need to light the cave up. She can't see it with her human eyes,' a voice says from beside me and by the annoyed tone I gather it's Falcon.

A large flame bursts out in front of me. I turn to run but Lazarus has a firm grip around my waist. The flying flame ignites a row of torches, lighting up the room, which I can now see is an enormous rock cave. The cave has a sharp edge ten metres in front of me, dropping straight down with the bottom nowhere in sight. It looks like I'm standing on a helicopter landing. This must be why the house backs onto the mountain—to hide the cave. It's surreal and looks like the cave out of a Batman movie.

I spot something moving in a dark corner and try to back away but I'm held firmly in place. Lazarus is standing behind me with his strong trapping arms wrapped around me.

'Trust me, Jazz, and try to take deep slow breaths. There is nothing more attractive than a pounding heart,' he whispers, warm against my ear.

'I want to introduce you to Corbin in his true form. Out of the three of us, he is the only one we can trust not to take a bite out of you, especially if you can't control that bloody heartbeat,' snarls Falcon.

I watch as an enormous creature emerges from the shadows. 'Holy cow!'

'Not exactly a cow,' sniggers Lazarus.

My eyes must be deceiving my brain because in front of me is a vibrant red, living, breathing dragon. It has the greenest eyes I have ever seen … not that I've seen a dragon in real life, just in my childish dreams.

The massive creature comes towards me with slow timid moves. Its clawed feet scrape the stone ground, like someone scraping their fingernail along a chalkboard. It sends a hair-raising shiver over my stunned body.

Lazarus tightens his grip around me and whispers into my ear, 'Keep your breathing calm and quiet or you will be a toothpick amongst his teeth.'

'You have to be shitting me?' I breathe.

'As much as I enjoy my arms around you, I need you to keep dead still. He would have eaten you by now if you had taken off like your sweet brain is telling you to do. Don't move suddenly and keep your breathing calm.'

The dragon moves so his nose is a metre away, giving me a clearer view. The back of his elongated head has a mane of sharp-looking spikes. He has small holes on the side of his head, which I presume are his ears. His mouth runs the full length of his head, displaying several fine sharp teeth which protrude even though his mouth is shut tight. Oh boy, I pray it's shut tight!

He breathes in through his oval-shaped nostrils, making my clothes draw towards him. Then he breathes out hot air and moves so his emerald eye is level with my face. I could fit my entire head into this animal's catlike eye.

He blinks and looks me over several times.

'Holy hell!' I feel as though my heart has pumped out of my chest and is now pulsing out of control in my hand. I take a deep breath and blow it out slowly and quietly.

The dragon shakes its head and snorts at me, covering me in dusty smoke.

'Hey bro, watch it, will you?' Lazarus chuckles. 'These are clean jeans.'

'You're doing well, Corbin. Her heart is beating faster than a steam train,' says Falcon, narrowing his eyes at me. 'Jasmine, try harder to control it!'

'Corbin?' I question. The dragon moves his eye next to me again and blinks. 'Corbin?' I repeat the question and he blinks again. I don't believe it—my dreams are a reality!

I reach forward and touch his skin. 'When I was a child, I lost my grandfather, whom I was very close to—he was my world. I'd have terrible nightmares until one day I found...' I hesitate, not wanting to show these men the pendant I'm wearing. I'd hate for them to take it. Then my nightmares would re-appear. 'I'd dream of dragons and other types of make-believe creatures. It was where my mind went to escape the sorrow of losing him and if I ever needed to escape life, I'd close my eyes and I see them. Am I dreaming now?'

'No, Jasmine, you're not dreaming and I'm more than happy to prove it,' snarls Falcon, sounding offended that I thought dragons were make-believe.

'Don't bully her, Falcon. Let her get a grasp on what's in front of her,' says Lazarus.

'Do you fear him?' asks Falcon.

'No.'

'Maybe that is because you've been around dragons before.'

'Dragons and other creatures exist only in my childish dreams; a fantasy world I live in to escape reality.'

'Are they dreams or memories? You should open your mind and dig a little deeper. You may be surprised at what you find,' says Falcon.

'I don't need to dig deeper. I like my mind exactly how it is.'

'I've noticed. Is that why you're running away from your home? To escape reality?'

I ignore him and concentrate on the beast in front of me.

'He's warm. I thought he'd feel like a blue-tongued lizard,' I whisper, hearing someone scoff behind me. I do what Lazarus said and move slowly so as not to startle the dragon. I remember, in my dreams, I was told to do the same. I can hear my grandfather saying, 'Slow, cautious and quiet movements around dragons at all times.'

I shake my grandfather out of my head and concentrate on the dragon in front of me. He could kill me with one quick swipe of his little-clawed finger. I run my hand along his lengthy scaled neck, keeping my movements to a minimum. His scales are tough leather plates of armour.

I stop at his pronged clawed foot which has three long deadly toes. I'm gentle and cautious when touching one of them. With a guarded move, he lifts it off the ground. I run my hand under his claw, feeling the sharp edge it carries. These claws could strip the meat off a cow in seconds.

I gasp out loud and stagger away from him, remembering the raw steak I ate this morning and spin around to gape at Lazarus. 'You're a dragon too, aren't you?'

'Yes, Jazz, I am.'

'And you, Falcon, are you one as well?'

Falcon nods. 'Yes. We wanted to show you this as we need your help.'

'My help! Look at the size of Corbin! He doesn't need my help. He could take on the whole Australian army,' I spit. Corbin lets another puff of dusty smoke escape his large nostrils. 'See? Even Corbin thinks it's a joke.

'I don't know what you're in to but I want no part of it. I'm trying to escape my past, my guilt and my nightmares. I was going along fine until you people—'

'We're not people, Jazz,' interrupts Lazarus. 'We are dragons.'

'Do you realise how stupid this sounds?' I shake my head and pace the length of Corbin's neck. 'What can I *do* to help you? That is if I'm willing to?'

'We need you to walk into Elyograg Castle during the day and slip a potion into Gabrielle and Malachi's drink,' explains Falcon.

'And who are they?'

'They're two angels we need quietened. The potion will not hurt them but it will put them to sleep for a good ten minutes.'

'Why don't you do it yourselves when you're in—what do you call it—human form?'

'Because we don't get invited over for afternoon tea,' he continues with a cooling tone.

'Why do you want them asleep?'

'That is our concern and none of your business,' he snaps.

'Well, if it's not my business, why should I do this for you?'

'Because my taste doesn't just lie with eating cows. My appetite ranges much further to horse. And we never eat our own horses,' he says, lifting one side of his lip to show a lopsided grin while his canine tooth lengthens several long centimetres.

'You'd eat my horse if I don't do this?' I spin to face Lazarus. 'Will you do the same?'

'I'm afraid Falcon is our leader and I do what's best for our family,' he replies, reaching his hand out to touch me.

'Don't!' I snap.

'Now that's a tasty heartbeat—anger. Haven't heard one in a long time,' groans Falcon.

'Yeah, well get used to it, because if you're around me that's what you're gonna hear,' I say.

He laughs and walks out of the room. 'Be careful, Jasmine. I also eat humans. You can sleep here tonight but be ready in the morning to go visit our dear neighbours,' he yells from the other room.

I continue to pace the room with Lazarus trying to grab my arm each time I pass him. I flinch away each time, not letting his warm touch soothe me.

I pace the length of Corbin for at least fifteen minutes with no one speaking a word. With several deep breaths, I calm my mind and try to take everything in.

Closing my eyes, I dredge up one of my dreams, keeping my focus on the dragons. One glides down from the sky and lands in front of me. It blows warm air over me, making me laugh. I feel no fear. If anything, I feel loved. I quickly flick my eyes open and grasp onto my pendant.

'I don't know what's real and what's fantasy,' I murmur to myself.

Lazarus moves towards me. I lift my index finger up to him as if to warn him to back away. He steps back and says nothing.

'You'd eat my horse?'

'No, I don't like the taste of horse,' says Lazarus. I huff and continue to pace.

After a long while, I calm and come to the conclusion I'm not in a dream. If I were, Grandfather and Sky would be in it.

But believing would mean that reality is my fantasy and all the creatures that fill my head exist.

I stand at the head of the dragon and admire his untamed strength and wild beauty. He is more amazing than the dragons in my dreams.

I walk closer to Corbin, who's calm and resting on the ground. With renewed confidence, I progress around his large head, stopping to stare into his large green eye.

'Can I touch your wings, Corbin?'

He blinks and with a calculated move, opens his wing. With a soft touch, I trace his massive body, letting my hand glide along his scaled skin and to let him know exactly where I am.

I glide my hand over his magical outstretched wing. It feels warmer and thicker than the gargoyle's injured wing. It sits behind his front shoulder and runs the full length of his body, finishing at the start of his tail. I can't see the end of his tail as he has it dropped over the edge of the cave and there's no way I am getting near it, especially with Falcon throwing around verbal threats. He may change his mind and push me over the edge.

'You'd better be careful. Corbin loves it when someone runs their hands over his scales.' Lazarus chuckles. Corbin jumps to his feet and snorts over Lazarus, letting a small flame escape his mouth. 'Watch it, you're not the only one who can play with fire!'

I step back in case these two have a testosterone clash. Corbin turns his head so I can see his eye and blinks. I presume it's a sign he won't hurt me. I move closer and continue to trace over his large wing.

'Do you want me to show you to your room, Jazz?' asks Lazarus.

'I'd like to stay here a while longer.'

'Suit yourself. I'll be in the house. Just walk in and I'll catch your scent.' He heads through the large timber double doors.

'My scent?'

'Hm, and what a lovely smell,' he purrs, before disappearing.

I return my focus to Corbin. 'You are enormous and could crush me with a flick of your nail but I don't fear you. Maybe I should, but I don't fear any of you. Plus, I gather Falcon wouldn't leave me here if I was in any danger. He needs my help.'

Corbin sits down, stretching out his front leg. In slow motion, I climb onto his foot and lean back against his heated leg.

'I hope you don't mind me lying on you but it's so chilly in here and you are toasty warm. Plus I fear I may accidentally fall off the cave's edge if I keep walking around you. I can't see the bottom so I presume it's a big fall.'

He turns his head and winks at me.

'Thanks, Corbin. I'm so confused. A week ago I left home looking forward to an exciting journey, but meeting you guys is a bucket load more than I had expected.'

I take a deep breath and relax into his warmth. Corbin inhales and relaxes the same way. 'Can you change into any-thing else?'

He shakes his head side to side, which I gather means no. 'Am I or my horse going to be dinner for one of you dragons?'

He snorts with a billow of dust coming out his nostril.

'I presume that's a laugh?'

He winks at me.

'Well, I hope you're laughing because you're not planning on eating me and not because you can already taste me between your teeth. Speaking of which, can I see how big your teeth are without tempting your taste buds?'

My curiosity is running wild. I want to know everything about these creatures and compare them with my dreams. I wait for his wink before sliding down his clawed toe and walking to his large mouth. He opens it wide enough for me to see the jungle of sharp teeth sitting there.

'Sheesh, Corbin, you are one mean killing machine.' I touch one tooth with my hand. Using my two hands, I hold one tooth and it's too large to fit in my grasp.

A sudden movement has me being propelling towards his razor-sharp teeth with my face stopping an inch away. There is a pair of heated hands on either side of my arms. I've been jolted towards Corbin's large teeth on purpose.

'Scare you?' Lazarus chuckles.

Corbin snaps his mouth shut and turns away from us. He releases a hellish belch of flame before slithering down the face of the cave into the darkness.

'You're an ass, do you know that?' I snap.

'And you sound delicious when you're angry, did you know that?'

'Yes, you dragons keep reminding me of how I sound!'

'Come and I'll show you your room for the night.'

'Where has Corbin gone?'

'He's probably gone to sulk. I think he was enjoying your company,' he says, bumping me.

'Again, you're an ass! I was just curious to know him as a dragon.'

'I can change form if you're still curious.'

I look up and he was serious. 'No! Apparently, you might eat me so I'm happy getting to know you with two feet, not four, and thirty-two teeth, not three hundred.'

'Come,' he says, holding his hand out. I stare at it. 'We're not that bad. We need your help and after you do what we ask, you will be free to go.' I place my hand in his and he gives it a firm squeeze. 'Good girl.'

'So, when I do what you ask, you'll let me walk away knowing what I know.'

'What is it you know?'

'That dragons live at Nogard Hollow and gargoyles are their neighbours.'

'You forgot the fairies, angels and sorcerers.'

'And no doubt the leprechauns, vampires, wolves and little tap-dancing gnomes.'

He stops walking and stands in front of me. 'Don't be naive, Jasmine. There's no such thing as leprechauns. But there could be wolves and vampires. I've never had the pleasure of meeting one… yet. And I've never seen a gnome tap dance but they can rock it.'

'You didn't answer my question—will I be able to walk away unscathed?'

'Xandria will cast a spell over you, making you think what you've seen is a dream.'

'Who is Xandria?'

'She is the little pain in my butt. A fairy who doesn't know when to mind her own business,' he snarls, then turns and tugs me to follow.

'So that's it? All I have to do is drug two angels and the fairy sprinkles her magical fairy dust and I continue on my travels as if nothing ever happened?'

'That is correct unless you want to stay here for a while.'

Breaking the tranquillity of the house is a vibrating roar which echoes and rolls around the room. 'Well, maybe I should ask Falcon first.'

'That was him?' Lazarus nods. 'How can he hear our conversation?'

'Dragons have ultra-sensitive hearing and can smell a scent we've locked onto up to ten kilometres away. Our eyesight is also different from a human and most animals, as we can x-ray through trees and structures. Our night vision is also extraordinarily clear. Hence, we can smell your fear, hear your delicious heart racing and even see it if I wish.'

'X-ray vision? So you can see through clothes?'

He blurts a boisterous laugh. 'Relax that heart of yours, Jazz, I'm being a complete gentleman, as you humans would say. That's not to say I didn't think about it.'

I gasp at his audacity. 'How dare you?' I lift my hand to slap his face. He grabs my wrist before it strikes his cheek. 'You're an ass!'

'That's the third time you've called me that, Jasmine. It might be wise for you to remember what I am. Dragons aren't known for their tolerance. If you raise your hand to one of the other dragons consider it bitten off. Physically!'

'And you'd best remember who I am, you oversized gecko,' I snap back, finding my backbone.

'Your room is there.' He ignores me and points towards an open door. He moves so his face is inches away from mine. He inhales deep and closes his emerald green eyes. When he opens them he stares hard into mine. 'Remember we can sense your every move.'

He kisses my cheek, long and warm. I hear him breathe me in—he's collecting my scent. I felt like pushing something out of my rear end for him to smell but behave the way my mother would want me too—like a lady.

He steps back and turns to walk away. 'Goodnight, beautiful.'

I watch him walk away then turn to enter the room I've been allocated. I close the door and admire the warm, homey furnishings around me. It is a huge room just like everything in this house, with a timber four-poster bed as the centrepiece. There is a matching long lounge running under a stained-glass window. It reflects a rainbow of colours over the floor. The room has a sweet floral smell, reminding me of lavender and jasmine. The space is welcoming, unlike its owners.

I push against the window but it only opens several inches and, from what I can see, there's considerable drop to the ground. I can rule this out as an escape route.

My bags are here but my clothes are scattered across the floor. Who keeps doing this? The fairy? I try to remember her name and scan my room for any little creature that looks the same as my Barbie doll.

'Xandria, are you here?' I whisper. There is no answer. I shake my head, feeling stupid. I bet the dragons are having a great laugh listening to me call out to a non-existent fairy.

I walk over to a door and open it, finding an elegant bathroom. It has a free-standing bath which looks inviting. I'm surprised when I turn the tap on and water flows from it. The water is warm so I let it fill the tub while I go back and grab fresh clothes. I close the door behind me and strip off my clothes, eager to rest my exhausted body in the warm bath.

I slide in so my shoulders are under the water. It's so deep it allows me to lean back and relax.

'Try hearing my heart now, dragons.'

'They can hear you,' says a small voice.

'Who said that?'

'I did,' the small voice says. I search the room again and out the corner of my eye I see a white glow. I turn to see a miniature person, no bigger than my hand. She flutters and hovers in mid-air, like an oversized butterfly.

'Xandria?'

'Yes, that is me and you are Jasmine,' replies the delicate little fairy.

With caution, she comes closer, her fragile wings flickering and glowing brightly. Keeping her distance, she lands on the far end of the bath, her small body dressed in a material I recognise. It looks like my satin pyjamas. I must remember to check them to see if she put a hole in them.

'I won't hurt you, Xandria. I think you have been watching me. I've seen your wings out the corner of my eye several times.'

'No, you didn't see Xandria. She was too quick. What are you, a gargoyle?'

'No, I'm human.' I laugh.

'Why do the dragons want you?'

'I'm not sure. I was hoping you could tell me.'

'You shouldn't kiss them, you know,' she growls, folding her arms across her chest.

'I didn't kiss them. They kissed me and it was only on the cheek. Are you jealous?'

'Fairies don't get jealous, you ridiculous human. What are you doing for the dragons?'

'They want me to go to the castle on the next parcel of land.'

'The gargoyles? Drake's family?'

'I thought two angels lived there?'

'Gabrielle and Malachi are angels and the rest are gargoyles.' She sits on the rim of the bath, making herself comfortable.

'Tell me about them.'

'It's pretty simple… well, maybe not to you, you being a stupid human. The angels protect the gargoyles during the day while they are in "stone sleep".'

'Stone sleep?'

'Yes, that's when they repair or heal any wounds that may have occurred during the day. When the sun sets they shed their outer layer of stone, returning to flesh and blood again,' she explains, swishing her small feet in the water.

'So gargoyles are living and breathing during the night and are concrete statues during the day. Is that correct?'

'You better not call them concrete if you want your head left on your shoulders. They turn to stone.'

'And can they take human form as well?'

'Yes, of course they can. You really need to get out more. You met Drake the other day in human form, didn't you?'

'Drake was the injured creature that turned to stone?'

'It takes a while for you humans to catch on, doesn't it?' she says, rolling her beady round eyes at me. 'Gargoyles are very strong, they are three times the strength of one human body-builder and have the sharpest teeth and claws. One bite from them and you'll know about it. But if they are in human form, they lose a third of their strength and can't protect themselves as much as if they were in gargoyle form.' She stands up and starts to dust imaginary lint from her tiny dress. 'Xandria must go now as she's told you too much already.' She laughs.

'What's so funny, Xandria?'

'It doesn't matter how much I tell you. When I throw my magic over you, you'll think this has been a wonderful dream.'

'Don't leave. I have so many more questions to ask.'

'Lazarus is on his way up with food, so you'd better get out of the bath unless you will let him sit on the edge of the bath like Xandria did.' She giggles and flutters away, sneaking between the bottom of the door and the floor.

What an amazing little creature! She looks nothing like my Barbie doll. I hear the bedroom door open so I scamper out of the bath, grab a towel, and wrap it around me firmly. 'Lazarus, you know I am in the bath!'.

'Sorry, I thought you might be asleep, your...'

'My heart has stopped racing.' I open the bathroom door with the towel wrapped around my torso. 'And you couldn't hear me.'

I stand in the bathroom doorway staring at Lazarus, who's only wearing his hole-pitted jeans, holding a plate filled with food. He is breathtakingly handsome, making me wonder how he looks in his dragon form.

'I can hear it now, Jazz.'

'Um, I'm hungry and that food looks delicious. Give me a minute to put my clothes on,' I say, blushing, knowing full well my heart is beating fast because he's standing in front of me.

'A towel or clothes. Makes no difference what you wear.'

'You better not be using that x-ray vision!'

He chuckles and runs his eyes leisurely up and down my body.

'Lazarus!'

'Mm, now that's the heartbeat I enjoy so much.' He laughs.

'You want me angry? You got it,' I spin and storm back into the bathroom. I'm quick to change into my clothes and sit on the floor, waiting until I hear Lazarus leave my room. I wait for at least fifteen minutes until can't hear anything.

As quiet as a mouse I stand up and open the door. Lazarus has left the plate of food on the bed. I walk out to examine it.

'Feeling better now, Jazz?' Lazarus is stretched out, lounging on the couch under the leadlight window.

'Sheesh! You scared me.'

'Yes, I can tell.'

'Oh, enough of the heartbeat stuff!'

'I'm sorry. Please sit and enjoy your dinner.' He smiles and points to the large plate of food.

'I can't eat all this. Why don't you come and share this with me?'

'Will that make you happy?'

'Packing up my horse and leaving here will make me happy,' I reply with a sarcastic tone and smile.

'Do you dislike me that much, Jazz?'

'No, I don't dislike you or Corbin. What I don't enjoy is being blackmailed by Falcon. Come and sit beside me and eat.' I sit on the bed and tap it with my hand.

'Now that is an offer I can't refuse.'

I glance over at him and roll my eyes. He moves to sit beside me. I pick at the food from the plate. It has fresh crunchy vegetables and, of course, meat. 'The meat tastes different. What is it?'

'Kangaroo. Do you like it?'

'Yes, it's delicious.'

He picks up a strawberry from the plate and places it at the tip of my lips. 'Bite,' he whispers. I do and it's fresh and juicy. 'I grow them myself.'

'Mm, mouth-watering!' I pick one up and place it close to his mouth. 'If I say bite, I mean the strawberry and not me.'

He laughs out loud and falls back onto the bed. 'You make me laugh, Jazz. It is so refreshing to have you around.' He sits up and grasps my hand, which still holds the stem of the strawberry. He draws my hand to his mouth and with a gentle action, takes the strawberry, with his warm lips closing over the tip of my fingers. My heart thuds hard and I try with all my might to slow its rhythm. His lips curve to a grin and his eyes glow their lime green.

'Well done, you're learning to tame your own heart. I'm impressed.'

'I'm the one impressed. Corbin in his dragon form is unbelievably beautiful. I can't do anything magical or change into another form. I'm just plain old me.'

'There's nothing plain about you, Jazz. You are unbelievably beautiful,' he says in a soft sincere tone.

'Whatever.' His comment and gaze are unnerving, forcing me to look down at my fidgeting fingers.

'You don't trust what anyone says, do you?'

'I trust my parents,' I reply, taking a deep breath to console myself as I remember them. I miss them and it's only been a week.

'You can trust me. I will never hurt or lie to you.'

'Trust is earned in my world,' I say, picking at the plate of food.

'As it is in mine. You will learn to trust me. Have I poisoned you yet?'

'No, and I must admit, you're a great cook. Thank you for dinner.'

'You haven't even touched it. Maybe I should leave and give you private time.' He stands up and moves towards the door.

'Privacy! You can hear everything I say and do.' I slide off the bed, throwing my hands on my hips.

'We sleep in the cave so I won't hear everything, as the walls drown out some of the noise. But I will sense if you leave the room.' He shrugs and gives a sympathetic smile.

'Did you hear Xandria talking with me?'

'Word for word,' he admits, dropping his head.

'Can your brothers hear us now?'

'No, they're in the cave. They can sense we are together but that's it,' he says, moving closer. I step back until my legs hit the base of the bed. He stands inches away from me, the heat radiating from his body.

'You're very hot. Um... I mean your body... as in temperature.'

His eyes narrow due to his large grin.

'I could have used your body heat the other night to heat my swag when I was camping. I froze out there,' I blurt. I'm not thinking rationally due to his close proximity.

'Are you cold in here? I could warm your bed for you if you wish.' His smile widens.

'Um, no! I'll be fine, thanks.'

He leans forward so his face is an inch from mine. His eyes are mesmerising as I flick mine back and forth, curious as to what his next move will be. He is so darn sexy. It makes it hard to breathe when he is so close.

'You were doing so well. You need to practice controlling your heart rate, as it gives away your feelings.' He turns and walks towards the door. 'Goodnight, Jasmine, from the outer suburbs of Melbourne. Sleep well.' He closes and locks the door behind him.

I fall back onto the bed. Oh, bugger! He knows what I am feeling and I don't even know what to call these feelings!

I sit up cross-legged and devour the food on the plate, my appetite suddenly ravenous. I stuff myself until I am bursting at the seams.

I snuggle under the bed cover, finding that the sheets are cold, making me wish I had taken up his offer to warm my bed. But lying beside a dragon could have its problems. Maybe I should have asked him to blow fire out his nostrils and light me a fire. I get the giggles as my mind runs away with me but it soon calms when I remember Drake and what I must do tomorrow.

I'm about to doze off when I sense someone. I sit straight up to see a mature woman leaning over me. In a blink, she places her hand over my mouth, smothering any sound that may come out.

'Jasmine, I won't hurt you. I need you to stay silent and still. If I take my hand away will you stay quiet?' she asks.

I nod my head. She slowly removes her hand as if not to startle me. 'Thank you. I don't have long and I can't be seen in this human form but I thought you might scream waking up to a gargoyle towering over you.'

'You're right. I would have shat myself. Who are you?'

'My name is Demona. You protected my son, Drake.' She smiles and clasps my hand with both of hers. 'Thank you.'

'You're welcome.'

'I need to be brief. Falcon has me captive here as he needs something from me and can only get it if I am in human form.

He is giving you a potion to give to our protecting angels so they will sleep and then the dragons can attack our castle.'

'What do you mean attack?'

'If they crush and burn us when we are in stone sleep we will crumble to ashes, leaving only our pure gold souls for the taking.'

'They want your souls, why?'

'I don't have time to explain. They will soon sense I'm in here. Please warn our guardian angels and tell Drake I will escape when it is safe. I don't need him being a hero.'

'Wait, I need to ask you so many questions,' I whisper, trying to stop her from leaving.

'You need to say Xandria was in here or they'll know it was me. And remember, they have your scent. They know where you are at all times,' she says, before disappearing out the door.

Minutes later, I hear footsteps outside my door.

'Bloody fairy better not come back. She doesn't shut up,' I whisper, knowing whichever dragon is on the other side will hear me whinging and think Xandria has returned to my room. I inhale deeply and try my best to rest my beating heart. It works as the sound of feet moves away.

CHAPTER THREE

I WAKE DISORIENTATED. My brain takes a few extra seconds to catch up with my eyes, realising that I'm in the dragons' home and everything that has happened is very real.

'Good morning, beautiful,' says Lazarus, sitting on the lounge.

'Are you going to be my alarm clock every morning?' I yawn, stretching my arms above my head.

'While you're here, yes. Did you sleep well?'

'I did when Xandria eventually left.' I may as well test the waters to see if they knew Demona was in my room.

'I'll have a talk to her if you wish.'

'No! She's a cute little thing. I was just tired, that's all.'

'As you wish. I have breakfast for you.' Lazarus points to a plate on the bedside table.

'Oh, please tell me there's no meat on it. I can't face any more meat.' I sit up to see a plate full of fruit. 'Oh, thank goodness.' He chuckles at my relief.

'Do you want to share this with me?'

'I ate earlier, as I need my full strength today. You need to eat and get dressed. Have you decided if you will ride over to Elyograg Castle or I'm happy to fly you there?'

'Fly? Um, no thanks. I'd prefer to ride Blue over if that's all right and if it's not too far for him.'

'It's not far. If you ride to the base of the mountain there's an underpass which comes out beside the Elyograg Castle.'

'What if they hurt me?' I ask, chewing on a fresh piece of fruit.

'They are angels, Jazz, they won't hurt a human. A

gargoyle might but they will be in stone sleep, so you're safe.' He stands up moving towards the door. 'Were you warm enough last night?'

'It was cold to start with and I thought about asking you to light a fire with the flame that comes out your nostrils.' I chuckle.

'My flame, as you call it, comes out my mouth. And I don't think I'd fit through the door. Plus, I don't always have control over what I do and I'd probably burn the place down.' He smiles. 'Get ready; Falcon is tapping his foot downstairs, waiting for you.'

'Tell him to take a chill pill. I'll be there when I'm good and ready.'

A loud roar rumbles through the house. I look up at Lazarus and he shakes his head. 'Really? He's listening to our conversation? Well, hear this, you slithering oversized snake with legs—I will be down when I'm ready!'

The house vibrates with a deafening roar.

'You must remember that he is in his dragon form so he's not as patient and polite as he is when he's in human form.' Lazarus holds his hand out for me to get out of bed.

'You're kidding me? That was his nicer side? Boy, oh boy, I'm gonna have a bad day!' I move quickly to the bathroom to change into my jeans and t-shirt.

Lazarus is still waiting for me when I open the bathroom door.

'Are you ready?'

'As I'll ever be.'

'Keep your distance from Falcon. He's not sure if he can hold his temper with you and might accidentally eat you.' Lazarus grabs my hand and tugs me towards the hallway.

'How can you *accidentally* eat someone? Really, you guys need to sort out a few serious issues.' I roll my eyes.

'You make me laugh, Jazz.' He kisses the back of my hand with his warm lips. 'Corbin has saddled Blue already. We will meet you over the other side of the creek and show you the hidden path.'

'Will you be human? Blue Boy hasn't seen a dragon, and I'd prefer to stay in the saddle.'

'He met Corbin in dragon form this morning, and he was fine.'

'Corbin didn't—'

'No, Jazz, he didn't eat him. Come and meet Falcon.' He continues to lead me down the hallway and back towards the two large timber doors.

I'm cautious when walking into the cave, making sure Lazarus is in front of me in case Falcon takes a swing at me for my earlier comments. A flame lights up the torches and I see two magnificent dragons before me. They are both candy apple red and in an instant, I recognise Corbin. He has a kinder eye than the other dragon and narrower features, as he does in human form. At a guess, I'd say Corbin is around nineteen years old and Falcon in his thirties, with Lazarus closer to my age, in his mid-twenties.

'Morning, Corbin.' I walk slowly but with confidence to his head. He lowers it and winks at me.

'Clever girl. How did you pick him?' asks Lazarus.

'Easy. He is better looking.' I snigger. Corbin blows out dusty smoke and I gather he is laughing.

But Falcon whips his head around bringing it centimetres away from me, snarling so I can see sharp teeth. Lazarus steps towards me as if he is about to protect me.

Falcon continues to snarl, blowing hot air over me.

'I think you missed a bit when you brushed this morning.' I pretend to pick food out of my teeth.

Lazarus pulls me away from his mouth. 'I'm not joking,

Jasmine. He will eat you and not even think about it,' he whispers.

'No, he won't because he needs me. I'm not intimidated by his size or his teeth.' I stand tall and square my shoulders. And it's true—none of them scares me, as I feel I've seen this all before, in my dreams.

'Mm, defiant, strong and angry. Now that's a delicious sound,' he hums.

'Enough about my heartbeat.' I hit his arm with a playful slap.

Falcon lets out a deafening roar making me jump. Okay, maybe he does intimidate me.

I quickly find Blue, who's saddled and standing patiently in the yard. I jump on and head off towards the creek.

Shortly after leaving Nogard Hollow, I stop and scan the land for dragons. I contemplate taking off in the opposite direction and pray I meet humans who can protect me from a huge village of killing machines. No human could stand up to these creatures unless they have an army's artillery behind them.

I turn back towards the creek and click Blue into a canter. I cross the creek, and since Blue hasn't spoken yet, I let him slurp the cool water as we go.

I canter on to the base of the mountain and spot two dragons sitting down. I approach slowly and calmly so they don't get excited and eat my horse. Lazarus is there in human form, holding what I presume is the potion.

'You made good time. Here's the potion and there's the passage through. It will be dark but Xandria has promised to guide you with the light from her wings.' Lazarus points to a small opening, just large enough to fit Blue and me.

'And what if she changes her mind and leaves me there in the dark?'

'She won't and if she does, I will personally de-wing

her,' he snarls at the little fairy who has just made her appearance.

'You better get going, Jasmine,' he says, passing me the potion. He grabs hold of my hand, encasing it in both his warm hands. 'I'll see you at Elyograg Castle. Trust me, Jazz.' His eyes hold sincerity and I'm not sure if he was trying to warn me or wish me luck.

Falcon's impatient and loud snort makes Blue jump backwards.

'Scare my horse again and I will de-scale you with a sharp knife,' I snap, then kick Blue on towards the dark tunnel. 'I'd just love a new red leather jacket.'

As I enter the tunnel, Xandria lands on the top of Blue Boy's head. He flicks his ears back and forth as if to push her away. She rubs his ears which, to my amazement, soothes him. She flutters her wings and they glow white, giving me enough light to see two metres in front of me.

My heart pounds a fierce beat. I can hear creatures moving around and above my head. 'How long is this tunnel?' I ask with fear seeping through my tone.

'Xandria has never travelled through this passage. Xandria is a very skilled fairy and can fly over the top,' she replies.

With slow, calculated steps we travel along the dirt track for what seems like hours. 'Xandria is getting tired.' She yawns, sitting on Blue's head. The light goes out of her wings and we are in darkness.

'Xandria, you need to keep going!' I say.

'Too tired.'

Blue is becoming agitated and I fear he may hurt himself or worse, me. 'Please, Xandria, I thought you were a skilled fairy. The dragons say you're the best around,' I say, appealing to her vanity.

'Xandria is the best around!' She flutters her wings, giving us back the light we so desperately need.

'I think you are too and I will tell everyone about the fantastic job you did.'

'Xandria is the fittest fairy. Most of the male fae want her.'

'I could imagine. A talented fairy like you would be on every male fairy's date list.'

'Fairies don't date. We—'

'No, stop! Please don't tell me what fairies do. I learnt so much in the last twenty-four hours I don't think I can deal with hearing the romantic relationships that go on between you creatures.'

'Look! Up ahead Xandria can see the end of the tunnel,' she sings.

My heart skips for joy, knowing this nightmare is nearly finished.

Within minutes, we are out the other side of the mountain and are momentarily blinded by the bright sunlight.

'Well, Xandria must leave. She will see you back at Nogard Hollow. Remember to tell everyone how amazing Xandria was.' She flutters away, not giving me time to thank her.

I look around and realise I am only a hundred yards away from the castle. My heart thuds, letting me know I am alive and I'm at the base of a castle full of gargoyles.

I reach into my pocket for the small vessel that holds the potion, wondering why I've agreed to do this.

I click Blue on and arrive at the massive entrance to the castle. I am greeted by a radiant blonde woman standing at the front door. I smile and dismount.

'Hello,' I say with a nervous quiver.

'Hello, are you lost?' she asks in an angelic, almost harmonic, voice.

'No, I was hoping to see Drake.'

'How do you know Drake?'

'We met the other day and he invited me to visit him.'

'During the day?' she asks, and I gather she is testing me.

'Oh, I know he will be asleep but I thought I could wait around. Plus, I didn't want to ride my horse home in the dark.'

'Why don't you come inside?' She smiles, pushing the front door wide open. 'Malachi will take your steed.'

I glance behind me. There is the most scrumptious blonde man, with too many muscles, walking towards us.

'Here, let me take him for you. I'll make sure he's properly watered and fed,' he says with a soft humming tone.

I can't speak due to my drooling mouth dropping open in response to his impressive features. If he is an angel, I can't wait to get to heaven!

'Please come inside and make yourself comfortable,' she says.

'Um, thank you.' I slip from the saddle. I watch Malachi as he takes the reins and walks Blue away.

'Your horse is in good hands. Please come and relax.'

'Oh, yes, I can see he is in good hands.'

I walk towards the immaculate blonde. In that very instant I realise that, yes, they are angels. It hits me swiftly and firmly with what I am supposed to do. Do I give them the potion or tell them what Demona said?

She walks me inside the enormous castle. The huge, three-level staircase takes centre stage, with soft comfortable lounges scattered around the room. This castle could also cater to a giant.

'Gabrielle?' I whisper.

She turns, smiling. 'How do you know my name?' Her brows crease but she still looks stunning.

'Do you have a pen and paper?'

'Do you mean documents?'

'Yes, so I can write a message?'

'I do but I can't read them.'

'Oh, God!'

'Excuse you!' She glares.

'I'm sorry. Can I have a glass of water, please?'

'Certainly. Follow me.'

I walk up the first flight of stairs and into the kitchen. She grabs a glass and places it under a spout of running water. I move next to her and turn the tap on full. I need my voice muffled so the dragons can't hear me.

'What are you doing?'

'Listen carefully to what I'm about to say. The dragons blackmailed me to come here to drug you and Malachi so they can get to the gargoyles during their stone sleep. With you two drugged it leaves the gargoyles unprotected.

'Drake's mother, Demona, came into my room last night and told me I had to warn you and to tell Drake that she will escape from them whenever she has the chance.' I pull out the potion from my pocket and show her.

She gasps and closes her eyes, holding them tight until Malachi is beside me.

'Did you hear?' she asks him.

'Yes, I did,' he replies.

'Sheesh, do angles have sensitive hearing as well?' I push the glass of water away, refusing to drink it. 'I'm convinced there's something in the water.'

The angels look at me for several seconds before taking off.

'You, stay in here where it's safe,' says Malachi, his sexy eyes locking with mine, adding a firm nod. I doubt any woman would argue with that handsome specimen.

I turn the running tap off and stand still, wondering what is happening. I walk to the staircase and see the angels on the top floor disappearing through a door.

I climb the stairs and enter the same door they had used. It leads me out onto the roof, where I am confronted with the two angels and four furious-looking gargoyles. They are flesh and blood and not what I had expected. They should be in stone sleep.

I freeze, as I don't want to startle these massive creatures. Four piercing pairs of glowing blue eyes lock hard onto me. I gulp in fear when one twists its head to get a good look at me, then opens its mouth and allows a long line of drool to escape. Oh hell—it's salivating at the thought of eating me!

I try to move my feet back towards the door, but they disobey my command. Behind them, I see a dark figure with a long black cape covering its head and body. It disappears before I can focus on it.

The sound of the dragons' wings flying overhead interrupts our staring contest. I glance up into the cloudless blue sky and witness a magnificent sight but also a terrifying one. I panic and crouch down, hoping I'm out of their way.

One of them swoops low, passing me by a metre, with its razor-sharp claws sticking out. The other two dragons fly past at a higher height.

I shoot up so I can see which dragon has just tried to skin me alive. It circles and in a swift motion returns, giving me the opportunity to recognise him as Falcon. He releases a loud roar, with a billow of flame shooting from his mouth.

I drop to the floor and pray I don't get burnt. I know I'm engulfed by the heat as it's mighty intense. I look up to see three of the gargoyles sheltering the angels, their large wings blanketing the flames. The fourth gargoyle is running straight for me. Oh no, it's attacking me! I cover my head with my arms to protect myself as best I can. It throws its bodyweight onto my legs. I kick and punch with all my strength into the hard gargoyle's back but I have zero impact.

'Get off me!' I panic. 'Help me someone, please, help!'

'Jasmine, stop.'

I look up and recognise the glowing blue eyes. It's Drake. I look at my legs and he is stamping out a fire with the pad of his clawed hands. My jeans are on fire and the instant my eyes see it I acknowledge the horrific pain. I scream, scaring myself with the sicking pitch coming from my voice box.

Drake keeps rolling his hands over my legs until the flames disperse. He flicks his eyes to mine with a sympathetic frown forming as my eyes flood with tears of pain.

'I'm sorry,' whispers Drake.

'Your mother told me to warn you. You must not rescue her as they are waiting for you. She is staying in stone sleep where they can't get to her and will escape when safe,' I blurt, wanting to relay the message before I forget or pass out.

He picks me up in his strong arms and I wince in pain.

'Look out, Drake! They're coming back,' yells Malachi.

We both look up to see Falcon coming towards us. He whips his razor-sharp tail at us and hits Drake hard across the face, making him stagger and fall. I'm thrown across the ground, rolling until I hit the edge of the roof. I grasp the edge of the guttering, praying I won't tumble over the edge. I look up to see Drake gaining his stance with blood streaking down his face.

'Drake, you're hurt!' I yell.

'No!' shouts Gabrielle.

Falcon flies past and hits me with his strong wing. I lose my grip on the guttering and fall from the roof. The unforgiving ground is racing closer towards me but I am calm. I see my grandfather standing before me and under his arm is my cousin, Sky, whom I love and haven't seen in years. I wonder if they are here to welcome me to heaven.

My body slams into something solid and I presume I have hit the ground. A soft cool breeze blows over me. Am I on my way to heaven? I can't be because if I were, I shouldn't be experiencing pain.

I open my eyes to see several large claws holding me by the waist.

'Ah!' I scream out in pain and fear. 'Put me down! Your claws are cutting into me.' I try to loosen their grip. I glance below and realise if I'm successful I will fall to my death.

I take a deep painful breath and try to calm my mind. I realise it's not Falcon or Corbin so this must be Lazarus. Fear surges through my veins as he told me he might not be able to control himself around me if he is in dragon form. I take a few deep breaths and try to shut out the excruciating pain racing through my body.

'Lazarus, you're hurting me. Please put me on the ground.'

He acknowledges he heard me by releasing a smothered roar within his belly. 'Falcon has burnt my legs, I'm in pain.'

He doesn't respond this time and keeps his wings flying a steady slow rhythm.

'Falcon tried to kill me, Lazarus,' I whisper. I lose the strength to talk; my body has used all the adrenaline I have. He vibrates in his belly with a rumbling roar. 'Please, you asked me to trust you. I'm trying to.'

He doesn't reply.

I'm becoming weaker and colder and am feeling faint. The only thing keeping me from passing out is the continuous flow of cool air on my face. He flies over the top of the mountain and lands close to where I camped on the first night. He places me on the ground and I scamper away from his large claws. I stumble and stagger, trying to stand up, praying my legs will hold me.

He's magnificent, with an intimidating size. His red scales glisten in the sunlight and his lime-green eyes are dominant on his face. He is the most astounding creature I have ever seen.

'Lazarus, I'm sorry I didn't drug the angels. I couldn't do it. It's not my nature to kill someone or help kill someone. Please forgive me.'

He drops his head and moves cautiously towards me. I step back, not sure if he is planning on eating me or whether I'm forgiven. He moves so his snout is inches away and he breathes me in. I lift my hand to touch him and gasp in horror. My arm is covered in blood. I look down at my stomach and I'm bleeding everywhere.

I lift my t-shirt up and see the damage his claws have created when he scooped me up, saving me from death.

He snorts and turns his head away. I know he didn't mean to hurt me but before I can reassure him I will be fine, I'm overwhelmed by nauseating light-headedness and need to sit before I fall.

Lazarus swings his head around, looking up at the sky. Falcon is approaching and lands with a thunderous thud. He blasts a deafening roar in our direction and Lazarus rises to stand tall on his clawed toes. He blasts back and I can tell by Falcon's defensive stance he wants me dead.

In a blink, Lazarus moves so he's between me and Falcon. Finding another hit of adrenaline, I scramble to my feet and run as fast as I can to the edge of the forest, trying to protect myself behind a tree in case they come crashing in my direction.

They circle each other, their bellows deafening, as though they are yelling at each other. They are both similar in size but Falcon's exterior is sharper and deadlier. He shoots the first burst of flame, hitting Lazarus' side, but he doesn't flinch. He retaliates by returning the flame.

Falcon lashes out with his tail, swinging it violently, hitting Lazarus square in the back, leaving a gaping bloody hole. The end of the dragon's tail has a sphere-shaped blade which I'd never noticed on Corbin when I'd first laid eyes on him.

'No!' I yell out. Lazarus turns his long neck to see me then whips it back to his brother. He swings his tail, connecting with Falcon's jaw, then he swipes him with his razor-sharp claws. Blood spurts from Falcon's face and neck and he bellows a heart-wrenching sound.

I hear another set of wings flapping above me and look up to see Corbin landing between the two fighting brothers. He lowers his long neck and growls a low thunderous sound, with flames flying out in all directions. The three of them roar wildly as if they are arguing and I pray it's not about who will eat me first.

My heart is pounding and my body shaking. I glance down at my torso; my t-shirt soaked with my blood. A dizzy swirl swishes inside my brain, my vision becoming fuzzy. Shaking my head, I try my hardest to hold on to the here and now.

'You don't look good, little human,' whispers a voice. I look up and Xandria is flying in front of my face.

'Help me, I'm hurt.'

'Yes, Xandria can see that. Help is on its way. You can trust Xandria,' she flutters.

The noise the three dragons are making is deafening. I glance over to Lazarus and see him looking in my direction. He releases a high-pitched roar as I drop to the ground. I see Xandria fluttering over my face.

'Help is here, human,' she whispers.

There's a cold hand on mine but my vision is blurry and I don't know who has hold of me. I'm being lifted into someone's arms as light fades from my eyes.

Chapter Four

I TRY TO open my eyes but my eyelids refuse to obey me. I hear the crunching of leaves and branches and only know I'm being carried.

'She's lost a large amount of blood,' a voice says.

'Why do you care about her? She was helping the dragons kill us. Let her bleed to death,' a female's voice says.

'We don't kill humans,' another snarls. 'Remember who you are.'

I try with all my might to speak but as I summon up every ounce of my strength, it pushes me further away, then nothing.

'Welcome back, Jasmine,' a sweet voice says as I flicker my eyelids open.

'Gabrielle?'

'Yes, but call me Gabby. How do you feel?'

'Confused.' I try to sit up straight but wince in pain, grabbing at my torso. 'Ouch! And sore.'

'Malachi, go get Drake and tell him she is awake,' she says over her shoulder.

'You had us worried for a while. There are some nasty puncture wounds on your upper body and your legs have burns on them. They are healing in an unusual way but they are healing. I will ask Raven to have a look at the markings that are forming on your legs.'

'Who is Raven?'

'She is the gargoyle's sorceress. She sensed that something was wrong and had already alerted the gargoyles, drawing them out of stone sleep into night flesh before Malachi and I had reached the rooftop.'

'Aren't sorcerers evil?'

'Not when their education is done correctly. I have had the pleasure of knowing Raven's teacher. He was one of the best and a skilled sorcerer.' Gabby tugs at the bedsheet, pulling it over my chest.

'So this sorceress can change them from solid stone back to flesh during the day?'

'Raven has many powers, one of which allows gargoyles to change to human form. They can change between stone sleep and gargoyle flesh without sorcery. Gargoyles are in stone sleep during the day where they repair and heal any wound that may have occurred the night before. They regain all their strength in stone sleep but if they haven't healed or gained their strength, they will be weaker than normal. Hence, Drake didn't have his full strength to fight Falcon and is devastated he couldn't protect you.'

'I don't blame him for this. I blame Falcon. He knew I was up there. He purposely tried to kill me,' I say, trying to slowly sit up. Gabby shakes her head, smiles and gently presses my shoulder back down on the bed. Her warm touch calms me.

'The dragons have been hunting Raven for years but she's talented enough to elude them. If they have control over her, she can disarm the gargoyles, rendering them helpless.'

'But I met Drake in human form. How does that work?'

'Raven has given each of them an orgle.' She lifts her hand. Her fingers hold a small colourful pebble. 'It's a magical stone which draws its powers from the earth. Gargoyles are nature-driven creatures. They wear them constantly, either in a necklace, ring or bracelet. They can draw on this power and change into human form at any time but they are only slightly stronger than the strongest human. It's the same for a dragon. It will be weaker in human form than in its natural dragon form.

'So if they don't have the "orgle" on them they can't turn into human form?'

'That is correct. They can also speak and understand several languages.' Gabby reaches over to a bowl and wrings out a wet sponge. She wipes the sides of my face, throat and chest. It's cool and smells of lavender.

'Do gargoyles have to turn to stone every day to reboot their systems?'

'No, they can walk around in human form but if an attack from the dragons occurs, they will not have the strength to fight. The dragons have a large family, spread around Australia and overseas. We never know how many to expect.'

'I don't mean to sound rude, but how can you and Malachi protect them?'

'It's written if any creature kills an angel their whole family will be taken to hell when the angel's soul is on its way to heaven. I have seen it happen and so has Falcon.

'He came to Australia, bringing his two cousins, Lazarus and Corbin, and met up with the Nogard Clan. Nogard took the lives of my parents and we watched as he and his family ignited into flames. Their souls were dragged below the earth by black ghostly spirits as my parents' angelic souls rose above the clouds. Because Falcon was not related to them in any way, he was safe but stayed here and took over their home with his father.'

'But Falcon tried to burn all of us, including you two,' I say, before lifting my arm for her to sponge.

'I found it disturbing that he attempted to burn my brother and me. He held no respect for his family by doing that. He must have been out of control with anger to attempt it.'

'Ah, that may be my fault. I constantly agitate him. Plus, I didn't give you two the potion.'

'It's not in your nature or your soul to do such an untrustworthy thing. You are here for greater things.' She smiles warmly.

'My soul? What do you mean greater things?'

'Jasmine!' shouts Drake, interrupting us. He runs into the room and drops to his knees to stare directly into my eyes. 'You're awake. That's great news.'

I study his face. There is no sign that he's been cut by Falcon's tail. I lift my hand to his face and trace where I saw him cut and bleeding. 'Your face, I saw Falcon slash it wide open.'

'I've been in stone sleep healing.' Drake smiles and moves his face so his lips are in the palm of my hand. He gently kisses my palm. 'I'm so sorry I dropped you. I should have protected you from them,' he says, bowing his head.

'Hey, you couldn't have done anything differently. They're too strong.'

'Like hell they are,' snaps a voice from behind Gabby.

'Jasmine, this is my eldest brother, Lysander,' says Drake. 'And my younger brother, Jarius, and beside him is my half-sister, Lolana.'

I lift my head to see the people he is introducing me to. Lysander is the same height as Drake with the same blue glowing eyes and brown hair. The others have similar features.

'Hello,' I squeak, feeling awkward with them staring at me.

'So you're the cattle thief,' spits Lolana.

'Thief! Me? I didn't steal any cows,' I say, feeling confused.

'No, you helped Lazarus herd them onto his property.'

'They were your cattle? I had no idea, he never said...'

'Well they *are* ours and we need them to survive. You're a thief.'

'Put your claws away, sis,' says Jarius, bumping her sideways. 'It's pretty funny when you think about it. You were rustling cattle and you didn't even know it.'

'Come on, everyone. Jasmine needs to rest. I'm sure there will be plenty of time to talk to her later,' says Gabby.

Lolana turns and walks out, with Jarius giving me a quick wave. Lysander nods his head on his exit.

'I'll sit here for a while, Gabby. You can go rest. And thank you for your hard work,' says Drake.

'Thank you, Gabby,' I add, smiling.

Thankfully, the room is quick to empty, leaving Drake and me alone to talk.

'I was so worried he would rip you to shreds for notifying us. When I saw you covered in blood, I expected the worse. Mind you, Gabby has been with you for several days and nights controlling a heightened temperature and cleaning your infected wounds. We were really worried about you.'

'Lazarus wouldn't have hurt me, not on purpose.' I try again to sit up but the pain forces me to stay lying on my back.

'You need to rest, Jasmine.' He runs his fingers over my forehead and down the side of my cheek. 'I wish I had done more to protect you. This is why I exist—to protect you.'

'Stop with the guilt trip!' I look into his glowing blue eyes for a long few seconds before I speak. 'Your mother is safe. I first saw her sitting in the dragons' lounge room. She was in stone sleep and looked mysteriously beautiful. Even Falcon said she was beautiful.'

'Huh!' he scoffs, rolling back his large shoulders.

'Oh, un-puff yourself. She doesn't want you to be a hero and rescue her. She has it under control.'

'If those overheated beasts touch her, I will—'

'Yes, they are quite warm.' I remember Lazarus' hand touching my waist and the heat from his body when close to me. Corbin also expelled a radiant of heat when I met him in his true dragon form.

'How close did you get to the beasts?' Drake's question drips with sarcasm.

I search his face, wondering why he's tone has changed. 'I

don't dislike them… except for Falcon. I could, with enjoyable ease, make a bag and matching shoes out of his hide.'

Drake laughs and relaxes. 'I should let you rest.'

'What part of the day is it?'

'Early morning.'

'Shouldn't all gargoyles be stone by now?'

'My family wanted to meet you in human form first. We thought you'd had enough excitement for a while. Waking up to four gargoyles staring down at you might stop that sweet heart of yours.' He smiles and stands.

'Don't tell me you can hear my heartbeat as well?'

'No, Jasmine. I look into your eyes. They are the window to your heart and soul.' He leans over to place his lips on my forehead. They are warm and soft.

'Your lips are warm. When I touched you that night under the trees you were cold,' I frown.

'I only had a few seconds to change from stone sleep to gargoyle to human. If I'd introduced myself as a gargoyle you'd have run screaming.'

'I probably would have stabbed you.'

'What, with the tiny twig you had in your small hands?' He laughs and I join him until the pain in my stomach stops me. 'You need to rest and I need to…'

'You need to sit on the roof and protect me,'

'Yes, I failed once and I won't fail again.'

I hold my hand up and he takes it in his. I pull it to my lips and kiss the back of his hand slowly. 'You didn't fail me, Drake. You took the brunt of Falcon's tail, not me. I'm here and I'm alive because of you.' He looks down with his magical blue eyes. 'Now go and turn into concrete,' I say with a cheeky tone. 'Or stone.' I wink.

'It's good to have you here again,' he says, leaving me to sleep.

'Again?' I question, but he's gone.

I MUST HAVE dozed off, waking late in the day. I slowly sit up, swivelling my legs out of the bed. I let any blood I have left circulate through my body before attempting to stand.

I gasp in pain when I pull myself into a vertical position. I take a deep breath and walk towards a long mirror.

I stagger backwards, trying to work out who it is I am looking at. Leaning forward, I touch the mirror to make sure it's me that is being reflected. My hand feels the cool glass but I'm shocked and bewildered at the person standing before me.

My brunette hair has a bright red streak running through it. I have black rings around my eyes and my skin is as pale as a ghost. I look to my legs and gasp out loud when I see my burnt legs. Gabby may be concerned about how my legs are healing but I'm horrified.

As my skin heals it's leaving a decorative mark, similar to what a tattooist would do if they were inking someone in white ink. The design is a vine growing up my legs, starting at my feet and finishing around my knees. It may be attractive as someone's wallpaper but not on my legs!

In a slow and anxious movement, I lift my top up, afraid of what I might see. There are six large puncture wounds on my stomach and several small ones. I spin around to see my back and find several more wounds.

There are no bandages or stitches but somehow they are knitting nicely together. Gabby has lacquered a brown ointment over each of them. I touch it with my index finger and lift it to my nose. I recognise the smell; it draws me back to fond memories of my grandfather.

Taking a deep breath, I wonder if I'm dreaming; a dream I can't control. Grabbing for my only comfort, I reach for my necklace. My pendant is gone! I search the bed, floor and benches trying to find it, with no luck.

My heart sinks and an uneasy feeling floods me. The necklace has been my security blanket for so many years and I fear my nightmares will return. Without my pendant, this may be a dream.

With steady legs, I cautiously head out of the bedroom, ready to investigate my surroundings. As I exit, I find myself on the top floor of the castle, the staircase narrowing as it leads to the roof. I grasp the hand-carved timber rail that leads elegantly up the staircase. I have a moment of déjà vu. I've touched this timber rail before and suddenly have an urge to jump on it and slide down it, even though I know I will get in trouble from my grandfather. I shake away the silly notion.

With a slow and steady climb, I eventually reach the door that leads out onto the roof, where there's one gargoyle in stone form, standing up on strong hind legs looking over the edge. The other gargoyles have positioned themselves at the opposite end.

I gingerly walk towards them, passing the broken guttering where I fell. I gulp and my heart thuds hard, reminding me I am still alive.

I walk up to the first gargoyle and it's not Drake, then the next, which I see is a female, so I presume it's Lolana.

'I know it was you that wanted me to bleed to death under the trees. Sorry to disappoint! Oh, what? No smart mouth comments? It's hard when you're a lump of concrete, hey Lolana?' I whisper as I pass by.

I reach Drake and run my hand over his large gothic wing. 'Hello, handsome. How has your day been?' He's standing tall and looking in the opposite direction. What a striking and powerful gargoyle he is and thankfully, one that would rather protect me than eat me.

I look around and the roof gives a heart-stopping three-hundred-and-sixty-degree view of rolling mountains and valleys. It is a magical and peaceful sight. I'm envious they get to witness this every day. I watch in awe as the sun drops behind the distant mountains.

I hear a large cracking sound like the sonic boom from a stock-whip. I look around and see Drake standing beside me in gargoyle form. I lean forward to see the other gargoyles standing and breathing, except Lolana. She stands in human form and moves in my direction.

'Call me concrete again and I will happily rip your head from your shoulders,' she spits.

Drake growls in his chest, which vibrates through his body, then pushes Lolana away.

'No, you won't, Lolana. You and your pathetic threat don't scare me,' I say, praying she can't hear my heart beating out of control.

Drake growls in his chest again and glares his darkening blue eyes down at me. I believe I have just been disciplined like a naughty child.

'Okay, I won't say another word.' I hold my hands up in defeat. I watch as she heads towards the open door. 'Rubble,' I murmur under my breath.

Lolana races back towards me, her eyes glowing navy blue, her features changing to black flesh and when she reaches me she is a full-blooded gargoyle.

'Do I scare you now huuumannnn?' She spits, towering over me.

I puff my petrified chest out. 'No gargoyle, you don't!'

'Enough!' bellows Drake. His chest is heaving up and down and his wings are held open wide, making him look the size and height of an elephant.

Lolana leaps to the edge of the roof and jumps off. Spreading her wings, she glides off into the darkening sky.

Jarius moves to the edge of the roof, spreads his wings

and lets out a growling chuckle before he jumps into the air and glides off in the same direction as Lolana. I join in the chuckle. I look up at Drake and instantly stop laughing due to his darkened eyes narrowing at me.

'Okay, okay, I'll stop,' I say with a smirk on my face. He shakes his head with a low rumble in his chest.

'Please remember you are a guest here,' says Lysander, standing in the doorway now in human form. 'I'd appreciate it if you didn't disparage the gargoyle race. We are made of stone, flesh, bone and blood. You are welcome to stay until you're well enough to travel.' He walks through the door, closing it behind him.

I blow out the breath I didn't know I was holding. I look up at Drake and he pulls his wings back in, folding them so they sit just behind his arms. He closes his eyes and takes a deep breath. I can see his flesh turning to a paler tone. He's changing form.

'No, don't change. Stay as you are, Drake. If you keep changing form it will weaken you. I will be devastated if something happened to you.'

He exhales and drops his head to look at me. 'Do I scare you?' His whisper has a hoarse tone.

'No, not at all. If anything, I believe the whole stone, muscle-bulging gargoyle winged thing is attractive.' I bump him in the arm with my shoulder, 'Ouch!' I should have realised he'd be solid rock.

'I don't think you can call gargoyles attractive.'

'Maybe you can't but I can. Anyhow, gargoyles and dragons have been a part of my life for a very long time. My mind uses them to help calm me. They protect me from any evil thoughts.'

'Come sit down,' he says, pointing his long fingers to a bench seat. I watch as he sits, lifting his massive wings over the back of the bench before doing so. I can't take my eyes off this magical creature. He tilts his head slightly sideways. 'I can change if it'll make you feel more comfortable.'

'Sorry, I didn't mean to stare. I've dreamt about you creatures for so long. I never really thought they existed. But here you are, living and breathing, with the occasion growl.'

'Lolana will come around. She's young,' he says, opening one of his wings when I sit beside him. He wraps it around me, and with a gentle draw, pulls me into him. 'Are you warm enough?'

'I am now, thank you. So what is her story?'

'Her family is in England. Her mother died at the hands of a dragon and her father sent her here so we can protect her, as she is his only child.'

'She must miss them?' I murmur, getting a sudden pinch to my heart, thinking of my parents back in Melbourne.

'I don't know, as she keeps her feelings hidden.'

'What about Lysander and Jarius?'

'They are my blood brothers. My father is in England at the moment, trying to calm a situation down. And you have met my mother, who is trapped at Nogard Hollow.'

'England! What situation is he calming?'

'A gargoyle clan has joined forces with one of the dragon clans. Unfortunately, the dragons double-crossed them and they are now either dead or trapped. I haven't heard from him for over a month.' He drops his head and his eyes start to glow a brighter blue.

I lift my feet up and snuggle comfortably into his wing. His wing expands then tightens to secure me to the seat and against his side.

I chuckle, making Drake flick his eyes to me.

'I'm starting to think Xandria may have sprinkled me with her magic dust many years ago and it's now wearing off. Every night I live this world, your world, in my dreams.' I watch for any reaction from Drake, but nothing. 'Are gargoyles tempted to eat humans?'

'You're safe, Jasmine. Humans are not on our menu.'

He lets out a growling chuckle. His chest rumbles. It increases in volume, vibrating throughout his body until a thunderous growl echoes out of his open jaw. I can see his lion-sharp teeth and feel the vibration tremble through his body and wings. I sit up with my mouth dropping open, staring at his natural beauty. He pants a few quick breaths then inhales one deep breath which seems to calm him. He draws me back in under his comforting wing.

'You scared the natural seed out of all the local birds.'

'The animals around here are used to it,' he snorts. 'You always make me laugh.'

'What do the dragons want with your mother?'

'You ask a lot of questions, Jazz.'

'Because you, my friend, have a lot of answers. Answer this last one and then you can ask me anything you want.'

'Our resident sorceress—'

'Raven?'

'Yes. She has taught my mother many of her sorcery secrets. The dragons have tried and failed to capture Raven. My mother was the next best thing. With the knowledge my mother has they can eliminate our clan.'

'But they can crush your mother while she's in stone sleep and take her soul. What do they want with your souls?'

'Hang on, it's my turn to ask the questions. We had a deal.'

'Weren't you taught it's polite to let the lady win?'

'No.'

'Fine, grumpy pants, ask away.'

'What brings you here?'

'Many things.' Drake frowns; he was expecting more of an

answer. I inhale deeply before speaking. 'I want to escape, be free of my nightmares. I want to learn how to control them instead of them controlling me. I want to forgive and to be forgiven and to stop feeling guilty. I want that warm feeling inside when you have a friend you can trust. I haven't felt anything in a very long time.'

'You can trust the angels and gargoyles and I know you can't trust a dragon.'

'Lazarus didn't mean to hurt me. I could see it in his eyes. He was sorry.'

'Why are you protecting him?' he snaps.

'Because I like him. But only in human form.'

Drake huffs, growls and looks away.

'Just as much as I like you,' I confess, elbowing him in his hard side, then wishing I hadn't. 'Ouch, you are made of rock!'

'Stonnnne,' he rumbles, and I giggle. 'The marks that are forming on your legs, do you know what they are?'

'I'm at a total loss but Gabby said she will ask Raven to have a look.'

I stretch out one of them. The burns have completely healed but instead of scars I now have a white vine running up and around my leg from my ankle to my knee. I gasp and pull out my other leg. It's matching, with the vine taking over my lower leg.

'Oh no! My legs are ugly. I'd rather have the burn marks.'

'I think they are very attractive.' I search his face but I can't tell if he is smiling or not. 'They remind me of Raven's markings, except hers are black and they are on her face.'

'Oh, the poor thing to have this on her face,'

'Drake, I am sorry to interrupt. But Jasmine should rest,' says Gabby, standing in front of the rooftop door.

'I left my mother at home, Gabby.' I'm annoyed I'm being told to go to bed at the age of twenty-five.

'Yes, you did, but you are in my care until your health is better.'

'Give me a minute and I'll be in.'

'One minute, Jasmine,' she says harmoniously, before leaving.

'Ooh, I hate being told what to do,' I say, jumping up, forgetting I have open wounds on my stomach. 'Ouch!'

'She's trying to help you, Jazz.'

Drake stands so I step back just in case his large frame knocks me. 'I know, Dad.'

'Now who's grumpy?'

'Fine, bend down so I can kiss you goodnight.'

Drake kneels on one large knee, his clawed toes scraping the tarred roof. He is still a monster of a size when kneeling and I notice he has rolled his sharp fingernails up into loose-fisted balls. He must be nervous about scratching me or worse, slicing off my entire hand, as the end of his fingers are as sharp-looking as the dragons' toes.

I approach him with confidence, wrapping my arms around his rock-hard neck and holding him tight. He unravels his wings, wrapping them around me, then gives a gentle squeeze. The hum of the night critters is drowned out, as is the whole world, blocked out by his large protective wings. In the confined space he has created I can hear my heart beating, or maybe it's his?

I lean back and look into his glowing blue eyes and kiss his cheek softly and slowly. 'Goodnight, handsome. Thanks again for saving me,' I whisper, moving out of his protective hold.

'I will always protect you.' He opens his large wings, releasing me from his cocoon embrace. Before I walk through the door he murmurs, 'Sleep well, my sweet Jasmine.'

'I guarantee I will, especially when I dream of gargoyles and dragons.' I grab for my pendant then remember I'd lost it. I fear my night's sleep won't be as pleasant as I had hoped.

Gabby has me tucked in bed after she applies another layer of brown ointment to my wounds. I want to question her further about the lifestyles of the gargoyles but my eyelids close and so does my mouth.

CHAPTER FIVE

'WE NEED TO *hide here until I can figure out what to do,' says Sky, her voice full of fear.*

'I don't understand! What happened to Grandfather? Why did Attor do that?'

'Greed! He wants something that is not his and Grandfather wanted to do the right thing and return it to the rightful owner. He was a good man who kept peace amongst all creatures.'

'I'm scared, Sky.'

'I know you are. So am I. We need to stay hidden until it's safe to leave.'

'Will Attor kill us?'

'I will protect you. I always have and I always will. You will be so powerful one day, more powerful than Grandfather and me. You must remember to keep your powers positive.'

'I don't understand. What powers?'

'Promise me if you choose this path you will stay true to yourself and stay positive.'

'I promise.'

I wake startled and twisted up in my bedsheets. I unravel my body to find Malachi sitting on the end of my bed.

'Hello, Jasmine, how are you feeling today?' He smiles that perfect white-toothed smile. Both he and Gabby could be on the front cover of a beauty magazine. Their movements are graceful, their voices harmonic and their looks hypnotic. There is a calm and peace when they're in my presence, drawing me to them.

'Great. Um, did you say today?'

'Yes, you have been asleep for two days. The medicine we

use makes your body rest to help it heal.'

'Two days?'

Gabby walks in with a plate of fresh fruit which she hands to Malachi. *Oh Lord, please let him handfeed me*, I silently pray.

'Morning! I have breakfast for you, Jasmine. Your wounds have almost healed. I'm very impressed with your recovery,' she says, walking back out the room.

'Um, good morning and goodbye.' I'm confused with her quick entrance and exit.

'She is heading upstairs to guard the gargoyles,' Malachi says, answering my silent question. 'I'll let you get up and eat. There are fresh clothes on the chair. I hope they are satisfactory.' He stands to leave.

My mind yells, 'Don't leave. Handfeed me, please.' But when my vocal cords rattle the only word that comes out is, 'Thanks.'

I eat every scrap of fruit and slip into a pair of jeans and a t-shirt which are a good fit. I walk up the stairs and out onto the roof. Drake is in the same position he was in the other day.

I turn to the first gargoyle. 'Good day to you, Lysander.'

Then I walk passed Jarius. 'Enjoying the sunshine, Jarius?' I whisper close to his ear, then run my hand over his head.

I walk up to Lolana and stop in front of her. I take in her stone sleep features. She is a little smaller than the others but she looks just as mean. I think about my parents and how much I miss them and decide to not make any disrespectful remarks. 'Hey, Lolana. I'm sorry about yesterday. I hope there are no hard feelings.'

'Good morning, Drake!' I wrap my arms around his overly large waist, trying and failing to give him a hug.

Strolling around the roof I take in the never-ending views, stopping when I spot Blue Boy in a paddock below. A person draped in a black cape is patting him. It looks like the same person who was on the roof the night Falcon attacked.

I race inside the castle, skip down the three flights of stairs and run for the entry. I pull the large door open and head out to Blue and the mysterious person in black.

'Hello,' I yell, keeping my distance, as I'm not sure what breed of creature is under the cape. 'Are you Raven?'

'Yes.'

'I need to thank you for the ointment you gave Gabby for my wounds.'

'You're welcome,' she says, not turning around, but still patting Blue.

'His name is Blue Boy. He's my horse.'

'I know his name. I remember him when he was just a foal.'

The creature turns around with a graceful spin. Her head is low and looking down. She lifts her hands and slowly pulls back the cape's hood, revealing her face.

I buckle over as if an imaginary fist has punched me hard in the stomach. Keeping my eyes on Raven, I open my mouth and force the air back into my lungs before I pass out. I slowly straighten, shaking my head before taking a longer look at the person standing before me.

She lifts her arm as if drawing a half circle over us.

'Sky?' my voice quivers. 'You're alive?'

'Yes, cousin. I am.'

'How can this be?' I stagger forward and touch her hand, gasping a sobbing gulp. 'I've cried myself to sleep wondering what happened to you.'

'I know you did and I'm sorry.' She opens her arms wide. I leap forward and fling my arms around her thin body. I squeeze her tight then pull back, trying to comprehend what I am seeing.

'It's me, Jazzle Dazzle.' She smiles.

As soon as I hear those words, I know it's my long-lost cousin, Sky. She and my grandfather gave me that nickname.

No one else knows it. 'It really is you, Sky!'

'Please don't cry. I will explain everything. Come sit.'

Sky sits down in the lush pasture from which Blue Boy never lifts his greedy head. I follow suit, still holding onto her arm. I don't want this dream to run away. 'I haven't seen you for over fourteen years. Where have you been? And why did you tattoo your face?'

'It's a long story and one you may find hard to believe but I need to explain it in great detail because you coming here has put your life in jeopardy.'

'Have you seen the puncture wounds on my torso? I think I'm already in trouble, cuz.' My fingers are still wrapped around her arm in fear this may be a dream.

'I promise I won't go anywhere.' She smiles and I reluctantly let go of her.

'Do you believe all this? I mean the dragons and the gargoyles, not to forget the angels and fairies?'

'Deep down, you have always known it to be true.'

'I dream of them every night. I thought they only lived in my head. Now seeing them in flesh and blood… it is so surreal.'

'I removed this from your neck when I was helping Gabby take care of you.' She holds my necklace in her hand. 'I didn't want anyone asking you where it came from.' She places it in my hand.

I flip it over my head to sit perfectly on my chest, where it has been for the last fourteen years. 'I found it one day when I was playing in Grandfather's room not long after he died and you disappeared.'

'You didn't just find it, Jazzle. I put it there for you to find. It keeps the positive memories alive and squashes the negative.'

'That makes sense. Gabby tells me you're a sorceress.'

'Grandfather was a sorcerer, just like I am. And just like you if you choose to be.'

'Me, a sorceress?'

'Let me explain everything, then you can ask questions,' she says, leaning over to caress my hand. Her gentle touch is warm, which reassures me she is real. 'Before Grandfather died, he was training me to understand the power I had inherited. You and I would go with him to visit local clans of both dragon and gargoyles. They were at peace with each other back then. As my powers became stronger, his started to diminish. We believe it was due to his age.

'Grandfather died at the hands of a dragon; one he considered a friend. It was unfortunate his death happened in front of us both. You closed off your feelings and had terrible nightmares. I saw the same dragon in human form in our local area and I knew he was hunting me.

'I had to leave to draw attention away from you and to protect myself. I watched from afar the pain you went through every night as you tried to sleep, so I returned and left you an orgle stone which I wrapped up in a sterling silver vine. I knew you would find it as you ventured into Grandfather's room to feel close to him. When you put it around your neck all the nightmares disappeared and the positive thoughts of the creatures reappeared in dream form.

'Your mother also has sorcery in her blood, but she chooses not to tap into it and refuses to believe in anything but human.'

'Who killed Grandfather?' It's the only question I want answered.

'If you can't remember what happened, it doesn't matter. Grandfather wouldn't want any form of revenge taken and by the look in your eyes, that's exactly what you want.'

'Why am I in danger?'

'If the dragons know the power you possess, they'll use it to disarm the gargoyles. They will do anything to make you join their clan.'

'Lazarus wouldn't do that. He isn't like Falcon.'

'You are either finding trust again or you have feelings for Lazarus.' She lifts her eyebrow, scrutinising me.

'I like him and I like Corbin, as I do the gargoyles. I have no ill-feeling towards any of them.'

'You always had a good heart, Jazzle, but now you need a sensible heart and a clear head.'

'Apparently, my heart gives off sounds the dragons enjoy.' I snigger. 'But I'm learning to control it when I need to.'

'If you decide to stay you will need to master that, and quickly.'

'As soon as you recognised me, I cast a silencing spell over us so no one can hear us. There are too many eyes and ears around. I can teach you how to do this and to remove your scent from the dragons' nose and many more wonderful things.'

'You must always keep your heart and soul pure, even if you leave. If you choose to move on, I can make it so you wake up thinking this is all a dream.'

'Why do the dragons want the souls of the gargoyles?'

'Falcon's father was beside his best friend when he died. He was a gargoyle. When he died, his body crumbled to ash, except his soul. It lay there in pure solid gold. He stole it instead of letting it rest in the gargoyle vault where we reincarnate it into the next newborn gargoyle soul.

'Falcon's father has infused it into Falcon to take as many gargoyle souls as he can get, for purely selfish reasons—to admire the gold. Sadly, Falcon obeys his father even though he has fled to England.'

'It seems a lot of creatures have fled to England.'

'The problem is they will return here and we need to be ready to protect Elyograg Castle.'

'Let me talk to Lazarus. I believe he will listen.'

'No, Jasmine. You can't go anywhere near them. One sniff

and they will trap you there for life, or worse, kill you.'

The panic in her voice tells me I should listen to her. 'Okay. Relax, Sky… or Raven, as everyone else calls you.'

'You must call me Raven. You must never have any link to your home or to your family. They will use it against us.'

'Tell me about the tattoo marks on your face and the ones forming on my legs.'

'It's hereditary; Grandfather had it on his chest. Can't you remember it? You would trace it with your little fingers. He'd lecture us, saying the day we received our markings is when we need to choose our life's path. Mine were white, like yours, and when I cast my first spell it changed to black.'

'Yes, I remember Grandfather's. The more you explain the more flashbacks and memories return.'

'Because you're allowing your mind to open to everything you've seen and heard.'

Blue Boy walks over and gives me a firm nudge. 'Ouch, Blue. Mind my wounds.'

'We should head inside. We have four pairs of gargoyle eyes staring down at us and they will soon be awake.'

'Does anyone know who you are or who you were?'

'Yes, the angels know everything, but they won't speak about it as they know it may put us in jeopardy. Plus, Lysander knows,' she adds with a shy smile.

'Lysander? Why him?'

She drops her eyes to the ground and blushes.

'Sky Pie, you cheeky little devil! You are getting it on with the eldest gargoyle!'

'He is a great guy… creature. Maybe you should try it yourself.' She flicks her eyes over my shoulder. I turn my head to see Drake walking towards us in human form. His biceps are bulging out of his tight t-shirt and his powerful blue eyes are bright against the background of green grass.

'You never know, I might.'

'Let me talk to Lysander regarding our relationship. He will guide us in whether to tell the others or not.' She flicks her eyes to Drake then back to me. 'Do you want to stay here where I can teach you everything you need to know?'

I shrug my shoulders.

'Remember, you can walk away and turn all this into a dream.'

'I'm not sure if I want to fight this battle.'

'Our family has fought to keep peace amongst the creatures for centuries. We are born for this world.'

'My head isn't in a good place. I'm carrying so much negative baggage of my own. I can't see how I can help.'

'You were drawn here for a reason. Maybe it's time to stop running and start standing up for something.'

'Can I have time to think about it? I don't want to lose you again but I need to make sure I'm here for the right reasons.' My skin chills as visions of why I left home flash before me. My unfaithful ex-boyfriend and best friend, Kelly, together!

My skin cools further, lifting the hairs on my arms, when I recall the traumatic affect my Grandfather's death had on me and Sky's disappearance.

My skin starts to warm, settling the hairs on my arm, when I picture my parents, Sky, Lazarus and Drake.

Drake jumps the paddock fence in one swift masculine leap and walks over to us.

'I wish I could wrap my arms around you, but I will wait until we are alone again. I missed you so much, Sky... um, Raven. I love you and Grandfather more than you will ever know.' A tear sneaks down my cheek.

'I know because I love you just as much and it killed me seeing you in pain.' She stands up as Drake arrives. 'Evening, Drake.' She smiles. 'It was lovely speaking with you, Jasmine. I need to track down Lysander so I will see you both later.'

Drake moves into my personal space.

'Good evening, Drake' I lift my head up to see his face.

He leans down and swiftly kisses my lips.

'Wow, what was that for?'

'I stood up on the roof watching you and Raven sit talking all afternoon. As soon as I could, I wanted to put my lips on yours.' He leans forward to kiss me again but this time it's slower and softer.

I blush and drop my head. 'You shouldn't have changed form. It leaves you vulnerable.'

'The others are staying unchanged so I can be with you in this form. It was nice what you said to Lolana. I know she appreciated it.'

My eyes shoot over to the castle where Lysander and Raven are talking. He towers over her small frame. He whips his head up and looks directly at me. I lift my hand and wave innocently, shrugging my shoulder as if to apologise for being a sorceress.

'How are you feeling today?'

'Good, thanks. Do you have your orgle on you?'

'Yes, how do you know about that?'

'Gabby told me about them.'

He holds up his hand, and there, embedded into a silver ring, is the same opal-looking stone I have around my neck.

'For a moment I thought Raven had been revealing her secrets. She is very tight-lipped when it comes to her spells. Even when she was training my mother they'd hide away for days on end.'

'Yes, I got the feeling she likes to be alone.' I'm glad he can't hear my heart skipping a lying beat.

'What were you two talking about? You were both very engrossed.'

'I asked questions about gargoyles and the dragons.' He

raises his eyebrow and I see another question coming so I quickly add, 'And girl stuff.'

'Oh, right. Well, I can answer questions you may have about us,' he says before turning away and walking over towards Blue Boy. 'He's getting a big belly eating this lush grass.'

'I'm hoping to go for a ride on him tomorrow. I'd love to explore this side of the mountain.' I run my hand over Blue Boy's soft coat.

'You should ask Gabby, to make sure you're well enough.' With one large step, he is back in front of me, holding the top of my arms, squaring me to him.

'I know my body better than anyone and I'm fine. I don't know how long I will be here. Lysander made it crystal clear he doesn't want me here. Plus, I don't want to miss out on seeing your countryside from the ground.'

'I'll talk to Lysander. You are our guest and can stay as long as you want, Jasmine.' He bends his head, lowering so his face is only inches away from mine.

I gulp and desperately try to calm my rapid breathing, but I can see out of the bottom of my eye that my chest is rising and falling at a great speed. I know he sees it too and he gives me a sexy smile. Drake releases my arms to slide his large hands around my back, pulling me into his muscled frame. Oh, boy!

I move my hands in unison to glide up the back of his arms. My heart is beating so hard I'm waiting for it to pop out my mouth. I haven't been passionately kissed by a guy since my ex-cheater-of-a-boyfriend but for some reason, I want Drake to kiss me. He looks back and forth between my two blue eyes. Is he waiting for a signal from me before he kisses me or does he need a rock to fall on his head to start the motion?

'You are a stunning woman, Jazz,' he purrs, close to my lips, too close without touching.

'Shut up and kiss me,' I whisper.

He presses his soft lips against mine. His arms tighten and he presses them again but this time his touch and kiss are more passionate. Drake's short facial stubble is tickling my face, adding to the sensation.

After a few long, heated seconds, he pulls back and searches my face.

'You kiss the same way humans do.'

'Yes, we do.' He chuckles.

'Does everything *else* work the same way as it does for humans?'

He throws his head back as if to look at the stars and chuckles. It vibrates through his toned body, the body I'm still clinging to. 'Yes, Jazz. Everything works the same.'

'Wow, Sky is one talented sorceress to conjure up that spell.'

'Sky?' Drake's expression alters with a frown crowding his brow.

'Oh, I meant Raven,' I squeak, but his frown remains. 'Let's go have something to eat. I haven't eaten since early this morning.' I reach up with both hands and pull his face to mine to kiss his soft lips once more. He takes heed and pulls me into him, accepting my invitation to kiss me passionately.

Eventually, I pull back and try to calm my increasing libido. 'Food!' I smile before I lose control and try to find out for myself how his human form works.

With a slow stroll, we walk hand in hand into the castle. He shows me around and I am in awe of what I see. There are a dozen bedrooms, all elegantly decorated with four-poster beds and lounges. It's set up like a hotel waiting for guests to arrive.

We arrive at the enormous kitchen which I only got a quick glance at last time I was in here. It's industrial; one you'd find out the back of a restaurant.

Drake opens the large walk-in refrigerator and it has

wall-to-wall food, with meat sliced and packaged, and fresh vegetables and fruit. He's proud when explaining that the vegetables and fruits grown here are all thanks to the two angels.

'They tend to the five-acre garden daily but often get called away if they sense a threat is coming and they need to be on the rooftop with us gargoyles,' he says. 'Unfortunately, the angels can't fly up to the roof and have to run up the stairs like you do. They are delicate creatures similar to the human race but with pure and unconditional souls, so they always do right by living creatures.'

We pull out several steaks and throw them onto the large sizzling hotplate. While cutting up vegetables we are soon inundated by the other gargoyles.

'Damn, human, that smells good. Can you throw some on for me?' says Jarius, standing behind me in gargoyle form. He moves in behind me, wraps his large wings around me and gives a gentle squeeze. 'Please, Jazzy.'

'Sure thing, Jarius.' I smile. But before I can open the refrigerator door Lolana enters. This massive kitchen doesn't feel as big when the gargoyles are in their true form.

'Could you add me to the list? Please, Jasmine,' she murmurs, her head dropping low.

'Sure can, Lolana. Should I cook for Lysander and Raven?'

'No, they have taken food into Raven's room.'

'Oh, she lives here?' I try to recall if Raven mentioned it in our afternoon conversation.

'She does but when those two talk we can't hear a word of it. She has a spell that puts a silent dome over her and anyone near her. Like today, when you and she were cosy on the grass talking. We couldn't hear a word you were saying.' Lolana looks straight at me as if to ask me what we were talking about.

I look around the kitchen and three pairs of eyes are staring at me. 'Nothing that will interest you guys. Just girl stuff.' I chuckle because suddenly the boys glowing blue eyes are awkwardly looking anywhere but at me. I love how that can shut grown men down, even big tough gargoyles. Lolana smiles and nods. She gets the hint—I don't want to repeat the conversation I had with Raven.

Drake and I busy ourselves cutting vegetables and fruit, and cooking the sumptuous inch-thick steaks. I lay it out on the dining table and we sit together to eat. Lolana and Jarius change form to human while eating.

The table talk has us laughing and, by the end of the meal, I feel more at home with these creatures than I did with friends I've known for over ten years. I don't need to live in my head, in my dreams, to be accepted here. It is refreshing to just be *me*.

Lolana, Jarius and Drake change form to perch themselves on the rooftop while I happily clean the kitchen.

'Jasmine, I was hoping to talk to you alone,' says Lysander, entering the kitchen with Raven two feet behind him.

'Sure. Can I make you a cup of herbal tea? I was just making myself one.'

'Thank you. That will be great.' He nods.

I look to Raven and hear her say, *'Thank you, yes.'* But her lips don't move. I frown and she lifts her index finger to her lips. I shake my head and think, *Did I hear Sky speak telepathically?* She nods and I hear, *'There's so much you need to learn, cousin.'*

I smile, wondering why I'm taking this all so calmly. I continue to make two extra cups of tea.

Raven lifts her arm and waves a half-circle above her head.

'Raven tells me you are her cousin,' says Lysander, getting straight to the point.

'Yes, that's true.'

'She wants to train you, here, at Elyograg Castle. She has mentioned you haven't decided whether to tap into your sorcery side.'

'A lot has happened since leaving home. A careful and well-thought-out decision needs to be made.'

'I understand that. You are welcome to stay here as long as you wish. We welcome your kind with open arms. What we have is yours.'

'My kind? I'm human, Lysander. Nothing more and nothing less.'

'*We are more than just human, Jasmine,*' Sky's voice echoes in my head.

'Sky, get out of my head!'

'Raven!' growls Lysander. 'You will put your parents and relatives in danger if you call her anything but Raven.'

'The dragons know me as Jasmine and they have questioned me about where I'm from and why I'm travelling,' I say. 'Oh no! I've mentioned I was from suburban Melbourne. Have I put Mum and Dad in danger?'

'I will send word to be on the lookout. But your parents refuse to acknowledge our kind or the existence of any creatures. This is a good thing. The dragons will sense they know nothing and move on,' says Raven.

'Take as long as you want to make your decision but keep close by the castle in case the dragons have worked out who you are,' adds Lysander.

'They would have attempted to grab her if they knew. Plus, the medicine running through her veins will mask her scent. I think she is safe for now, but you should stay close, just in case,' says Raven.

They both stand, with Lysander nodding as he leaves. Raven smiles at me and enters my headspace again, '*I missed you, Jasmine.*'

'*I don't want to lose you again Sky, um, Raven, but I need to think hard about this,*' I echo in my head. She nods and leaves me to finish cleaning the dishes.

After finishing up in the kitchen I join the gargoyles on the roof. The three of them are growling with laughter when I walk up in between them. 'What's so funny?'

'We appreciated you cooking dinner for us, but I suppose we should have let you know one little steak doesn't do it for us. We eat at least three or four,' says Lolana with a boisterous giggle.

'Oh, boy! I had trouble finishing one piece. They were huge.' I laugh, rubbing my swollen belly. 'I should have realised. I mean, look at the size of you guys.'

We sit on the rooftop sharing stories of their lives and mine. I lay back in Drake's warm wing, staring at the countless numbers of stars. Uninterrupted by the city lights, they shine so brightly.

My eyelids drop and before I know it, I am being tucked into bed. I half-open my eyes to see Drake pulling the top blanket over me.

'Did I fall asleep?' I murmur.

'Yes, gorgeous, you did. I carried you down.'

'You should have woken me. I would have walked.'

'You looked so peaceful. Plus, you're as light as a feather, Jazz. Go to sleep and I will see you in the morning.' He kisses my forehead before leaving.

Chapter Six

I wake with a spring in my step, surprising Gabby, who is bringing my breakfast up the stairs.

I take the plate filled with fresh fruit and head for the rooftop. The four gargoyles are in the same position. I presume they have their own spot to sleep as dogs do.

I chuckle, keeping my lips sealed as I don't think they'd appreciate me calling them well-trained dogs. I greet everyone along the way and stop squarely in front of Drake.

'Good morning. Stay in stone sleep. I'm happy to sit beside you and enjoy the view,' I whisper, reaching up to kiss his cheek. I sit at the base of his feet and lean back on his strong sturdy legs to eat my breakfast.

The sun is shining, warming my skin, making my pores open to accept its rays. I love spring and can't wait to saddle Blue Boy and head out exploring.

On completing my breakfast, I saddle Blue Boy and am on my way to discover this magical land. I stay close to the base of the mountain so I don't get lost, even though the size of the castle makes it hard to miss. We hook up to the creek and dawdle along its snake-shaped line.

My friendly wedge-tailed eagle has decided to visit. He flies overhead and at one stage, lands close by to watch me clean out a stone from one of Blue's hooves.

'Hello, big fella! I haven't seen you for a while and boy, do I have stories to tell you.' He moves cautiously towards me, flicking his head side to side, always on alert.

I sit cross-legged on the ground, letting Blue Boy graze,

and blurt out everything that has happened. Amazingly, the eagle stands still, except for his twitching head. Only after I have finished my long story does he fly away. For some silly reason, I'm relieved for venting to him.

A cool breeze blows over me, letting me know the day is coming to an end. I should head back before dark. On a loose rein, Blue Boy treks back along the track we'd previously made, sneaking a mouthful of tall grass as he goes. I close my eyes and let my mind go blank, tilting my head to the sky so I can soak in the last of the sun's rays on my face.

Blue Boy stops dead still, his ears pricked and his head held high. He has spotted something under a group of trees next to the creek. I gather my reins in case he shies and takes flight.

I spot two people under the tree in a romantic embrace. Blue Boy breathes out a loud neigh and they both turn and see me. I recognise them both but am bewildered. A dragon and a gargoyle together?

I stare in disbelief. Lolana and Corbin? Corbin keeps his eyes on me, his posture growing taller. He takes off running, faster than the wind, in my direction. I panic and give a hard yank on the reins. I spin Blue Boy around and jab my heels into his sides. He leaps into a frantic canter but before he can get his third stride in, he stops and rears. I lean forward grabbing for his mane so I don't fall off his back. He lands and I see Corbin standing in front of me.

'Jasmine?' he says, with doubtful eyes. 'You died. We saw you drop to the ground dead. Your scent disappeared but I can smell you and hear your healthy heartbeat.'

'Dead? My heart is very healthy and I'd like to keep it pumping that way, Corbin.' I pat Blue Boy's neck to calm his shaking and rapid heartbeat. I don't want him to think he sounds delicious and take a chunk out of him.

'I wasn't thinking about your heart that way, but I am now

you mention it. You know you can trust me. I showed you that in the cave.'

'I do trust you.' I shock myself when the words pass my lips.

'Lazarus is devastated. He thought he killed you when he carried you. He presumed he punctured a lung or worse, your heart. But I can hear it.'

'Yes, we have already concluded you can hear my heart beating. I'd be happier if we got off the topic.'

He nods.

'Would you like to explain what you two were doing? And I don't mean the kissing side of it. Trust me; I can work that part out. I mean a dragon and gargoyle duo.'

'We've been together for the last twelve months. Plain and simple, I love her and she loves me. But neither of us can divulge this to our families.'

'Have you tried to talk to them? I think Lazarus will understand.'

'Are you kidding me? He'd love to get his hands on her soul.'

'No, I believe you're wrong. It's Falcon you need to worry about. Lazarus will stand by you.'

'You don't know them the way I do.'

'I know Falcon wanted me dead and tried his bloody hardest to do it, but Lazarus stopped him. I'm here because of him and the angels' medicine.'

'I don't know what spell you've cast over Lazarus but he is obsessed with you. He hasn't eaten since your death.'

'Hello, I am alive. Flesh, blood and beating heart, remember?' I lift my arms out wide.

'Yes, thanks for reminding me.' He smirks and licks his lips. 'He hasn't spoken a word to anyone and if he doesn't eat soon, he will deteriorate and Falcon won't have a useless dragon living around him. He will finish him off as he is useless to the clan in that state.'

'Falcon will kill his own cousin? I need to go see him, show him I am not dead. But what if Lazarus suddenly feels hungry and I'm the closest thing to his mouth, especially if he hasn't eaten in such a long time?'

'We still have several cows on the land, and he knows that. I don't think he will attack you. He cares for you as I do Lolana.'

'Ah, yes the cows. Remind me to discuss that particular subject with him. Speaking of Lolana, where did she go?'

'She ran back to the castle. She's worried you'll tell her family, or worse, Raven.'

'Why is she scared of Raven?'

'She can take the orgle from her, then we wouldn't be able to be together in human form,' he says running his hands through his hair. 'It would be very difficult to have a relationship with a gargoyle. We could never…'

'No need to explain, I understand. Let me talk to Lolana when I get back but right now, I need to see Lazarus to bring him out of his depression. I don't trust Falcon and nor should you, cousin or not.'

I gather up my reins and kick Blue Boy forward. 'Why does Falcon call you brothers when you are only cousins?'

'As brothers, we must follow his orders but as cousins, not so much.'

'What a control freak!'

'If you knew his father, you'd understand why Falcon is the way he is. I'll run ahead and keep Falcon entertained but he will sense you, just as I did. You won't have much time before he comes to find you and Lazarus isn't strong enough to protect you. Jasmine, you're taking a big risk.'

'You didn't hear me until I was under your nose. Falcon won't be expecting me and apparently, my scent has changed.'

'My senses were overloaded with… Lolana. Falcon is clear-headed no matter what he is doing. He will sense you.'

'And if I don't go to see Lazarus, Falcon could kill him. So I have no choice.'

'Can I ask you why you care for him so much?'

'Maybe he cast a spell over me.'

'Be careful, Jasmine. I can only help you to a certain extent. Falcon is my leader and I must obey.'

'If he tells you to jump off a cliff will you do it?'

'Yes, we jump from high surfaces all the time.'

'I mean in human form, Corbin.'

'No, of course not.'

'Right! Because it's dangerous and wrong. Think for yourself, Corbin, and do what's right. Come on, let's go. I'll race you.' I smile and he's gone in a flash.

I keep my leg on Blue Boy, asking him for a constant firm canter. My head is telling me to turn back towards Elyogarg Castle and get help from the gargoyles but my heart is telling me that Lazarus needs me and only me. I came out today for a ride to clear my head but now it's filling with more unanswered questions.

By going to see Lazarus am I deciding to stay? And why do I care that he is miserable? Do I have feelings for him or am I under a spell? I kissed Drake last night and, for a reason that baffles me, I want to kiss Lazarus as well. Crikey! I bet it's the water I drank! I knew I should have boiled it!

Walking up to the house I have my heart in my hand and try desperately to inhale through my nose and exhale out my mouth to calm my nerves. Falcon will smell me a mile away with the large amount of adrenaline racing through me.

I see Corbin near the corral and he waves for me to go to him. 'Falcon's grazing on a cow out the back so he's not expecting you, but you need to move quickly. Lazarus is in the cave where you first met me. Please be quick. I will take Blue for you.' He grabs the reins from my hands and gently pushes me towards the house.

I run into the house and head straight for the two large doors. I try to push one of them open, but they are extremely heavy and I can only open it enough to slide through. It's dark and I pray I'm not near the edge of the cave as I don't know how far the drop is.

'Lazarus,' I whisper and listen for any noise. Nothing. 'Lazarus,' I say louder. Still nothing. I take a deep breath and yell, 'Lazarus, its Jasmine! I am alive.'

A sudden deafening roar and a gust of wind vibrates my body. I don't move. I can hear someone breathing beside me and I pray it isn't Falcon.

'Lazarus, it's Jasmine.' The snout of a dragon breathes me in, then a flame shoots from its mouth to light the torches. I freeze so I don't get burnt and am glad when I turn to see Lazarus beside me.

'Oh, thank heavens it's you. I haven't been well enough to come to see you. Plus, I don't think Falcon has the welcome mat rolled out for me.'

He moves so his wide green eye is beside me.

'Corbin says you haven't been eating. Falcon will rip shreds off you, or worse, kill you.'

I look into his eye and move my hand slowly to run it over his large red scales. 'I wish you would turn into human form. I really need to talk to you. Plus, I'm worried you might eat me if you're hungry.'

He steps back and breathes me in again, then opens his mouth. I panic and take a step back. He lowers his head.

It dawns on me that he wants me to trust him, so I step forward and he opens his razor-sharp mouth. With a gentle touch, I run my hand over his large teeth. His tongue skims my fingers. I stand still and look into his eye. He blinks and I know he is controlling himself.

I stand in front of his two large nostrils, open my arms wide and lean forward to hug his scaled nose. I instantly get the same warmth I did when he was human. 'You're so warm, Lazarus, please eat.' I rub his head before adding, 'But not me, okay? I have enough puncture wounds in me.'

With that he takes off, distinguishing the torches. I am standing in total darkness. I slide my foot backwards and pray that I am going in the right direction to reach the door. I jump and gasp when a warm hand reaches out and touches me.

'You are alive,' says Lazarus. He moves so his body in alignment with mine, the heat intense. 'I thought you were dead. I thought I'd killed you.'

'You gave me a few extra holes but I'm recovering. Can we move to another room with light? I want to see your face.'

Before either of us could move, the double doors fly open and Falcon stands square-shouldered in the middle. 'Smells like we have someone for dinner,' he purrs.

'I thought you'd be full after mauling a cow,' I snap.

Lazarus grabs my hand, giving it a gentle squeeze. Is he reminding me he hasn't eaten and won't be strong enough to fight Falcon if I need his help? Or have I got it wrong and he will never go against Falcon?

'You eat meat. What's the difference?' Falcon says, wiping his lips with his hand then picking something from his teeth.

'Humans kill them humanely, not savagely, like you.' I turn to Lazarus, 'Can we go somewhere to talk in private, please?'

'Of course.' He guides me past Falcon, who refuses to move.

'I haven't finished with you yet, Jasmine. You need to answer for what happened the other day!'

'I need to answer questions? What about you shooting flames at me and making me fall from the roof? I don't need to answer to you. You should be the one answering questions!'

'How dare you defy me in my house!'

'Shut up, Falcon!' yells Lazarus, pushing me towards the same bedroom I was in before.

'Oh brother, you better remember who you're talking to,' snarls Falcon.

'Correction, he is your cousin, not your brother, you control freak!'

'It sounds like someone has been telling stories. I'd be interested to find out what else you know.'

'I've got nothing to say to you, you overheated, oversized snake.' Lazarus pushes me into the bedroom before I spray more insults at Falcon.

'Put a leash on your pet, Lazarus, or I will. She is not to leave until I say so,' he says.

Lazarus closes the door and pushes me up against the wall. His hands are holding my face. 'If thinking you were dead didn't nearly kill me, I can guarantee you smart mouth will.' He looks exhausted and drawn.

Our eyes flick back and forth for several long seconds before he says anything. 'I'm so sorry I punctured you. I saw you falling from the roof and I dove from a great height. The impact of my claws connecting with you must have done it.

'When I saw you soaked in blood, I knew then I had hurt you. When Falcon landed, I couldn't change form or he would have killed us both. I had to defend you and I could only do that in my dragon form.'

I lower my voice, knowing the other two dragons can hear every word. 'I'm okay… well, I am now.'

'When you dropped to the ground, I imagined the worst. I saw Drake and his family pick you up and disappear into the forest, but I had a furious Falcon to deal with. If I turned my back for a split second to follow them, I wouldn't be here.'

'Why do you stand by him if you know he would snuff out your life that easily? A family trusts and cares for each other, they don't fear each other.'

'Enough about him. Let me look at you.' He smiles and stands back to admire me.

I jog around in a circle, cheekily swinging my hips.

'You are my angel, Jazz.'

'And you are far too skinny. Look at your big muscles. They're dropping off your bones.' I poke his arms and chest, which are still very toned.

'Is that so?' He chuckles and gently pushes me back against the wall.

'Yes,' I whisper. He leans forward and kisses my lips firmly. He springs back with his eyes shooting wide open.

'Who the hell have you been kissing? Which gargoyle is it?'

'Excuse me?'

'I can taste him on your lips, Jasmine!'

'Jasmine is it? What happened to Jazz?'

'Don't play games!' He throws the chair closest to him across the room. 'Who?'

'If you're going to act like a child, I'll leave.'

'Oh no, you're not going anywhere. Answer my question.' He paces the room in a ridiculously quick time.

'I didn't know we had a contract! I can kiss who and whatever I please!' I stamp my foot, giving strength to my words.

'Well, why did you come back here?'

'Because I saw Corbin when I was riding and he said you were distraught thinking you killed me. I couldn't let you think that and I was worried for you.'

'So you care for me?'

'Yes.'

'But you kissed a gargoyle?'

'Yes.'

'Argh! Why?' He yells and throws the bedside table across the room, shattering it to pieces.

'Stop doing that. It's scaring me.'

'Oh, I can tell and it sounds delicious.' He inhales deeply and calms when blowing out. He stalks his way over to me.

I walk backwards until my back is against the wall. I'm the deer and he's the lion. He leaps and in one stride, he has me encased in his heating body. 'You are mine, Jazz.'

'Excuse me, but nobody owns—' I don't finish my lecture as Lazarus presses his lips firmly against mine, his body pinning me to the wall.

I push at his shoulders to get him off me but he isn't easily moved. He continues to kiss me and I stop struggling to enjoy his hot mouth on mine. His lips leave mine and trickle soft kisses along my neck. I roll my head back, giving him room to devour me.

Jazzle, where are you?' a voice in my head echoes. Damn telepathic cousin!

'Not now,' I echo back.

'Everyone is worried. Have you left?'

'No, I'm at the dragons' cave,' I echo, before my mind drifts back to enjoy Lazarus' warm lips. He returns his hot lips to my mouth. *'Oh, hell yes!'* I accidentally echo.

Jazzle, are you trapped! Are they torturing you?'

If this is torture, I never want to be saved! *'No torture. Can't talk now. I'm fine. Trust me.'* I squeeze an echo through the heated adrenaline my body is receiving.

'If they know who you are they will trap you.' She continues to cloud my head.

'Get out of my head!' I yell loudly. Lazarus stops his glorious kissing and stares at me with a dark frown growing across his brow.

'What's going on, Jazz?'

'Nothing. Your kissing is driving me crazy.' I try to cover the truth then feel like a complete fool.

'I hope it does, but I believe there's more to it than you are saying.' He moves away from me, leaving my body to cool. He sits on the edge of the bed and folds his arms in a negative posture.

I smile and shrug my shoulders.

'Are you thinking of the gargoyle you kissed? Is he in your head?'

'No, he's not. Well, he is now you mentioned him.'

'Which concrete bolder did you kiss?'

'That's my business, Lazarus.'

'It's mine when I'm kissing you and he is in your head!'

'He wasn't in my head, you were! You asked me to trust you and I do. I need to talk to you alone.'

'We are alone, Jazz.'

'No, we aren't. I can sense your cousins sensing me.'

I soon as the words leave my mouth I know they are true. I can feel them sensing and listening to our conversation. It's a cool chill that fills the air.

Why didn't I sense that before? Has Raven unleashed a part of me by telling me what I am, a sorceress? Is my mind tapping into that side of me without trying?

'I can carry you to the base of the cave where no one will hear us, but it will be dangerous. The descent is too steep for you to climb and I'd hate you to fall trying.'

'I trust you.' I move to stand in front of him.

'I need to be in dragon form, but I haven't eaten and I don't trust myself. 'He reaches out and holds my hands, returning the heat I was missing.

'I trust you so let's go.' I nod.

He stands up, looking straight into my eyes. 'I don't think I should. If I hurt you again…'

Reaching up to caress his cheek, I pull his face to mine and kiss his warm lips. 'I trust you.' I tug him towards the door. He stops me before I open it and holds me tight in his arms. He kisses me hard and desperately, then he squeezes me in his arms. I think he is reassuring himself that he can do it.

We walk quietly to the cave and in a heated flash and gust of hot air, Lazarus' dragon form is standing gloriously in front of me. He's quick to move to my side. I freeze to let him settle before I clamber over him. His nostrils are large and flare as he inhales a deep breath, sucking me forward. He closes his eyes then flicks them open, staring at me. He closes them again and inhales, maybe confirming my scent. When he opens them they are only half-opened.

I drift my hand along his long neck, running it down his scaly side. I reach his front leg and step up onto his foot, but his back is too high for me to reach. He swings his head around and, for a split second, I believe I've made the wrong decision and he has decided to have me for breakfast. I hold my breath, anxious for his next move.

He nudges me under my bottom, lifting me up his body until I am sitting on his back just in front of his frill-like wings.

Sitting on top his back gives me a different perspective of his amazing body. He is twice as wide as Blue Boy, with his neck thinning into a wedge-shaped head. I can see his small ears and wonder how he can hear so well.

Lazarus opens his wings wide and they remind me of a stingray's pectoral fin I've seen skimming the ocean floor. He lifts them high then drops them low. He repeats the motion several times; I can feel them move against my bottom. I presume he's testing his wings to make sure I'm not hindering them in any way.

I turn to look along the length of his back; his long tail lies dormant. At the end of it, there's a sphere-looking dagger. I shiver, remembering the fight he had with Falcon when he'd lashed out, striking Lazarus with this weapon, gutting him a bloody hole. And Drake's grazed face when Falcon whipped him with it. One end of a dragon is as deadly as the other.

Lazarus snorts and moves, finishing my observation. I place my hands on his neck, wishing I had a set of reins to occupy them and to control him. He moves to the edge of the cave and allows me to see what we are about to dive into—an enormous black endlessness. He opens his wings and holds them high.

With one downward thrust, he lifts off the landing and surges forward into the darkness. He circles once at the landing's height before descending, keeping his wings stretched open. It reminds me of a hang glider who jumps off a cliff and soars through the air.

The already dark cave is soon pitch black. I lift my hand, holding it in front of me, but I see nothing. Trying to keep balance and stay on top of Lazarus' back, I close my eyes. In an instant, my hearing, sense of smell, touch and taste are all heightened. The smell the cave's damp walls remind me of the mouldy shower my grandfather had. He would never clean with chemicals, saying they kill the Earth's powers.

Lazarus flaps his wings quickly as his feet touch the ground. I pray this is the bottom of the cave. The fear of sliding down his side only to fall off another cliff face scares me. He drops his wings to his side, then pulls them in tight.

'It's too dark Lazarus. I can't see.'

He walks and I grip hold of his back with my thighs, hearing a growling breath from him.

He rounds a corner and a brilliant golden light brightens the cave. Lazarus stops and, with caution in his movement, sits. I throw my leg over his back and slide down as I do on Blue Boy.

I panic, waiting for when my feet will touch the ground; it's the longest descent I have had from an animal. Not that I ride dragons on a regular basis. My heart sings when my feet touch the cave floor.

Lazarus growls and snorts, a small flame escaping his mouth. Within a flash and a warm welcome breeze, he is back in human form. He looks exhausted; more than before.

In a swift move, he is back at my side, embracing me in his hot arms. His lime green eyes radiate in the golden light. He kisses me passionately for several wonderful minutes and then pulls me back to arm's length as if to distance himself.

'Feeling you slide down my body like that…' He shakes his head.

'You want to eat me?'

'Not exactly, Jazz. Let's just say I needed to change out of dragon form quick so I could kiss you. If I tried to kiss you in dragon form, you may not be talking to me right now.'

'Oh! I'm sorry I didn't—'

He silences me with another kiss. 'So what are you, Jasmine? As soon as I was in dragon form, your scent differed from before. I've never known anyone's scent to change unless they have given birth to a child. And by the look of your slender figure, I doubt that.'

'Can anyone hear us?' I glance around at my new surroundings. The cave is lit up by a golden glow coming from behind a large boulder. The cave floor is wet and I can hear water trickling as if a small stream is running through it.

'No, the cave walls drown out our voices. How are you connected to Raven?' He steps back and folds his arms across his chest, waiting for my answer.

'Why do you say that?' I wonder if I am doing the right thing by telling him what I am. Have I trusted the wrong creature?

'Falcon and Raven were together for several years. Her scent changed as she became stronger in her sorcery. Sorcery has a very distinctive aroma mixed into the individual's scent. I can smell your sorcery, Jasmine.' His eyes widen, with one brow lifting in question.

'Raven and Falcon were together... as in boyfriend and girlfriend?'

'Yes, Jasmine. We *are* capable of having relationships.'

'I understand that. I believe you've shown me what you're capable of.'

'Oh Jazz, I haven't shown you anything yet.' In one quick stride, he is next to me, embracing me in his warm arms. I'm glad for his heat, as it's extremely cold. 'Is she your mother?'

'Huh! She'd love to hear that. No, she is my cousin. My grandfather taught her and I am starting to remember the things he taught me when I was younger. I blocked out my memories of him. Raven believes it's because I saw him being murdered by a dragon. My grandfather would take us to visit dragon lairs and gargoyle castles.'

'Raven's parents aren't sorcerers. It skipped a generation. Are your parents sorcerers?'

'My mother is, but she refuses to acknowledge creatures not known to man.'

'So that makes you stronger than Raven. Hell!' He throws his hand in the air, grabbing and holding his head.

'Why are you yelling?'

'If Falcon knows of your connection to Raven, he will keep you here and use your powers against the gargoyles. Then he will have no further use for Drake's mother, Demona, and will destroy her.'

'Why do you care about Drake's mother? The night Falcon burnt me you were there to kill them.'

'I was there because Falcon is our leader and I must follow. If you took any notice, Corbin and I were flying higher than Falcon, keeping a safe distance. He is determined to collect all the souls of the gargoyles, making his father proud of him.'

'But what use is a gargoyle soul to dragons?'

'To my knowledge, it's pure greed that makes his father want them. The gold colour is extremely attractive to us, just as attractive as you are to me. But I won't kill to have a golden soul.'

'Would you kill to have me?'

'If it came to that... yes.'

'What if I took the golden soul back to the gargoyles? Would you stop me?'

'I'm not sure but in my weakened state, I'll ask you not to attempt it today. I couldn't fight Falcon to protect you, and the way you antagonise him, he will definitely be fired up. No pun intended,' he says, with a small curve of his lip.

'The gargoyles need the soul of a fallen gargoyle to be reincarnated into a newborn.'

'Not exactly, Jazz. The gargoyles are born with a soul but allowing a wiser and stronger soul to join it accelerates the aging process. It will be mentally and physically stronger like Jarius and Lolana are.'

'Do you see me in a different light now you know what I am?'

'No, far from it, gorgeous. But I will be careful not to make you angry. I remember seeing Raven accidentally throw Falcon's human form across the room when she was practising her sorcery. Corbin and I fell over laughing.'

'I bet she'd love to "accidentally" throw him now.' I chuckle.

'I think part of his hunt against the gargoyles is because he knows she is with Lysander.' He moves closer, with half-hooded eyes. 'Which means the only other gargoyle there for you to kiss is Drake, as Jarius is too young!' He grows another foot taller in front of me.

I roll my shoulders back and stand firm before him. I listen to my heart and to my surprise, I can hear it loud and clear. It is thumping hard and angry.

'You look and sound so delicious, especially standing in the glow of a golden soul,' he says, quietening his tone. I hear another heartbeat and I shoot my eyes up to his lime green ones.

'I can hear your heartbeat and my own,' I gasp. 'But I don't want to eat it. Sheesh, I knew I shouldn't have drunk the water!'

'You can hear my heartbeat?'

I nod.

'I need to get you out of here.' His eyes flick back and forth as if he is listening for something. 'You are stronger than Raven ever was. You need to confide in her with all the new things you're tapping into. You need to learn how to keep a cool head when in danger.'

'I do keep a cool head!' I hear my heartbeat skip.

'You're so easy to read, Jazz.'

'As you are now, Lazarus.'

'I will remember that in the future but right now, and I don't believe I'm saying this, I need to take you back to Elyograg Castle for your own safety. But I warn you of one thing—if I smell or taste Drake on your lips again, I will rip his head off and put his soul in a chandelier in the middle of my dining room.' He pulls me tight into his arms and kisses me.

'You don't own me!'

'You are mine and I am yours. We have a connection I can't explain.' He moves his lips to whisper in my ear. 'How'd you feel if I passionately kissed another woman?' His warm breath flows around my neck, giving me a body-rippling shiver. My heart disobeys my head and thuds hard at the thought of another woman in his arms.

'I wouldn't mind.' I lie and pray he didn't hear my heart skip.

'You are, and by the sound of it, will always be a terrible liar. I need to feed before I attempt to get you out of here. Will you be all right if I go for half an hour to feed and strengthen?'

'Yes, but does that mean you're dining on a live cow?' As soon as I ask, I'm unsure if I want to hear his answer.

'We're not cruel. Remember, we are also animals. The cow is happily grazing and doesn't lift its head from the grass before it hits the ground, dead. More humane than what you humans do.'

'Don't tell me any more. Just go quickly.' I squint my eyes shut, trying to block out the images of him eating a whole cow. He kisses my lips and with a warm gush, he is gone, leaving a lit lantern beside me.

I look around at my Arctic surrounds and take a peek at the golden glow behind the boulder. It gets brighter as I approach. I can hear my heart pounding with fear, or is it excitement?

I round the side of the boulder to see not one but two golden souls. They are different from what I had imagined. I pictured them to be gooey messy lumps of mush but instead, they are glittery, shiny, bright golden balls.

One is fading in colour and I wonder if it's dying. I'm cautious when reaching for it, expecting something unusual to happen. However, when I touch it, nothing happens so I pick it up. It sits comfortably in my palm and is no bigger than a kiwifruit. It is light to hold and warm to touch, unlike a gargoyle in stone sleep.

'You're stunning.'

Leave me and take the other soul, I hear, echoing in my head.

'You're telepathic?'

I am weak. Take the other soul and return it to Elyograg Castle. Lysander knows what to do.

'Why are you weaker?'

'I have been here for a very long time. Falcon's father was my closest friend and when I died, he stole my soul.'

'That's when there was peace. We need your soul—we need help to bring peace between creatures. Your soul may have the key to that. I won't leave you here. You're both small enough to carry out.'

I pick up the second soul and hold them both in one hand. I look for a pocket in my t-shirt and there's none. I have an idea and pray these souls don't have eyes. *'I will put you underneath my shirt. Don't go into my head until I tell you you're safe. I had someone in my head at a time I needed to concentrate and it made it difficult to do so. Do you understand?'*

'Yes. Can I ask who our saviour is?' another voice echoes.

'My name is Jasmine.'

'Little Jasmine, who came with her grandfather to visit the clans?'

'I visited the gargoyles' castle with my grandfather before his death.'

'His death was a sad day for all man and creature-kind. He kept the balance between us and the dragons.'

'Lazarus will return shortly so please be quiet.'

I slip one soul into the cup of my bra then the other into the other cup. I slip my top over and their glow is hidden but my cleavage looks amazing. I move so I am beside the lantern Lazarus kindly lit for me. I look around for somewhere to sit but the cave floor and rocks are cold and wet.

The lantern blows out and the heat from a dragon's nostril is beside me, breathing me in.

'It's me, Lazarus,' I whisper. 'Do you want me to climb onto your back?' I get a nudge to my side and work my way along his neck to his back. He sits and I climb awkwardly onto his leg. 'Boost me up with your nose, big boy.' I giggle.

He does but with a forceful nudge. 'Ouch! Take it easy.' I sit straddling his back just in front of his wings, as I had done earlier. 'Okay, I'm ready.'

He lets out an enormous roar, with flames shooting out of his mouth. Why the hell is he making so much noise? Falcon will definitely hear him. But as soon as the flames light up a dozen torches around the cave I realise that I am not sitting on Lazarus. I have climbed onto my worst enemy's back.

Falcon leaps into the air. I lean forward, holding on with every muscle I have. He flies with no respect for my safety and I know my death will be something he'd take great joy in achieving. I grasp onto a clump of his scales with both hands, hoping it won't break off and leave me nothing to hold onto.

His powerful wings have us at the landing in no time. There is a woman standing on the landing and I recognise her. It's Drake's mother, Demona. What the hell is she doing in human form? That's exactly what Falcon wants.

'Demona, change back into stone sleep. He will kill you!'.

'I can help but you need to jump off his back or I could hurt you,' she yells.

Falcon roars and, with great speed, dives for Demona, picking her up in his large clawed feet. I hear her skin pop when his claws pierce her flesh. She lets out a gut-retching scream. Her skin pops again but this time she's silent. He must be squeezing her to death.

'Falcon, stop. I will do you want. Please stop crushing her.'

He roars a deafening sound and flies higher into the cave. I lean forward, still gripping my legs tight as I do on my horse and praying he's not going to crash through a stone wall with me on top and Demona in his claws.

He winds through the large cave tunnel until I can see light up ahead. As the daylight gravitates towards us it's difficult to keep in focus. My dilated pupils are taking too long to re-adjust. I shut my eyes tight then slowly try to re-open them. It takes a good few minutes to gain my sight again.

I glance around, trying to make out any landmarks below

us. There's nothing I recognise. He's heading for a large mountain. There's a cave halfway up the side of the mountain. He folds in his wings as he glides in, dropping Demona first before stopping to shake me from his back. I fall unceremoniously to the hard cave floor.

He spins around and roars wildly at Demona. I scamper to my feet and race towards her, throwing myself in front of her to protect her. She pulls me to the side, placing her body in front of mine to protect me.

Falcon spins and in a heated swirl of red particles, is standing in front of us in human form.

'Isn't that sweet, Demona. The human wants to be the protector. Maybe you are a gargoyle, Jasmine,' he snarls.

'If I were, I would have ripped your heart out by now, lizard!'

'Be quiet girl,' snaps Demona.

'I'm not frightened of him.' I confidently walk from behind her and away from her protection.

'You should be. You're human. He will kill you in the blink of an eye.' She moves to protect me again.

'You should listen to Demona. But you are right, I won't snuff you out, not just yet anyhow. You are more valuable alive.' He moves closer to us.

'Demona, don't you have a magical power to do something?' I ask.

'I haven't eaten for months and he knows I'm too weak,' she whispers, even though we know he can hear us.

He continues to move closer with the eyes of the devil. I jump in front of her and throw my hand out in front of me with the palm of my hand facing him. An energy surges through my veins like I've never felt before. It feels as though the ground is coming up my legs, through my body and out of my hand.

He flies back against the cave wall and collapses to the ground.

'Holy hell! What just happened?' I say.

'You! You *are* Raven's family,' Falcon spits viciously. He jumps to his feet and in a blink, is standing inches away from me. 'I wasn't sure if what I smelt and heard was true. Having Raven's cousin will be a great bonus to the dragons and, on my father's return, we will destroy every gargoyle at Elyograg Castle.'

I lift my hand again and try to draw on the same feelings as before. But nothing happens. I try again and again but nothing.

'You may be a sorceress but you're yet to master your powers,' he says.

'What makes you think I'd help a slithering slug like you?' I snarl, leaning forward into his personal space.

'I will kill Lazarus right in front of your stunning blue eyes. Hell, I should have recognised those eyes when I first met you. But instead, I smelt your sorcery all the way from the base of the cave. It had Raven written all over it.'

'What dumbfounds me the most is that she once loved you. But I am glad she woke up and is now madly in love with Lysander.'

'Let's see how your smart mouth survives without food and water. You are still a mere human. There's always another way to eliminate the gargoyles.'

'Lazarus will sense you've taken me,' I snap, feeling Demona's hand on my arm, drawing me out of Falcon's face.

'Give me a little credit, Jasmine. I waited until he was engrossed in his prey before I made my descent to the base of the cave. He will have sensed your fear when we were outdoors flying but now, you're in this cave he will lose any connection he has.'

'He won't have sensed fear, only anger, you fork-tongued gecko!'

'Believe me, Lazarus is a dragon first and human second. He will choose me over you.'

'He is nothing like you! Your blood runs in the opposite direction!'

'Enough of your insults or I will break every bone in your body and let you die a slow, painful death!' Falcon's movement is too quick for my eyes to see; I only know he moved when his face is inches away from mine, letting a small amount of smoke escape his breath covering me.

'Blow your smoke out your backside, Falcon.'

'Jasmine!' snaps Demona, pulling me backwards and staggering as she does.

'Put her on a leash! I will return when my father does. It could be a month or two,' he says, turning and walking towards the entrance. In a heated gust of red particles, he is back into dragon form. He forces a large boulder across the entrance, blocking it. I shut my eyes and concentrate, willing my mind to talk to Raven.

'Raven, please hear me.'

'Jazz, I hear you,' she echoes in my head.

'Falcon has Demona and me trapped in a cave halfway up a mountain.'

'Where?'

'I don't know but he is shutting us in with a large boulder. I may lose contact with you but trust Lazarus.'

'Lazarus? Is either of you... Jazz can you hear... Please...' Her echo disappears as the boulder closes the entry.

'Bugger! I had Raven but now I can't hear her.'

Demona falls against the cave wall, sliding down to its wet floor.

'Are you okay? How can I help?'

'I am weak and I fear if I return to stone sleep I won't have enough energy to return to help you. And with these new puncture wounds in my torso, I doubt I will heal in one stone sleep. It will take several days or a week to heal as I haven't eaten for such a long time.'

'Can these guys help you?' I lift my t-shirt to expose the two golden souls.

'They are beautiful.'

'Normally standing like this, I'd be proud of a comment like that.' We both chuckle but hers is weak. I pull the souls out one at a time, handing them to her. 'I knew them both when I was younger. I came here with my grandfather and Raven.'

'Yes, I remember you and Raven as children.' She stares at the small golden souls glowing in her palm, with a small smile curving her lips. 'If Falcon had caught you with these, he would have definitely killed you. You're an extremely brave woman.'

'Lucky for me he's not a boob man.' I laugh, and she joins in. 'So can you use them to gain your strength?'

'If I do, then the soul will truly die.'

'But it will live within you.'

'That's true but I am old and they should be reincarnated into a newborn. It would be selfish of me.'

I roll my eyes exasperatingly at her.

'That's the way our life's circle works.'

'I'm sure no one will mind if it saves your life. I can ask the golden souls, as they're telepathic.'

'Gargoyles can also hear a golden soul speak. I'd rather die and let my soul go to another as written and as it should be.'

'I don't understand your way and I won't interfere, even though I believe the lack of food has made you go mad.' I look around our new home. 'Can I be rude and ask to borrow one golden soul? I want to venture further into the cave to see where it goes. I would have brought a torch if I'd known what my day would hold.' I giggle and Demona raises her eyebrow at me. 'I should have woken up this morning and reminded myself to pack a backpack full of food, a torch and to mind my business when I saw Corbin and Lolana kissing under the trees.'

'They were kissing?'

'Oh, hells bells! Me and my big mouth! Please say nothing to Lolana. We've only just got talking as we didn't hit it off that well at the start.'

'I won't say a word.' She forces a smile through her pain. 'Who she loves is her business. It sounds like you're fond of Lazarus.'

'I am but I also have a connection to Drake, just to confuse everything.' I shrug my shoulders.

'I can't help you with that. Put your head and heart together and your soul will work that one out. Good luck, as they are both lovely men.'

'You think a dragon is lovely?'

'Jasmine, I have nothing against them and when we were at peace, I was great friends with the dragons at Nogard Hollow. Drake and Lazarus were inseparable and had a great friendship.'

'I'm falling in love with best friends?'

'I'd hate to be in your shoes. Loving one person is hard enough.' She smiles sympathetically before handing me one of the golden souls.

'Raven can cast a spell that will make all this a simple dream. If I can't decide what to do, I will ask her to do so and leave them both to live their lives and fall in love with one of their own kind.'

'That would be sad and drastic move to make. You were drawn here for a reason. Make sure you think long and hard on it before jumping into something you may regret.' She smiles, rubbing my shoulder with her hand.

'I will.' I notice her glowing blue eyes are fading to a dull grey. 'There must be something I can do to help you heal, Demona. I will do anything to help. Do you want to drink my blood?'

She chuckles. 'I'm not a vampire, Jasmine. There's nothing you can do but thank you for caring.'

'Why don't you rest and I will see how far this cave goes? I won't go too far. To be truthful, dark wet caves scare the poop out of me, plus, you've just mentioned vampires.'

'I will be here. All you need to do is yell and I will come as quick as my body allows.'

'And I will come if I hear you yell, not that I know how to control my sorcery yet.' I remember the shock I got when I shot Falcon across the room.

I hold the little soul out in front of me so its glow radiates onto the walls as well at the cave floor. It would be pitch black if I didn't have my golden friend. I glance back at Demona and pray she's able to heal those nasty puncture wounds.

CHAPTER SEVEN

I HAVE BEEN walking for what seems hours and the rapid beating of my heart is starting to scare me. I'm cold and a little damp due to water constantly dripping on top of me. The cave narrows, making me feel claustrophobic. A flood of chilled goosebumps floods my skin.

With no exit in sight, I fear we may be trapped underground until Falcon lets us out. With fear flooding my veins and a quickened stride, I backtrack to Demona. When I eventually return, she has gone into stone sleep. She needs all her strength to stay alive. I sit beside her and look up at her gargoyle features. She is a remarkable-looking creature. She has a golden soul sitting between her arms. I place the one I have beside it.

'I didn't find an exit. It felt like I was walking for hours but my return trip was too quick. I'm sorry I was a chicken and came back. But please stay in stone sleep. I understand you need to heal. Trust me, I need some alone time to sort out my emotions and comprehend what has happened over the last few weeks.'

I lie on the freezing ground and shiver myself to sleep. I wake several times, but the chilly conditions force me to sleep.

I wake with a jolt, not knowing what the time is and where I am. I glance around and see Demona in stone sleep with the two golden souls between her solid front arms.

I'm slow to stand; my body cramped due to lying on the damp cave floor. I walk to the boulder and push with all my might, trying to force it open. There is no way in hell it will move, especially with my weak girly arms.

I stand back and draw up the energy I felt previously. I hold my hand out but only several large rocks fly around the room, making me duck for cover. The boulder remains unmoved. Well, at least I know how to throw a rock at someone.

I try to use my mind to contact Raven, but I hear nothing. Then I pray to grandfather, asking him to help me, but nothing.

Placing a pile of rocks on the ground, I try to move them from one place to another. I jump with glee when they do. Eventually, I can move them without worrying if I will lose an eye.

I remove my shoes and the chill of the cave floor shoots through me. I lay them in front of me and, closing my eyes, I picture them in my head. I pick them up and twirl them around in circles, then flip them upside down and place them gently on the ground.

I do it again, but this time with my eyes open, and before me, I witness true sorcery at its finest. My shoes spin and flip on my command.

I continue to practice until my brain shuts down.

'Did you see that, Demona? I'm getting the hang of it.'

Without warning, my body drops to the ground. I am exhausted and it feels like I have run a ten-mile race. I reach for my shoes. My feet are now blue and my toes are numb and motionless. I roll my body into a tight ball and shiver myself into a numbing sleep.

I wake with a fright when the large boulder rolls open. Falcon is standing square-shouldered with a man I don't recognise.

They enter the cave and I try to stagger to my feet, but my limbs are sore and ache due to the Arctic floor stealing my heat. I lift myself up on one arm and try to warm my legs with my other hand.

'She resembles her grandfather,' says a male voice. 'They

kept her well-hidden all these years.'

'She is still learning to use her powers,' says Falcon, moving towards me.

The two silhouettes stand straight in front of me. I raise my hand to shadow the sun shining through the cave's entrance, the small amount of warmth welcoming.

I notice Falcon and then let my eyes glaze over the other male standing confidently beside him. He moves closer and squats in front of me.

I can see his face now. He looks like Sean Connery in his younger days, with the added black stubble running along his jawline. I've seen this face before and search what little memory I have of these creatures. It hits me like a cricket bat to the head!

'Attor!' I say out loud.

'You remember me, Blue Eyes,' he says.

'I remember your face and your voice, but...' A sudden flashback races through my mind. I see grandfather in the grand lounge room of Nogard Hollow. Attor is standing beside him and there's a gargoyle's glowing golden soul sitting on a table between them. They are in a heated argument over it.

'You must return it to Elyogarg Castle, Attor. It is a part of the gargoyles' ritual, their circle of life, to be reincarnated into a newborn's soul. You mustn't interfere with their life's cycle,' insists my grandfather.

'Maybe their cycle needs a little interruption,' Attor snidely replies.

'This will cause a war between the gargoyles and dragons. We will end up like Europe, with unnecessary fighting. We have kept the peace here for centuries and now you're willing to give that up so you can have a shiny glowing soul; a trinket?'

'Oh no, my dear friend, it's more than a shiny glowing trinket. It controls the strength, wisdom and knowledge of the newborn. This soul was my best friend for the last ninety years and he is wiser, stronger and more knowledgeable than anyone I know. His soul entering a fresh young body of a newborn will create a very powerful gargoyle, one of the finest. I won't allow it!' Attor snaps close to my grandfather's face.

Grandfather stands unhindered. 'I have been speaking to my relatives over in Europe and they are weakening the gargoyles by taking their souls and are using them as slaves to protect the dragon lairs. The gargoyles feed and protect the dragons—putting themselves in danger so our race can survive.'

'You want to make the gargoyles slaves? You're being poisoned by your relatives' twisted minds, Attor. Here in Australia we respect each race and allow each to live their lives as they wish.

'I will not allow this to happen. We are all equals, Attor.' Grandfather frowns, placing his hands on the golden soul. 'I will return the soul to Elyograg Castle and no one will be the wiser to your innocent misjudgement.'

'My innocent misjudgement! You misjudge me if you think I will let you leave with that soul in your hand. I will take it from your cold dead body, my friend. I will give you two seconds to put it back on the table, then leave to never return!'

'I know deep down in your warm heart you will never kill me. Our friendship is worth so much more to you than—' Grandfather's words halt. In slow motion, he falls to his knees. Attor's lime green eyes stare directly at me. He is holding a bloodied red heart in his hand. But his hand isn't human. It's his dragon claw with the red scales shooting up his forearm and taking over his whole arm. The scales continue to race up his body as he changes into dragon form before me.

Grandfather falls to the floor, dropping the golden soul. A white light radiates from his body then shoots quickly up in a fluorescent stream and through the roof towards the heavens.

Attor is in full dragon form when a violent tug of my arm shoots me backwards. Raven is here! She drags me, running out of Nogard Hollow and into the nearby forest. She waves her hand over her head and I know she is blocking our conversation, heartbeat and scent from the beast that has just killed my grandfather.

I blink several times and return to the present. 'You mongrel! You killed my grandfather and he was your friend,' I spit through gritted teeth.

'Ooh, watch out son, I believe I've just awoken a sleeping devil.'

I stagger to my feet; the adrenaline surge flooding through my body gives me the courage to face this beast head-on. Anger rolls and circles inside my gut, joining the earth-drawn pull spiking up my legs. It floods down my arms to my hands. I open my palms to see two swirling white ghostly balls.

I lift my arms and feel the weight of them, like holding six oranges in each hand. I throw them directly at Attor.

He drops to the ground, dodging them. They hit Falcon solidly in his chest, the force throwing him back several long metres before he lands violently on his back. He screams out in pain while his father looks on, laughing.

'I thought you knew how to duck a sorceress' white rage, son.' Attor turns back to me with his eyes wide open. 'You are stronger than Raven. I have plans for you and me, my blue-eyed baby.'

'I'm not and will never be your "blue-eyed baby". And the only plan I have for you is to turn you into a handbag, matching belt, jacket and shoes! It looks like you've put on a few extra pounds, so I'll make a pair of pants as well.'

'Obviously, you need more time locked in here without food or water to realise who is in charge.'

Within a blink of an eye, he is standing shockingly in front of me. He grabs both my arms and lifts me up so our faces are equal. His emerald eyes are blazing an eternal flame and the heat from his body is fierce. He needs my help otherwise I'd be dead, like my grandfather.

'You need me, Attor!' I spray into his face. 'Weaken me now if you wish but I will take my revenge on you.'

He bursts out into laughter and drops me. The ligaments and muscles in my legs have fallen asleep and I fall hard to the cave floor. 'You will do everything I ask, baby blue eyes, because I have the biggest weapon against you. Lazarus!'

I gasp hearing his name. Is he threatening to kill Lazarus if I don't join him in whatever sick twisted venture he has planned?

'Ah, I see I've hit a nerve,' Attor snidely says.

'Jasmine! Don't say another word,' threatens Demona.

She moves next to me into human form. I shake my head at her, as she is making herself vulnerable to the dragons. She doesn't have the golden souls and when I look behind her its dark. She's cleverly hid them.

'Well, hello Demona. How nice of you to make yourself present,' says Attor.

'Attor.' She gives a short sharp nod. 'Leave the girl and take me.'

'I can guarantee you I will keep you close. If Jasmine keeps on with her spiteful tongue, I will revoke her invite and use your skills, even if they are a little second-hand.'

'Why don't you tie a knot in that forked tongue,' I snap.

Falcon is slow to stand, and with a slight stagger, heads towards his father.

'Looks like you took the wind out of his sails, Jasmine.'

Attor laughs at his son's pain. 'With practice, she will pierce a hole right through you, my son.'

'Give me one minute with her, Father, and she won't lift those ball-wielding hands again,' snarls Falcon.

'Settle, son. You can do what you want with her when I have everything I need.'

'Let me talk to the girl and explain how things work in our world, Attor,' interjects Demona. 'She's hasn't been amongst us in a long time.'

'You were always the one who brought calm to the table, Demona. I must confess I miss your company. I will return in a week and, if you are alive, I will give you an opportunity to apologise for your outburst today, Jasmine. Otherwise, I will bring back Lazarus and rip him to shreds, scale by scale, in front of you. Then I will wrap you in his stripped leather skin, giving you the jacket and pants you so desire.'

'You are a beast!' I pull my legs into my chest as the chill from sitting on the cave's floor takes control.

'Demona, teach her some manners or I may let Falcon have his way with her,' says Attor, turning and walking towards the cave entrance. I watch as Attor changes form with a welcome, heated gust.

Falcon takes double the time to change and I gather that's because I 'white ball' soccer-punched him. They close the entrance with ease, using the same large boulder.

'You need to control your thoughts as you don't have a filter on your mouth. He will take your life without blinking that green eye. He still has me and even better, Raven,' she says, pulling the golden souls out from under the dirt hole where she must have hidden them. 'Even though I tried not to laugh when you threatened to turn him into your new wardrobe.'

'The power I felt surge through my body when I produced those balls was unbelievable!'

'Raven will help you control your power but for now, you need to listen and think before you speak. We call the white balls anorics and they will be your main threat to the enemy.' She picks up the two golden souls in her small human hands. 'We need to head further into the cave. It's freezing and damp in here and you won't be alive in another week. Your skin is looking grey. I'm scared I can hear a rattle in your chest.'

I close my eyes and listen to my heartbeat. She is right. My heart sounds wet, as do my lungs, which have a noticeable rattle in them. 'I hear it too. Are you well enough to walk?'

'Yes, I haven't totally healed from Falcon's claws. But the puncture wounds have closed enough for me to move. Normally I'd heal over one day but with no food, it has taken me longer.'

'It's only been one day.'

'You've been asleep, off and on, for three days. Come on let's go. The golden souls will be our guiding light.'

Demona pulls me up by my arm. My legs take hold and I stand, eager to seek an escape route. She walks in front of me, holding out the two golden souls which lighten up the dark, dim cave.

As the walls narrow, I fear it may be a dead end. I don't have the energy to walk back to the cave entrance.

We walk for several long hours until the walls of the cave are rubbing against my shoulders. A claustrophobic feeling floods me, with Demona a short metre in front of me and the walls closing in on us. I hear my breath shorten with panic and my heartbeat quicken like a drum roll in a scary movie.

'We need to turn back,' I say in a whisper, my voice fading.

'There's a light up ahead, Jasmine. It's small but it's definitely daylight.'

'Oh, thank heaven!' We both bend over and scrape our bodies against the cave walls. 'I can't see past you. Is there an exit?'

'It's blocked by fallen rocks. We'll have to dig them out.'

Demona punches the rocks, breaking them to the size of basketballs. She passes them between her bent legs. They're still too heavy for me so I roll them through my legs like a game of tunnel-ball.

My back, legs and arms ache. It feels like we've been passing rocks for ages. 'I can't fit anymore behind me. Please tell me we can get through and not that we've just made a grave for ourselves.'

'It's only a small exit but I reckon we can crawl out.'

Demona drops to her knees, placing the golden souls into her top. She crawls out the small exit on her hands and knees.

As her backside disappears, I take off on all fours through the petite hole. I scamper away from the cave's exit, stopping at Demona's feet.

I inhale a deep rewarding breath only to hear a rattle vibrate loudly through my body. I have definitely caught a cold, or worse, pneumonia.

I instantly try to contact Raven, but my head is clear of any voices. I echo to the golden souls to see if I have lost my power and hear them loud and clear.

'I can't hear Raven. Something must be blocking us. I pray that Attor doesn't have her.'

'If he had Raven, he would have killed both of us. I think the cave's thick walls and these large mountains are interfering with your telepathy.'

'We need to find shelter for the night as it looks like a storm has just passed and with those hovering black clouds, it will return soon. You need to keep warm; I can hear your rattle from here, Jasmine.'

'You should be in stone sleep. You need to heal. I won't risk your life, Demona.'

'I'm the protector here. Are you sure there's no gargoyle blood in you?'

'Trust me, my parents are both very human.'

'You're not strong enough to travel. I will rest in stone sleep during the night and pray we don't bump into anyone during the day. Once we are clear of this mountain you should be able to contact Raven and she can send help.'

I get to my feet shakily and glance around, taking in our cold, wet surroundings. There are at least fifty kangaroos grazing amongst the gum trees and shrubs. Every one of them is standing tall in fear we might come near them.

There is a thick scrub area a fair distance away. I point my index finger to show Demona. 'Over there the shrub is thicker. I can blanket under broken shrubs to keep warm.'

'Good thinking. Let's go before that sky drops its load.'

We trudge through the long grasses, soaking my jeans and shoes even more. We arrive at the bushy area within the hour. Half the kangaroos have decided we are a threat and have scattered, with the other half staying to see what we are doing.

We break off large branches that are covered with thick foliage. We lie them on the leaf-covered ground and break several more to pull over my body. I lay down and Demona helps to cover me with branches.

My body is trembling, with the chill now reaching my bones. My lungs release a winter breath, white vapour flowing past my lips. I bury my head, lifting my t-shirt to my mouth, and blow warm air onto my chest.

'You're freezing, Jasmine. I will hunt and bring you back the skin to keep you warm.'

'No, don't kill for me,' I stutter through my trembling lips.

The crunching of branches tells me she's ignored my plea. My warm breath is becoming cooler, bringing down the temperature of my already chilled body.

I hear the crunching of leaves and presume that Demona has returned. I gingerly lift my head and see several curious kangaroos scratching at the ground we have disturbed. There is a small joey half hanging out of its mother's pouch, scratching the ground and picking up leaves. It tastes the leaves then chews on them with the scissor action of its jaw.

'Hello, little joey,' I echo in my head.

'Hello, little human. These leaves are delicious and I'm so toasty warm in my mother's pouch!'

'I'm cold and a friend to all creatures. Would you ask your mum to lie beside me?' 'No, she is too busy to help you. Maybe it's your destiny to die here camouflaged by these branches. No one will ever find you. At least you won't have to make a decision about which man you love—a dragon or a gargoyle,' it says before its mother hops away.

'No! Come back.' I try to stretch my hand out but it's frozen closed. I blink several times to see Demona squatting in front of me. 'Kangaroos are telepathic.'

'No, sweet girl, they're not. You must be hallucinating.' She puts her warm hand on my forehead. 'Oh, God help me! You're as cold as an ice block.' She pulls off the branches and replaces it with a warm blanket.

'Thank you. It's warm,' I murmur, through my chattering teeth.

'I need to leave you and go get help, Jasmine. You won't survive the night,' she says, rubbing my body. 'I have eaten and am already stronger. Promise me you will hang on until I get help.' She places her warm lips on my forehead before she covers it with the warm furry blanket.

My body trembles and the only noise I can hear is the

chattering of my teeth. I try to trick my body into thinking I am lying on the beach, soaking up the warm sun rays but my skin lifts as goosebumps race over it.

I drift in and out of sleep, waking only to hear my body scream out in painful chills. Is it day or night? There's not enough strength left in my body to lift the blanket and peek out. Maybe the joey was telling me the truth and I will die here under a bunch of bushes.

Jasmine, my dear granddaughter, dying here is not your fate. You came to this place guided by your loving soul. You are meant for better and greater things. Place your trust in your own mind and soul. Shut down your mind, sleep now and keep your breathing calm, as tomorrow you will be the strong granddaughter I have taught you to be.' Grandfather's voice echoes in my head.

He is right. He made me strong-willed. I refuse to let this be my fate. I listen to my heart and, together with my soul, we calm my rattling breaths. I shut everything out of my mind, my grandfather being my last vision. I am pain-free and warm.

'I pray we aren't too late,' says Demona.

'Jazz, it's me, Lazarus.'

I hear his voice, but I can't answer or move. I don't want to come out of my pain-free zone.

'Jasmine! She is stone cold, Mum,' I hear Drake say.

'She is too weak to move, and with Attor and Falcon looking for us, we need to keep a low profile. We need to get her body temperature up. Lazarus, I need you to lie with her but your human form isn't big enough to cover her so I need you to change to dragon form. I know you won't hurt her.'

'No! I will lie with her,' snaps Drake.

'This is not a contest for her love, boys. She needs heat and gargoyles don't generate as much as dragons do. She doesn't react to our voices or touch. I pray that we aren't too late.'

I hear the familiar gush of air and then a cocoon of heat envelopes me. It is deliciously warm and deathly quiet. Have I floated to heaven?

CHAPTER EIGHT

'HELLO, JASMINE. YOU are making quite a habit of waking up in my care.'

I flick my eyes open to see Gabby smiling down at me. 'Gabby? Am I in heaven?'

'No, sweet girl, you are safe in Elyograg Castle.' She wipes my forehead with a cool, refreshing cloth.

'Demona, Drake and Lazarus? What about Blue Boy?'

'They are all safe. Blue Boy is still at Nogard Hollow, and to my knowledge, is unharmed. Lazarus heated your body, thawing it back from the brink of death. Then when it was safe, Drake carried you in his arms for several days and Lazarus would warm you at night until they reached the castle. They have both been guarding the castle day and night, waiting for Attor and Falcon's attack, but nothing has happened as yet.'

'Day and night? How long have I been out of it?' I try to sit up and look out the window.

'You need to lie down and rest. You have been in a comatose state for two weeks. You've had pneumonia.' She pushes my shoulders back on the soft bed. 'Raven tried to search your mind, but you shut it down. She hoped you were protecting yourself and would soon return. She fears she's lost you. I will be happy to tell her you are perfectly fine.'

Jazz!' echoes Raven.

'No need to tell her, Gabby. She's already popped in my head to say hello.'

'*I hear you loud and clear, cousin,*' I echo back to Raven.

I hear footsteps racing up the staircase before Raven bursts through the door.

'Oh, Jazzle! You had us so worried!' She runs over, draping the top of her body over mine and squeezing me with her arms.

'Don't overdo it, Raven. She needs to rest,' Gabby threatens sweetly.

The next second I hear swooping of large wings and feet racing down the staircase.

'Jazz,' screeches Lazarus, still changing form into human as he squashes through the oversized door.

'Jasmine, you're awake,' says Drake, with lumps of stone still falling from his frame.

'Yes, I am thanks to you both and Demona.'

'Okay everyone, you can see she is fine. Now she needs to rest,' says Gabby.

Lolana, Lysander and Jarius all come racing in the room. They stand shoulder to shoulder around the bed.

'What the heck, no one listens.' Gabby throws her hands in the air.

'It's good to see you, Jasmine,' says Lolana, taking a step forward while holding eye contact.

'Everything is fine, Lolana.' I smile, reassuring her I won't tell her secret, except to Demona, who I told accidentally. 'Where is Demona?'

'She's fully recovered and refuses to leave her post on the roof. She knows you're awake and sends her love,' says Jarius.

'Listen here, everyone,' snaps Gabby with her hands on her delicate hips. 'If Jasmine doesn't get the rest she needs to heal, I will blame every one of you for putting her back into her coma.'

'Right. Come on, everyone. You can come and see her later in the day,' says Lysander.

One by one, they kiss my cheek or forehead before leaving. I feel like I am part of one big happy family—a family I never want to leave.

'That wasn't so bad,' says Gabby, dusting herself off nervously.

'Are you all right, Gabby?'

'I am an angel, Jasmine. I don't lose control, ever.'

'When did you lose control? Do you mean asking everyone to leave?'

'Yes, I had to use an annoyed tone. Angels don't use annoyed tones.'

'If it makes you feel any better, it sounded extremely polite with a magical angelic sound.'

'Really? It didn't sound rude?'

'You are beautiful inside and out, Gabby. Thank you again for taking good care of me.' I reach for her hand and clasp it in mine.

'You are welcome but please take better care of yourself.' She leans down and kisses my cheek. 'Now sleep and I will check on you later.' She smiles and floats elegantly from the room.

I pull the blanket up and over my chest. It's so nice to be toasty warm. I wiggle down and listen to my heartbeat. It is calm and content but there is still a small rattle coming from my lungs.

'Raven, sneak back in as I have so many questions to ask,' I echo.

'I'm right here, Jazzle. Great minds think alike,' she says, loud and clear, standing next to the bed. I flip the bed sheet off my head to see her smiling down at me. 'Move over and let me snuggle in, just like we used to do as kids.'

I open my arm and lift the blanket. She jumps under and pulls it over the top of our heads. We snuggle into each other, fitting perfectly, as if we were still children. We giggle uncontrollably until we remember the harmless threat Gabby expressed about me needing to rest.

We lie for hours while I fire question after question, picking her brain for spells and how to control and use my new power.

'I'm worried about Blue Boy, even though Gabby says he's fine,' I say.

'Corbin won't let anything happen to him. He loves horses too much to let Falcon hurt him.'

'I pray you're right.'

'I am. The gargoyles will bring him back here when it's safe.'

With my index finger, I gently trace the tattooed marking on the side of her face. Her eyes watch me for any reaction.

'Your markings are attractive,' I say, once I've completed trailing them.

'You're trying not to hurt my feelings.'

'I really like them, I promise.' I hold my pinkie finger up which she quickly wraps with her pinkie.

'I've missed this. I've missed you.'

'Dreaming about you and our childhood kept me sane. I'd often escape to those memories so I felt close to you again. I needed to feel the warmth of your love and the sisterly connection we had, even if it was only for an hour.'

'You have me for more than an hour now, Jazz. I watched you from a distance until it got too dangerous for both of us. It killed me the last day I saw you. I was saying goodbye to a big part of my heart. I cried for days, with no creature able to console me. But I did it for your safety because I love you.'

'I wish you'd taken me with you.'

'You were too young. A decision was made amongst the elite creatures and your parents that you should be hidden.'

'It all makes sense now. My mother tried to talk me out of travelling. They were both reluctant to let me go.'

'It's taken the strongest sorcerer to keep a covering spell over you, hiding you from the European creatures that will kill to have your powers.'

'I'm safe here and I'm stronger than I was then.'

'I fear for your safety more now than before. You're stronger than Grandfather and me put together and you'll be sought out by greedy creatures. I fear and pray you never side with Attor or Falcon.'

'I can assure you, that day will never come. And if there was enough leather left over after killing Attor I will be happy to make you a pair of shoes and a matching handbag.'

We both giggle, with Raven snorting, making us giggle louder.

'You also need to make a decision about Drake and Lazarus, as both men are infatuated with you.'

'I have strong romantic feelings for Lazarus but I'm drawn to Drake. There's a bond there like I've known him all my life.'

'Maybe Drake was in your past and that's what draws you to him. Your memories are slowly returning, so perhaps they will reveal your connection.' She twirls several long strands of my long hair before braiding them together. As children, we'd often enjoyed playing hairdressers.

'I'm getting a lot of flashbacks but they mainly relate to our past together.'

'Lazarus approached Drake asking for his help to find you when he realised Falcon had abducted you. He abandoned his clan for you and joined forces with his so-called enemy, the gargoyles,' says Raven, grabbing another section of my hair to braid. 'The two of them were distraught but it brought two old and best friends together again. It's a bond that should have never been broken.'

'Many bonds were broken by Attor's greed.'

She nods. 'For some reason, Lolana was a mess with nerves. And Lysander stayed in stone sleep the whole time, ready to fight with full strength. The angels mixed every concoction they knew, ready to use them without delay.'

'I definitely know how to make an entrance into their lives.' I smile.

'It's more than an entrance, it's an explosion.' She giggles.

We move the conversation away from the drama, giggling and reminding each other of the fond memories we have of our grandfather.

'Can I get in on this conversation or do I have to snuggle under the blanket? I am more than happy to do so,' says Lazarus.

We flip the top of the blanket off our heads. Lazarus is standing in his jeans and t-shirt and of course, bare feet. His happy handsome features are a welcome sight.

'I'll leave you two to catch up,' says Raven, slipping out of the bed. I feel the cool air as she leaves and a shiver rattles my body.

'Are you cold, Jazz? I can jump in and give you more body heat than Raven did.' Lazarus smiles.

'Behave, dragon.' Raven chuckles, leaving us alone.

I pat the bed, indicating that he can sit beside me.

He smiles and nods then sits down. 'Your skin has a lovely pink glow. I feared I'd never see it that colour again.' The smile drops from his lips.

'Thank you for keeping me warm. Gabby told me what you all did for me.' I reach for his hand and feel his warmth instantly.

'You had me worried for a while but it was my great pleasure keeping you warm.' His smile is cheeky.

'I'm sorry I don't remember any of it. Were you in dragon form or human?'

'Which one would have you preferred?' His tone is light and playful.

'Just tell me.' I roll my eyes, deflating his ego.

'A red hot-blooded dragon.' He raises an eyebrow over his lime green eye.

'Well, I'm glad about the hot blood side but you could have just snorted me a fire.'

'Snorted!' He laughs. 'I had you wrapped tightly under my wing, pulling you against my body. You were as cold as a—'

'A gargoyle?'

'Yes, a gargoyle.'

A deafening silence falls between us. I watch his expression—one of doubt and insecurity. I wonder if it's because he has left his family, his clan.

'Is something bothering you, Lazarus?'

'You forget I can hear extremely well. Raven didn't put up her silencing shield, and I heard you talking about Drake and myself. I am honoured that you have feelings for me, as I do you. But Drake and I were best mates not that long ago and we swore an oath to each other that we would never let a woman come between us. The look on his face when I said Falcon had kidnapped you was like he had just lost his greatest love.

'When I asked him to join me in the hunt for you, he didn't hesitate, throwing out his hand in friendship and forgiving all that had happened in the past. I could only presume he didn't know I had kissed you. I wished I didn't know *he* had kissed *you*; I was full of jealousy the whole time he carried you in his arms. The only thing that stopped me ripping his head off his shoulders was knowing I would be the one wrapping my warm wings around you at night.'

'What about your family? Corbin? It must be hard living here under the protection of the gargoyles.'

'Let's get one thing straight—I am here to protect you. They are not protecting me,' he explains with a slight raise in his voice.

'Oh, don't go getting all macho on me, lizard.' A smirk creeps onto my lips.

'You have a way with words, Jazz. Demona was telling us what you said to Attor and how you'd turn him into your new wardrobe, and the fight you had in you, even though your body was shutting down. You're a strong woman.'

'Don't change the subject. I need to know how you feel about leaving your family.'

'What does it matter? Demona told me what Attor and Falcon had planned for me—to slowly kill me out in front of you if you didn't join them.' He pulls his arm slightly away from me.

'It matters to me because you gave up your family, Nogard Hollow and your lifestyle to find me. You walked or *flew* away from it all because of me! That is why it matters.'

'Since you have woken, all I think about is Corbin. I fear his life may be in jeopardy if he doesn't comply with what Attor has planned and I know he will have something planned.' His green eyes narrow. 'Anyone approaching Nogard Hollow will be sensed, sniffed out and eliminated before getting anywhere near Corbin. I pray he escapes and does it soon.'

'I may know of a way to get in contact with him.'

'How?'

'He might meet me down at the creek in the next week.' I wonder if Lolana has plans for meeting Corbin soon. She could tell him he is safe here and needs to escape Nogard Hollow before Attor uses him as a tool in his wicked plans.

'Don't tell me you're kissing him too!' snaps Lazarus, jumping to his feet. He paces the room, back and forth, his eyes darting between me and the door. I'm not sure if he is contemplating leaving or if he can hear someone coming.

'I can't explain it so please don't ask me to. Please, you need to trust me,' I whisper.

'Are you kissing Malachi as well?' He places his hands on top of the bedside table.

'Don't you dare throw that!' I remember the last time he lost his cool. Several antique furniture pieces were destroyed. 'Do you think that little of me? You know what? Don't answer that. I think you should leave.' I'm hurt he thinks I would kiss more than one guy. Well, two guys. Oh hell, he has a point!

'Yes, Lazarus, I think you should leave and let Jasmine rest,' says Gabby, entering the room. He glares at her and I can see the fire in his eyes. 'Do I need to get my rude voice out again or are you going to leave quietly like you have been asked to?' Her voice is as soft as a breeze.

'You're playing a deadly game, Jasmine. Remember, two men who wanted the same thing got your grandfather killed and started a war amongst us creatures.' He walks towards the door.

'No, it was pure greed that killed my grandfather. I was there and saw Attor kill him so he could steal the golden soul that never belonged to him. My grandfather wanted to return it to its rightful owners. The stories you've been told are fabricated and were told by a heartless and hideous red dragon.'

'Is that how you see us? No, wait. Don't answer that. I'll do as you ask and leave.' His tone is laced with sadness.

'Don't leave like this. Please come back and talk.' I hear his feet skip the stairs at a great speed. It sounds like he wants to put distance between us and I can't blame him.

'Hell, hell, hell, hell!' I yell, flapping my arms and legs wildly under the blanket.

'Excuse me!' says Gabby in a shocked tone. I look up and she is glaring at me. 'Mind your language.'

'Sorry, Gabby, but I have the worst case of foot in mouth. I didn't mean he was hideous, just his uncle.'

'Why did you let him think you were seeing Corbin?'

'Because I have earned someone's trust and I refuse to let them down. I know how painful that feels.'

'You are full of emotions, young Jasmine. All of them you will need to learn to put under control. Push away the negative emotions and draw on the positive, that way your sorcery will always appear as a white light. You must never tap into your dark side and believe me, you do have a dark side. All humans do, even gifted ones like yourself.'

'Do I have the devil inside me?'

'Oh, sweet girl, there's no devil in you. You radiate the most positive light from your soul. I was just warning you to turn every situation, whether it's good or bad, into a positive and leave the negative for others to worry about.'

'I'll keep that in mind. Thanks, Gabby.' I smile, and then try to sit up.

'Oh, no you don't. Back to bed. From the moment I left, you had visitors sneaking in here. Angels know all.' She taps the side of her temple.

'Well if you know all, tell me which guy I should be in love with.'

'Oh, I know the answer, but you need to listen to your heart and soul. They will guide you and help you make the right decision. Now close your eyes and sleep. Malachi is stationed outside your door so no one will interrupt you.' She grins, kissing my forehead before leaving.

'Gabby…'

'I know, Jasmine, and you are welcome.' She smiles.

I close my eyes and blank my mind as previously taught by my grandfather. I instantly feel my body relax and sag into the bed, and before I take another breath, I drift off to sleep.

I WAKE TO the smell of cooked bacon and eggs, which sets my stomach rumbling.

'Good morning, Jasmine,' says Drake, standing before me with a tray full of food. 'I wasn't sure what you'd like to eat so I've got a selection for you to choose from.'

'Thank you, I am starving. I could eat a horse.' I lick my lips and slowly sit up. I look up at Drake and he has one eyebrow lifted. 'Well maybe not a horse,' I add, making him chuckle.

He places the tray beside me and there's a mountain of bacon, several poached eggs, spinach, tomatoes, several pieces of toast and freshly cut fruit.

'I will never eat all this. Please sit and join me,' I say, trying to stop the salivating dribble from rolling out my mouth and down my chin.

'It would be my pleasure,' He smiles warmly before sitting beside me. 'You look brighter today. How do you feel?'

'Oh, it's daytime?' He nods. 'You should be in stone sleep, especially with Attor on the warpath. Stop putting yourself in danger for me.' I reach out for his hand.

He accepts my hand and, lifting it to his lips, he presses a soft gentle kiss on the back. The warmth from his lips radiates up my arm and towards my soul. I hear my heart thud hard.

'I will be fine. My family have my back and are all upstairs on guard. They know I am here and in human form.'

'It seems everyone knows what I'm up to.' I roll my eyes. I take a bite out of a slice of bacon and it's delicious. My mouth waters and I chew it slowly, savouring the flavour. It is as if I haven't eaten for weeks. But then, I suppose it has been weeks. I gasp, wondering how much weight I have lost and quickly scamper out of bed.

'Where are you going?'

'I want to see myself in the mirror. I must have lost so much weight because I haven't eaten in three weeks.' I gasp in horror when I see a gaunt-looking girl standing in front of me. My face has lost its roundness and my skin is hanging off my bones. A hot flush floods me and my legs wobble.

Drake has me in his arms, lifting me into his chest. 'I am a rake. I'm hideous!'

'No, Jasmine, you are beautiful. A little underweight, but beautiful. Please don't cry,' he whispers in my ear.

I take a deep breath and calm my emotions. 'Can you take me to the bathroom please?' He smiles and carries me, flinging open the door and gently placing me back onto my feet. 'Thank you, I won't be a moment.' He smiles and leaves, closing the door behind him.

I quickly refresh myself and clean my teeth. I look at my reflection in the mirror and shake my head at my small outburst. Drake must think me to be so vain, especially when his whole family turn into gargoyles. I roll my shoulders back and head out into the bedroom. Drake is standing by the window gazing towards Nogard Hollow.

'Sorry about that. Let's eat.' I smile.

'Sure.' He pulls back the blanket so I can slip back underneath. 'So Raven is your cousin.'

'She is and I am a sorceress. My grandfather was one as well and was great friends with your family.'

'I remember him well and I remember you when you were a child. I didn't connect you to Raven. When I met you there was no sign of sorcery. But now, when I look at you both together, I see the magic in your blue eyes.'

'Unbeknownst to me, my childhood memories of the elite creatures was blocked by sorcery. But I found them in my dreams, hence I thought they were exactly that. Dreams!

It was somewhere I would go to escape the sadness of losing Grandfather and Raven.

'Coming here and seeing Raven again has brought back a few memories but when Attor confronted me, everything came crashing back. I saw him take my grandfather's life. He reached into his chest… and took his heart.' I struggle to speak while forcing back my tears.

'My mother has explained everything. You don't need to talk about it if it upsets you.' Drake smiles, rubbing my arm.

'I need to talk about it and often. I will take revenge on Attor when the time is right,' I say through gritted teeth.

'Revenge is not a good trait if you're a sorceress. You need to keep positive, Jazz.'

'Oh, I'm positive all right. I'm positive I will rip out his heart when the time is right.'

Drake shakes his head. 'If he sees you full of anger, he has won, as that is what he wants. A sorceress who can tap into her dark side is more valuable to him than his own sons. Once you go down that road it's hard to return. My advice is to stay true to your soul and forget Attor and Falcon.'

'That is easy for you to say. It was my grandfather's heart that was ripped out.'

'You're right, it was your grandfather, but he was also a part of our family and his death hit us all very hard. He'd want you to stay positive and follow in his footsteps.'

'How do you know what he wants me to do?' I snap, then instantly feel guilty for my outburst. 'I'm sorry. It's just that I miss him every day. I would sit in his room day after day, smelling his jackets and lying on his bed, just so I felt close to him.' I quickly wipe an elusive tear from my cheek.

'I know. I protected you then as I will now. I would watch over you at night and see you cry yourself to sleep,' he admits, dropping his head.

'I never saw you.'

'We were close friends when you were young. I hope those memories return, as we had a special bond.'

'I may not have the memories, but I can feel the bond.'

'I would visit every night for several months after his death. Your mother approached me, asking me to never return. She said she had a sorceress coming to give you a magical orgle stone so everything you knew would be as if it were a dream. I returned a week later to see you happy, playing and sleeping without tears. I knew then the spell had worked and I left you to live a normal life.'

I kneel up in bed and lean over to kiss Drake's cheek, 'Thank you for caring for me.'

'If I'd known you'd be so beautiful, I would have never left your side.'

Lifting both his hands to my lips, I kiss them softly. He cups my cheek in one hand. I turn and kiss his hand again. His blue eyes glow brightly, hypnotising me. I hear his heart beating rapidly. I smile and he cocks his head to the side, questioning my reaction.

'I can hear your heartbeat.'

'That's not fair.' He blushes.

'Oh, I don't know. You can climb any building and glide for hours over the most picturesque land, change form at a whim, not to mention your handsome looks and the copious amounts of muscles bulging out of your skin and your adoring glowing blue eyes. Me—I am a sorceress who can throw white balls around and listen to your heartbeat. Big deal!'

'You forgot to mention your large amazing blue eyes, the red stripe in your brunette hair that matches your spritely per-sonality, with a heart and soul that draws everyone towards it. I would mention your soft rosy lips, but you have just revealed that you can hear my heartbeat.' He smiles widely.

'Eat.' I smile and slide back under the blanket. 'I need to get my strength back or you will have sore arms carrying me around everywhere.'

'It would be my pleasure.'

'And I need to sneak back to get my horse, Blue Boy, from Nogard Hollow.'

'No, you're not to go anywhere near them. Lazarus and I will work out a way to get your horse back.' He grabs my shoulders and sits me square to him. 'Promise me you won't go back there.'

'I won't promise you as I don't want to lose your trust if I happen to stumble over there.'

'You are one frustrating woman. Well, promise me if you happen to *stumble* anywhere off our land you will let either Lazarus or me know.'

'Okay, I promise.' I give him a cheeky smile. He huffs and shakes his head before releasing his grip on my shoulders.

'I wish I could lock you up,' he mumbles.

'I was locked up in a cold cave. I never wish for that to happen again so I'll do what "his lordship" asks. Now eat up, as I am desperately in need of a warm bath and then I want to stretch my legs and go for a walk. And I'd be happier if you'd change form. I worry about your safety.'

'Sounds like you want me out of the way.'

'I promised you I would behave, plus, I don't have the energy to walk down one flight of stairs, so Nogard Hollow is safe from my rant for now.'

'Lord help any man who has to listen to Jazzle Dazzle's rant,' sniggers Raven, walking into the bedroom.

'Morning, cuz!' I smile.

'I'll leave you to shower, Jazz. I will be on the roof. Just call me if you need me.' Drake stands up and kisses my cheek before leaving.

'Change form! I will be sitting right here when you wake,' I yell before he leaves the room.

'Did I interrupt something?' teases Raven.

'Maybe.'

'Well, tell me everything.' She giggles.

'I am having a bath and then, my sweet cousin, we will sit outside and bake in the sun where you can show me the spell to silence my conversation.' I slip out of the bed to head for the bathroom.

'Ah yes, I forgot Lazarus can hear everything we say. Morning, Lazarus!'

'He heard our conversation yesterday which made it easier for me. I didn't have to explain everything twice. But I need to learn the silencing spell so I can control who hears my conversation.'

'Hurry and have your bath. I'll sit here and finish your breakfast. You left so much food on the plate, were you preoccupied?'

'You will never know, cousin!'

I fill the bath to the brim, sliding into the warm water, letting my body and bones relax. I close my eyes and tilt my head back against the bath. Oh, I'm in heaven!

A small scratching sound breaks my tranquillity. With reluctance, I open my eyes to see Xandria flying above my head.

'Xandria?'

'Shh, I need to turn the basin tap on so Lazarus won't hear me.' She flutters over, pulls the tap on and flies back, stopping on the bath's brim near my head.

'What is so important?'

'Attor and Falcon need to talk to you, but you must come alone or they will murder Corbin.'

'Corbin? They wouldn't kill him. He hasn't done anything wrong.'

'Yes, human, they will. Have you forgotten how they were going to kill Lazarus in front of you?' She sits down, swishing her small legs in the warm water.

'Don't get me wrong, I'm concerned for Corbin, but I'm worried about Blue Boy.'

'Xandria has seen your horse. He is fat and in one piece.'

'Thank goodness! What do they want from me? To kill me, as they did my grandfather?'

'They promise not to hurt you. They only need to talk to you.'

'Like hell they want to talk. Why would they kill Corbin if they only need to talk? They want more than just talking and you know it. Don't play me for a fool, fairy!'

'Hey! Xandria is only the messenger. Don't pluck her wings if you don't like the message,' she snaps, jumping to her feet. 'Xandria doesn't care if you go or not. She has delivered the message, now she goes.' She stands with her small hands on her hips. 'Do you have a return message or shall Xandria tell them you don't care about Corbin?'

'I'll meet them, but at the end of the week. Today's the first time I've been out of bed. I need to regain my strength and learn a few tricks of the trade.'

'Xandria can smell you haven't been out of bed or showered for a while.' She sniffs, turning her nose up at me.

'What? I smell? How badly?' I panic, remembering every-one in the bedroom and the close encounters I've had with Drake and Lazarus.

She buckles over, laughing hysterically. 'It's all right, human. You smell fine. That was just a fairy joke. Gabby and Malachi bathed you every day.'

'Malachi bathed me?' I blush.

'Yes, you are one very lucky human. Xandria would love for Malachi to bathe her,' she flutters.

'Hang on, I have no transport over to Nogard Hollow. My horse is over there.'

'Xandria will meet you at the edge of the treeline. She will have your horse so you can ride to Nogard Hollow.'

'You'll bring my horse?' I scoff.

'Fairies may be little but Xandria is strong and he likes her.' She throws her hands back onto her hips, tapping her toe at me.

'Do you think I'm doing the right thing? Maybe I should ask the gargoyles to come along for security?'

'They distinctly said to come alone. Xandria is not an angel who can see into the future, but she does know they don't want to hurt you. They have kept your horse alive so that must count for something. The worst thing that can happen is you get your fat horse back.'

'Fine, I will meet you Friday morning at dawn when Drake is in stone sleep.'

'Remember, you have a dragon here who has your scent.'

'Leave that for me to worry about, fairy.' I slowly stand up to get out of the bath.

'Xandria will leave and return your message to Attor and Falcon. Xandria will see you on Friday.' She flutters her wings and flies to the window, where she squeezes out a small gap. I must take a mental note to remind myself to plug up that hole so she doesn't come back.

I dress quickly and am back out with Raven, picking her brains for answers from all the questions in my head. 'How do I do the silent spell?'

'Grandfather taught us this spell when we were little. I'm amazed your memory hasn't picked it up as you were always using it to cheat while playing hide-and-seek.'

'I never cheated! You just couldn't find me.'

'I'll describe it to you the same way Grandfather did—it

may help unlock your memory. Imagine that you have a colourful crayon in your hand and you are going to draw a rainbow. Start near your hip and draw a rainbow up over your head and down the other side. It creates a dome over you and whoever is with you.

'You can use it to cover your scent as well, but you must do it regularly, as it wears off after an hour. Try it and you will see a faint dome cast over you.'

Doing as she says, I imagine a colourful crayon and, with a slow steady hand, draw a rainbow over us. When finished, I can see a faint dome surrounding me. I'm proud and amazed at how easily this comes to me.

'Well done, cousin. Now let's go outside and steal some of those warm sun rays. We can talk more out there.' She clutches my hand in hers and we walk out of the bedroom and slowly down the long staircase.

'This is when I wish Elyograg Castle had modern amenities, like a lift!'

'Just imagine how terrific your backside will look after running up and down these steps.' She winks, slapping her bottom with her free hand.

We sit for most of the day and talk about the spells and powers I have inside me. I throw large rocks and broken branches around the paddock with a flick of my hand. At one stage, I even lift my horse float off the ground by a metre.

To our amusement, I lift a cow up and watch its shocked face when it tries to run away, its little legs kicking wildly in the air. When I place it on the ground it takes off at a great speed.

I occasionally glance up to the roofline of the castle to see all the gargoyles staring out in the direction of their enemy. Lazarus sits on top, wrapping his amazing red dragon form around a large pillar. He never lets his lime green eye drop down to mine and I get the feeling he is not happy with me.

Gabby interrupts us with more food, which I take willingly, as I need all the strength I can get if I'm confronting Attor. I continue to question Raven about the spells I can use on dragons to inhibit their movements or disarm them.

By the end of the day, I am exhausted, my head swimming with spells. I pray I don't mix up the spells and turn them into tyrannosaurus rex.

I return to my bed, exhausted, and wish Lazarus would come down from the roof to visit me, but he doesn't. All the gargoyles visit one at a time, with Lolana asking me to use my silent spell so she can talk about Corbin.

'Thank you for not saying anything to my family,' she whispers.

'You don't have to whisper. No one will hear us. But don't thank me because I accidentally slipped to Demona when I was weak and locked up in the cave.'

'She hasn't mentioned anything.'

'She is happy for you and said it's your business and no one else's. Maybe now you can confide in her.'

'But I have something urgent I need to discuss with you. Corbin needs to get out of Nogard Hollow. Attor has threatened to kill him.' I keep my tone gentle, but her face shows pure fear.

'That's his family; his uncle. How do you know this?'

'Please don't ask me that. I'm putting my trust in someone and I need you to do the same. When are you meeting him again?'

'Not until Saturday.'

'Bugger! Can you get a message to him before Friday?'

'I could try to sneak onto his land and hope he senses me before the others do.'

'No, that's too risky. Saturday will do.' I don't want to put her in danger. Plus, since they're using Corbin as leverage, they may have him locked up somewhere and unable to meet her.

'You have me worried, Jasmine. What if they hurt him before I get to him?'

'I believe it's only a threat to make me do something. Corbin stands beside Attor so they have no reason to kill him. You must trust me, as I will trust you not to do anything stupid.' I pray that I can get to him before they see me and use my silence spell to tell him to escape to Elyograg Castle. I hope I'm not too late to save Corbin and steal back my horse.

'What do they want you to do? You're not putting yourself in danger?'

'Let's say I've declined their offer.'

Lolana face is grim and I say the only comforting words I can. 'You and Corbin look like a lovely couple.'

It works; her face lights up like a Christmas tree. 'I love him so much it hurts when we aren't together.'

'I can imagine. Why didn't Corbin come here when Lazarus did?'

'He didn't think he was in danger and was constantly listening for clues to your whereabouts. He followed them night after night, but they seemed more interested in hunting other creatures for food and game. Corbin feels he's let you down, as he knows you trust him.'

'I do trust him. It's Attor and Falcon I don't trust.'

'It sounds like you protect your heart with a steel shield.'

'In the past, I put my faith in people only for them to abuse it. So I put up a wall protecting myself from being hurt. There are three people I've let in, as they have proven to be trustworthy—my parents and, oddly enough, my schoolteacher, Paul.' I roll my shoulders back and block out the memories of my ex-boyfriend and Attor.

'But recently, I'm trying to drop my wall and trust you and the other elite creatures. Life's going to have its ups and its downs; humans and elites are going to sometimes fail me, as I will them. I need to learn from their mistakes and mine, keeping my focus on the good in them. If I don't allow myself to trust, I'll become bitter and alone.'

'I understand. Is that why you're torn between Drake and Lazarus?'

'I'm not torn. I care deeply for both of them.'

'You can't have both of them, Jasmine. It's not fair on either of them.'

'As much as it will hurt, it might be wise for me to leave and join another clan where I can continue my training. I don't want to leave either of them but if I can't make a decision, I'll do just that.'

'I'd hate to see you go but I'd do the same. Laz and Drake have a special bond. It would be a shame to see it broken again.'

'You're right, I don't want to be the one who comes in between them.'

'I'm glad I'm in love with one fiery red-hot dragon who will need my support very soon, especially if he's leaving his clan.' She smiles.

'Yes, you are his rock! No offence or pun intended.'

'Don't panic, I won't change form and sit on you for the day, even though I thought about doing that the first day I met you.'

'If that is your way of telling me you're happy to be my friend, I'll take it.' I smile, then I open my arms to invite her in for a hug.

She jumps forward and holds me in a warm embrace. 'Thanks, Jasmine. It gets boring around here with all the boys and Gabby keeps to herself.'

'You're very welcome. I enjoy your company as well, but I

need to lift the silence spell as people will wonder what we are talking about.' I wave my hand over the top of us as if I'm wiping the rainbow away. 'And because Lazarus is being a child and not talking to me.'

A loud rumbling roar echoes from the rooftop.

'Come down and talk, Lazarus. Stop being so childish!'

He releases another rumbling roar.

'Suit yourself, lizard.'

'Wow, you really know how to woo the guys.' Lolana laughs.

'He is shirty because he thinks Corbin and I are an item.'

'Did you tell him that you're not?'

'Yes, but I won't lose the trust I have with a certain person to explain the truth.' I wink at her.

'I'm sorry this has caused you grief, but thank you.'

'He needs a bucket of water thrown down his throat to calm that fiery temper,' I yell, making sure he can hear me.

Drake walks in, making us both jump. 'I think Lazarus heard you loud and clear and has taken off into the forest,' he says with a cheeky grin. 'You love to stir the pot, Jasmine.'

'Well then, my job is done!' I clap and dust my hands.

'Gabby asked me to tuck you into bed. You need your rest, Jazz.'

'I am in bed,' I say cheekily.

'I will leave and let you sleep. Thanks for the chat, Jazz.' Lolana smiles and kisses my cheek before walking out of the room.

'What were you two girls chatting about?'

'You sexy men, of course.' I flutter my eyelids.

'Is that so?' His voice is steamy. Drake moves gracefully towards me and stands strong and tall beside me. He bends so our faces are inches apart. He stares those amazing glowing eyes into mine—blue on blue. I listen to his heartbeat and it's racing fast. He wants to kiss me. 'You have feelings for Lazarus.'

'Yes, I do.'

'But you kissed me.' He frowns.

'Yes, I did. I have feelings for you that I can't explain.'

'Does he know you kissed me?'

'Um… yes.'

'Did you tell him?'

'Not exactly.'

'How exactly did he find out?'

'He tasted you on my lips when he kissed me.' I cringe.

'You kissed Lazarus?' He steps back as if I had pushed him.

'Once, before you and I actually kissed. I mean, I kiss you all the time, but we have only just kissed… passionately. Oh boy, this conversation is embarrassing.' I drop back into the bed, pulling the blanket over my head.

'I won't fight with Lazarus over a woman. We made a pact many years ago and I still stand by it.'

'I know. He told me the same thing and he won't fight you either. He missed your friendship, and you're both right—a woman shouldn't come between two friends.'

'I missed his friendship and am glad it's returned.'

'It may be best if I leave. I can always join another clan in Australia and continue my training there.'

'No, neither of us wants that. If you choose to be with Lazarus, I will accept it and enjoy your company as a friend, as Lazarus will if you choose to be with me.'

'I refuse to be the wedge that comes between you both.' I drop my head in shame. 'There's something I need to do before I leave.'

'Jasmine, please don't leave,' he says, kneeling beside me.

'I'm tired.'

'Please think this through carefully before making a dramatic decision. I walked away from you once, I don't want to do it again.' He kisses my forehead. 'Goodnight.'

'I will always have you in my dreams, Drake.' I roll over so my back is to him.

As soon as the door closes, a flood of tears run down my cheek. When Attor abducted me, it rekindled a fractured friendship, but now my presence is going to fracture it again.

The decision to leave is easy. As much as I love and feel a part of this family, I need to leave to keep the peace amongst the elites. I will keep my word and see Attor on Friday, only to lure Corbin away from his evil claws and retrieve my horse.

CHAPTER NINE

I cry myself to sleep and wake tired and disorientated. I walk around in a small daze until Gabby stands firmly in front of me. She places a comforting hand on my shoulder and smiles. A warmth flows through me, followed by a feeling of peace with myself and the decision I have made. Whatever magic she has I'm glad she's sharing it with me.

I walk upstairs to the rooftop and see the gargoyles in their stone sleep positions. I inhale a deep breath, drawing in my emotions and putting on a confident, cheery demeanour.

'Morning, Lysander,' I shout to one end of the roof. 'Good morning, Jarius. It's lovely to see you smiling.' I giggle, as he has his tongue poking out in a rude gesture. He is obviously teasing one of his family members. 'Morning, Lolana. Nice to see you've filed those nails. Demona, it has been a long time since I've seen you. Thank you again for bringing me back home… um, I mean back here.'

I move towards Drake and run my hand over his large wing. 'Good morning, handsome. How's the day looking?'

I hear a loud sigh and turn to see Lazarus perched on top of a concrete pillar in dragon form. Damn, he's absolutely incredible to look at. 'And good morning to you, Lazarus.' I smile but he keeps his lime green eye staring out and away from me. 'Are you going to ignore me again?'

He roars, leaps off the top of the pillar and lands beside me.

'You don't scare me, Lazarus, even if you are a ten-tonne killing machine.'

He moves his head so it's before me. He raises his red

scaly lips; something a snarling dog does.

'Do you have something in your teeth you'd like me to get out?'

He roars, leaps into the air and flies around screaming on the top of his lungs. What an attention seeker! I move to the edge of the roof and watch his rant play out.

He lands on the ground and looks up at me. 'Well, at least you're looking at me now.'

He bellows out a roaring flame which falls short of the castle and me. I know it's a childish threat and nothing more. But if he wants to play with fire, I can play with my anorics.

Holding my hands out to the side, I draw energy up through my feet and body, allowing it to flow to my hands. I feel the surge before I see the white swirls ignite. I draw up more energy and let it flow. The balls increase in size and I glare down at the glorious creature below me.

I lift my hands and he huffs at me, letting smoke escape his mouth. He is laughing at me. I hurl both hands towards the ground, aiming so they'll land next to his clawed feet but won't hit him. They explode when they hit the ground.

He jumps sideways and glares up at me before releasing an almighty rumbling roar. I lift one hand to my mouth, holding my index and middle finger together as if I had just shot a bullet from them. I blow on it and holster my hand into my jean pocket then I repeat the action with my other hand. 'Who's laughing now?'

He spins, and with a violent gush of hot air, he is standing in human form. 'What the hell was that?'

'Oh, so now you want to talk?' I throw my hands on my hips before skipping down the stairs and out of the castle. Lazarus is pacing back and forth, his lime-green eyes staring deadly daggers at me.

I slow my pace as I exit the castle, trying to judge his mood before I approach. He's angry and a dragon—not a good mix.

'You think firing your white fury at me is funny?' he yells. 'I'm not used to being attacked and not taking revenge. I could have lashed out and ripped your head off your shoulders.'

'And then you could stick my head on the mantelpiece and walk past it every day and *not talk to me!*' I shout. 'Anyhow, I wasn't going to hit you with them. You fired first, remember?'

'I know how far my flame will go. You don't know your strength or what your powers can do. You could have killed me! Or was that your plan?'

'Don't be so stupid! Why on Earth would I want to kill you? The anorics landed exactly where I wanted them to— close enough to show you I too can be scary.'

'Do I scare you when I'm in dragon form?' his voice taking a softer tone. 'When have I ever hurt you in dragon form? I've proven to you I can control my urges.'

'You punctured my torso, remember? I leaked like a sieve.'

'You think I meant to hurt you? Was I supposed to let you fall to your death?' He paces back and forth, kicking the stones along the ground.

'You don't scare me in any form, human or dragon. I know you'd never burn or hurt me, not on purpose. I don't fear any of you creatures, only the beasts at Nogard Hollow.' I bring my voice back to a more civilised tone.

'Don't mention them. It reminds me of the danger Corbin could be in. Plus, the fact you have been seeing him and Drake.'

'I've seen Corbin but not in the way you think. I can't and won't explain our connection but it's not what you so rudely suggested!'

I glance up to the gargoyles still in stone sleep. I wonder if they are enjoying the cabaret show Lazarus and I are putting on.

'Do that silent spell.'

'Why?'

'Because I don't need everyone listening to our conversation,' he spits through gritted teeth.

I close my eyes and pick up my spiritual coloured crayon and draw my rainbow.

When I open my eyes, Lazarus grabs me by the shoulders, lifting me off my feet. In one swift stride, I am backed up against the castle wall.

He presses his warm heated body against mine and forces his hot lips onto me. He kisses me hard and angry, bruising my lips, but I don't stop him. If I'm leaving at the end of the week, I may as well enjoy it.

His hands eventually lose their firm grip and slowly slip around my waist, pulling me tight in into him. I hear his heart racing at the same speed as mine and it brings a small curve to my lips.

'You're smiling while I'm kissing you.' His emerald green eyes blink in question.

'I'm listening to our hearts.'

'Try being a dragon. It's deafening.'

'Can I ask you something without you getting upset?'

'Trust me, I'm quite calm now I have my arms around you.' He smiles the devil's grin.

'The first time I came to Nogard Hollow, you weren't certain you could control yourself, when you were in dragon form, to keep from eating me.'

'Dragons have been known to roast a human, then eat them. You taste like pork with crackling, apparently. I haven't had the pleasure of tasting it. What I do know is how delicious your scent is.'

'Well, you'd best keep that flame dowsed and those teeth in your head and away from me, mister.' He releases a laugh and it's angelic to my ears. 'Anyhow, it may only be a myth and humans may taste like leather. No pun intended.'

'None taken. I once saw Attor rip out a heart from a human and swallow it. Apparently, he then consumed the body after roasting it with his flame. I didn't hang around to watch, as it made me sick to the stomach. Animals I can deal with, but not taking a human life,' he says, loosening his hold on me.

'Maybe I should fear Attor more than I do.'

'You don't have to fear him because you will never be near him again. We will protect you from him and anyone else who threatens you.' He kisses me again.

I lose my train of thought as his heated body presses against mine and his lips, which have softened, caress mine. I let my hands slide over his toned arms and across his large pectoral muscles, letting one hand rest comfortably over his beating heart and the other to continue to examine his back. Talk about mind overload! He is pure muscle and when he moves his hands to caress my back and waist, I can feel them contract under my fingers.

His firm hold keeps our bodies aligned. The heat between us is incredible, and his kiss is intense. The heat from his body moves into mine, warming me on the inside. There's a pull like gravity, starting in my feet and surging up through my legs into my stomach. It slithers through me and stops at my heart.

Lazarus continues to kiss me, awakening all my senses, sparking a heated current in my head. I let all the energy in my body collide and feel as though I am about to explode.

'Ouch!' Lazarus flies backwards several steps. 'What was that?'

I chuckle with embarrassment. 'I'm not sure.'

'It felt like I was kissing an electric fence and the light that came out of you was… it was beautiful.'

'So kissing me is like kissing a fence?'

'Oh no, Jazz. I could get lost in those lips all day.'

'I'm sorry about the electric shock. I felt it brewing but I didn't know what it was. Part of it came from the heat of your body, which mixed with the same energy pull I get when creating my anorics. I may need to discuss this with Raven.'

'If you need a reenactment, I'm a willing participant. What better way to spend my days than kissing you?'

'I need to tell you something but with your hearing, you may already know. I've decided to leave and continue my training elsewhere. I refuse to come between you and Drake, especially since you have re-established your friendship.'

'No, you can't leave. It's fine if you want to be with Drake. As long as I can see and talk to you, I will be happy.' He pulls me back into his arms.

'That is a lie and you know it. You flew off the handle when you thought I was kissing Corbin. If you see me in Drake's arms every day, you will end up hating me, or worse, Drake.'

'I can handle it. Please stay.' His green eyes soften.

'I have made my mind up. Let's enjoy the last few days I have here. Please.' I force a smile to my lips.

'I won't let you go, Jazz.'

'Then I will leave without you knowing.'

He taps his nose and grins. 'I will sense you.'

I wiggle my fingers in front of him. 'I have my ways of sneaking around undetected.'

'You won't leave without saying goodbye? Promise me, Jasmine, that you won't do that?'

'I cross my heart.' I symbolise a cross over my heart using my index finger. 'And I promise with my soul that I will never leave you without saying goodbye.'

He grabs the hand that has just pledged my promise and lifts it to his lips. He places a soft kiss on the tip of my index finger. 'I'll take that promise. Now, I know what I would like to do today but what would you like to do today?'

'Have you eaten recently?'

'An odd question, but yes, I had deer, thanks for asking.' He breathes through his teeth as if still tasting the deer.

'I'd really like to see the countryside from up there.' I point to the sky.

'You like living life on the edge.' He sighs. 'Your wish is my command.' He steps away, giving himself enough room to change form without knocking me. He drops his head slightly, giving me a cheeky green-eyed grin. In seconds, a gust of warm air circles around me.

'Wait! What was it you wanted to do today?'

'I wanted to lock you away in your bedroom and kiss you until you couldn't breathe.'

My heart kick-starts into top speed. A wide smile covers his face; he heard it too.

'I wouldn't have said no,' I yell, watching his form change before my amazed eyes.

It is a beautiful thing to witness. Bright red misty swirls of cloudy dust come together in a squall of hot air to create the exceptional creature we call a dragon.

He shakes his long scaly body, like a dog shaking its coat after being washed, and moves slowly towards me, careful not to tread on me. He moves so his nose is nudging my waistline. With a long and slow breath, he breathes me in, then opens his mouth, showing his crocodile-sharp teeth.

I place one hand on the tip of his tooth and gently run my hand over the tips of several of them, letting him know how much I trust him. His tongue follows my hand, tickling my fingers as I reach the larger teeth at the back of his mouth.

I watch his eye as he studies me. I move back to his two large nostrils and he inhales another long breath. I lay my chest between his two oval nostrils, spreading my arms wide, hugging his large head.

His breath on my legs is warming as I relax into the small dip in between his nostrils. He sighs and, with gentle hands, I glide them over his face.

I look up to see his two lime green eyes watching me intently. 'Let's go flying, baby.'

I move around to his front leg. His nose is under my backside, slowly pushing me up to his back.

'I must admit, I enjoyed your nose nuzzling my cheek when we were kissing but having your nose nuzzle my butt to get onto your back has me a little embarrassed.' I pull myself up between his shoulder blades and wings. He lets out a smoky rumble and I know he is laughing.

I grip with my knees and he stretches his wings wide open, lifting them up and down as if testing them with me sitting at the base of them. He turns his head and winks his eye.

'I'm ready when you are.' I smile and, out of habit, I rub him on his shoulder with my hand like I do Blue Boy.

He rumbles and it vibrates through his body before he expands his large wings and, with a vertical gush, we are in the air and flying.

He circles the castle, which shows its true size. If someone were to tell me that there was a castle of this size in Australia out in the middle of nowhere, I would have thought they were loopy. Seeing it for myself is unbelievably surreal.

'The castle is so big. I knew when I climbed those stairs it was big but seeing it from up here, it's jaw-dropping huge!' I say loudly, then remember he can hear me when I whisper.

He takes off in the opposite direction from Nogard Hollow. I presume he doesn't want to have an encounter with his deranged family. 'Good choice of direction.'

He gains height, then opens his wings wide and glides over this amazing country. The hills and pasture are lush with green grasses and I can smell the difference when passing over the top of gum trees from when we pass over the top of wattle trees. The bush aroma sets my olfactory system into overload.

We soar above wild Brumbies, who are oblivious to Lazarus' large frame above them. To see them wild and free makes my heart sing. Lazarus must have heard my heart, and he releases a loud roar similar to a lion. It spooks the Brumbies and they gallop off, elegantly jumping over clumps of bush with their heads held high, swinging their necks side to side, clearly trying to spot where the noise came from.

After a while they stop, turn and stand tall, looking in the direction they came from with ears pricked, listening for any more frightening sounds.

Lazarus turns and heads towards the river which feeds the creek that runs behind the castle and near Nogard Hollow. The river is wide, with a number of large lakes that branch off in several directions. Its blue veins give life to the earth.

There is an abundant array of wildlife feeding below us, with birds taking off in flight when we drop to glide metres above the river.

Kangaroos join in the flight and scatter off, changing their route with every second stride. A group of emus drinking on the side of the river move away at a locomotive speed, evading the tips of Lazarus' wide, spanned wings.

Cattle graze close by and are unmoved by our presence; no wonder they are easy prey for dragons and gargoyles.

Out the corner of my eye, I spot small creatures scattering under bushes too quickly for my eyes to see. Lazarus gradually slows and flaps his wings, hovering as if his prey were underneath him. I pray he remembers I'm on him and doesn't dive onto an unaware animal.

'Hey, remember I'm on top,' I whisper, rubbing his shoulders gently with my hands.

He lands with a small jolt, then sits. I presume he wants me to get off. I throw my leg over his back and slide down his shoulder, leg and foot, until my feet hit the soft ground. I remember his reaction the last time I slid off him and chuckle at the thought. 'Am I getting too heavy for you?'

He snorts and I gather he is laughing but it doesn't answer my question. He winks his eye and he gently pushes me away with his nose.

With a gush of warm air and the red collection of particles I have become to know so well, Lazarus is standing in front of me in human form. With one stride, he is right beside me, his lime-green eyes darkening and his chest rising and falling at a rapid speed.

He stares at me for a few long seconds before encasing me in his strong arms. His lips are on mine, hot, heated and hard.

He pulls back and shakes his head. 'We need to find another way to get you off my back. If you keep sliding your body down me, I'll combust.'

'Oh,' I say shyly, dropping my eyes to the ground. He puts his index finger under my chin and softly lifts my face up to look at his. 'Please don't leave me, Jazz. I'm falling in love with you, if you haven't noticed.'

'I'm not changing my mind so can we change the subject?'

'No!'

'Lazarus!'

'Jasmine!'

'Why did we stop?'

'Apart from listening to your delicious heart jumping around with excitement every time you saw something new, I thought you might enjoy a cool swim in the river. It's safe here and I'll sense if anyone's coming.'

'I thought you said you weren't interested in eating me?'

'You are very tempting, Jazz, but I know I can control

myself in the dietary department. If I had to withhold from kissing you, it would be a totally different situation. Speaking of which,' he purrs, leaning into me for another kiss.

I accept his soft lips and, for a split second, I wish I weren't leaving at the end of the week. I shake the thought out of my head. The clans have come together again and with me being here, it will put undue pressure on the relationship.

Pulling back, Lazarus opens his eyes and gives me an assessing look. 'What's that head of yours thinking about?'

'Nothing,' I lie.

'Rubbish.' He taps his ear. 'Your heart was pumping beautifully then it nearly thudded to a stop.'

'Stop over-analysing everything. Men will never understand a woman's emotions so don't try to start now. Let's go for that swim. I was getting quite hot sitting up there between your wings.'

'Mmm, were you now?' he says with the cheeky grin. 'I was getting hot kissing you.'

I smack him on the arm. 'Behave, dragon!'

He releases a boisterous laugh, scoops me up into his strong arms and carries me to the river's edge. 'Shall I throw you in or would you prefer to enter at your own pace?'

'No, don't throw me in! I'd like to walk in nice and slowly to let my body adjust.'

'To hell with that!' With one giant leap, he jumps into the middle of the river with me still in his arms. We hit the cold water fully clothed.

I pop up to see his face wearing the largest grin. I splash him and, within a second, he disappears underwater.

I wait for him to tug me under the cooling water or jump up to scare me, but his warm hand touches my leg and I feel the heat from his body before he surfaces inches from my face.

He treads water, holding me afloat with his warm arm around my waist. The heat from his body is a welcoming and an unusual feeling, especially when the cold river water is trying to lower my temperature.

He kisses me softly, then passionately. He releases me and floats me on my back with my ears just underneath the water.

I lie motionless, gazing through the canopy of trees to see the odd bird fly past. The sky is a magnificent royal blue dotted with the whitest puffy clouds I have ever seen. I close my eyes and let my nose explore the surroundings. The Outback doesn't disappoint, giving me an amazing mixture of aromas.

I can feel the heat from Lazarus as he moves around my floating body as if he is heating the water around me.

After what seems like hours, we swim to the edge of the river and slowly climb out. Lazarus removes his jeans and wrings them out, throwing them over a tree branch to dry. He confidently stands in front of me in his underwear. I shyly remove my t-shirt and jeans, wringing and throwing them over the same tree branch.

'The bra I'm quite enjoying, but the granny undies!'

'Hey, I like my cottontails. They are comfortable when I'm riding my horse *or my dragon.*' I smile, looking at my underwear, which is nearly the same size as a pair of shorts.

'You have tattoos similar to Raven's,' he acknowledges with sceptical eyes.

'Yes, you dragons aren't the only ones fond of ink.'

'My tattoos appeared by themselves.' He glances down at the red and green dragon wrapping around his large bicep.

'Mine appeared after Falcon burnt my legs. They were white in colour to start with, but since I have tapped into my sorcery, they have changed to black. Every time I bathe I forget they are there and get a shock. I suppose I'm still getting used to them.'

'It's nothing to be embarrassed about. It's a part of you and you should embrace the fact that you are different from the person next to you.' He says before slowly moving towards me.

'Oh, I am definitely different!'

'What a boring world it would be if we were all the same, Jazz. You and I are amazing creatures that make this world exciting and unique. I believe that out in this large solar system there's another planet like Earth, where living and breathing creatures reside. They may be more intelligent or less. They may be four-legged creatures or three-legged razor-sharp toothed beasts. But they will be different.

'Humans are so shallow-minded as they believe dragons, gargoyles, fairies, vampires, werewolves and sorcerers are all created in their minds. How wrong can they be? You've seen that for yourself now.' He smiles, moving me into his warm arms.

'I suppose it's my vanity that is consuming me. I don't want people to point and stare. But I don't want to live my life as I did before leaving home. The repetitiveness of waking up, working, returning home to sleep, then up again is a life I left behind for a reason.'

'And when those people come to their last day in life, they'll look back and see how humdrum their lives have been, and believe me, they will. You can look back and say, "Hell, yeah. I had fun!"

'To be different means you are an original; one of a kind. To be different is to be *you*!' He locks his warm green eyes with mine. 'You can also say what a great time you had falling in love with Lazarus and how he was such a great kisser.' He smirks, leaning forward to place his soft lips on mine, halting any further conversation.

'Oh, I can definitely say that!'

He scoops me up in his muscular arms and gently lies me on the ground. The soft cushioning of the grass supports my body and I watch with wide eyes as Lazarus lies beside me. He rolls onto his side, his arm reaching over me so the top of his bronzed chest towers over me. His face halts several inches away from mine.

I search his eyes, wondering why he isn't kissing me. He gazes at me for several painstaking minutes. 'You can't leave me, Jasmine.'

'I don't want to talk now. I'd prefer it if you were kissing me,' I say, a smile tickling the sides of my mouth.

I slide my hand up his arm, letting my eyes follow what I am feeling. I slowly glide my fingers over his rounding bicep, up and over his solid shoulder, stopping at the nape of his neck.

I place a small amount of pressure, encouraging him to lower his amazing soft lips to mine. He gives a lopsided smirk before heeding my command.

I give a sigh of relief when I feel the warmth of his lips and the heat from his chest which is now pressing against my breasts.

He rolls his body so he is lying on top of me, holding most of his weight on his elbows, with his long legs slipping between mine. His black hair falls forward, outlining his handsome features.

With his toned body encasing mine, my body temperature automatically rises. I'm not sure if it's from Lazarus' natural warmth or the excitement rising inside of me.

His kiss becomes more passionate and I welcome it, encouraging him by running my hands firmly over his toned bronzed back muscles.

My body absorbs the heat Lazarus' body is exuding. The same energy I felt when I gave him the electric shock is again building up through me.

I try to control my heartbeat because between my electric shocks and Lazarus with his flame, we could set the whole countryside on fire.

I slow my beat and Lazarus lifts his lips from mine. His eyes question me and I smile, sneaking my hand from his glorious back to make it travel to the nape of his neck where I can persuade him to continue his assault on my lips.

He growls, and it rumbles through his toned body, vibrating through his chest into mine. When he is this close it's as though we are one and, for a split-second, I wonder if my soul is trying to tell me he is the one.

As soon as I stop concentrating on my heartbeat, it accelerates. I hear Lazarus', which is pounding out of control. He rolls, flipping me, so I am lying on top of him.

Now I have the control. I sit up and gaze at this poster boy I am straddling. Once I catch my breath I lean down, my hair cascading around my face, as I continue to kiss him.

The heat radiating from his body is intense and mine seems to crave it, drawing it into my core. His large hands race over my body, eager to know me better.

I sit up and stare at his handsome face. He softly runs his coarse hands from my knees to my thighs, watching my face intently.

I lift my arms and bend them to behind my back, undoing my bra.

'Jazz, no!' gasps Lazarus.

'You're saying no? You don't want to make love?' I'm shocked. I leave my bra hitched and flop to the side, rolling off him and onto the grass. 'Ouch! That's the most embarrassing thing that has happened to me.'

I lay on my back with one arm thrown over my face to cover my eyes and my embarrassment.

'Trust me, every inch of my body is saying yes and if my hand could reach the back of my head, it would slap me hard for being so stupid!' He pulls my arm slightly to the side of my face so he can see one of my eyes.

'Maybe you should change form and the sharp end of your tail could slap you one,' I grunt.

'But you've said you're leaving, so if that is true, I don't want to be the one to take your virtue.' He sits but never loses eye contact.

'Who said you would be taking my virtue?' I childishly snap, trying to cover the embarrassment of his rejection.

'What are you saying? Have there been other men? Who was it, Drake?' In a blink of an eye, he jumps on top of me, straddling me, holding my arms away from my face, pinning them beside my ears.

'No, I haven't made love to Drake! I have kissed him, which you know.' I try to wriggle my arms free. He loosens his hold but doesn't let go. 'I have had boyfriends before you.'

'Who are they and how many?'

'Who is my business and so is the number.'

'Don't make me ask again, Jasmine,' he growls.

'Oooh, back to calling me Jasmine.'

He rumbles deep in his chest and I can feel it vibrate through his entire body. His eyes flicker and darken to a sinister green. 'Now if you had smoke coming out your mouth, I'd be scared.'

He puckers his rosy lips and blows out half a dozen smoke rings, then smirks one side of his mouth. His eyes narrow and I know his silence is because he is stopping himself from blowing his stack.

'One serious boyfriend!' I say.

He inhales a deep breath and narrows his eyes again. He wants more information. He releases my hands and crosses his arms across his chest. I shrug my shoulders. He leans closer and blows smoke into my face again.

'I do believe what I did with my ex-boyfriend is my business.'

'Maybe I should visit this young man and ask him myself. I can be very persuasive.'

'As I can be,' I purr. I walk my fingers up his stomach, over his crossed arms to his chest. His hand snatches at mine, holding it firmly while grasping my other hand and placing them both beside my ears.

I open my mouth slightly and lick the top of my lip, teasing him to forget my past and concentrate on the present. With a deep breath through his nose, I hear his heart change from a bass drum to a softer tambourine sound.

'I hate thinking someone else is kissing and touching you. I want to rip his heart out for having the pleasures only I should have,' he says greedily.

He drops his face to mine and forces his lips to lock firmly onto me. His kiss is bruising but I don't complain—his urgency and want are engraved in his powerful kiss. I wrap my arms around him and pull him harder into me. It's like it's our last kiss and maybe it will be.

He sits up and turns his head so he is looking at me from the corner of his softening eyes.

'You said you'd had boyfriends before me. Does that mean I am your boyfriend?' A small curve lifts the corner of his lips.

'It was a slip of the tongue.'

'Mmm, and what a wonderful tongue it is.' He kisses me again.

We lie in the warm sun, Lazarus on his back with his eyes closed, but with a continuous smile upon his lips. I cocoon into his side, and glide my fingers over his chest, tracing the outline of the tattoo he has over his heart. It's a small yin-yang symbol with a red dragon curving through the middle.

The tattoo on his arm is more tribal, with sharp distinctive edges, whereas the one on his chest is softer and, because it sits over his heart, I imagine it has some significance to the balance of his race. I try to remember if I've seen a tattoo on Attor's chest but my skin lifts with goosebumps when I think about it.

'Get it out of your head,' whispers Lazarus, rolling onto his side so we are face to face. 'Your heart just blew an extra valve.'

'Sorry, I was thinking of Attor.'

'I thought me lying beside you might trigger a more exciting thought than that.'

'Oh, it does.' I give him a quick kiss. 'The tattoo on your chest; does Attor have one?'

'Yes, we all do. But his and Falcon's have a black dragon, as do a few of our overseas relatives. Corbin's is the same as mine—a red dragon clambering through the balanced yin-yang.' He pushes a few loose strands of my hair back from my face.

A cool breeze blows over us, making my body shiver.

'We should head back before the sun sets, not that I want to take you anywhere near Drake,' he says, jokingly snarling, then pouncing on me and my waiting lips.

Within minutes, we gather our dried clothes and re-dress. I watch in awe as Lazarus changes form, drawing his natural form from the earth. He sits his large frame down and waits for me to climb on board.

I walk to the tip of his nose and run my hand slowly down the length of his leathery red skin. I am speechless every time I see this magnificent creature before me, and unfortunately, I fall in love with him with every breath I take. I reach the tip off his tail and, with a light touch, run my hand over the sphere-bladed end. It has four sharp edges running to the tip, like four sharp butcher's knives tied together. This weapon can easily pierce a hole through another dragon. I walk back towards his front leg.

'I've changed my mind about you hitting yourself in the head with the end of your tail.'

He snorts a puff of smoke, laughing with me. He turns his head and moves his nose towards my bottom.

'I think I'd prefer to climb up by myself if you don't mind?'

He shakes his head and rumbles a loud sound within his huge body.

'Thank you.' I climb up his leg, using his scales to pull myself along. It's like rock climbing but I daren't mention the words 'rock' or 'stone' when he is in dragon form. His jealous tantrum in human form was tough enough to handle. I could imagine him, a full-grown dragon rolling around the ground, stomping his legs and swishing his tail, pulling out trees and throwing them across the valley, not to mention burning everything in sight.

When I reach the top of his shoulders, I wiggle my bottom to sit against the base of his wings. I rub his shoulders with my hands and he makes a sound as if he is rumbling a purr; a noise I imagine a contented lion makes.

I grip with my legs and he stretches his wings, testing or feeling for where I am. With several downward thrusts, we are in the air and moving forward. His long neck moves downward when his wings are high and lifts when his wings lower.

Lazarus is quick to gain height and glides most of the way back to the castle where the gargoyles are starting to come out of sleep. His body tenses underneath me as he flies in a circle over the castle.

'Relax, Lazarus. If it makes you feel better, I love you. But I am still leaving,' I whisper.

He lands as gently as he can, but I still jolt forward onto his neck. He sits, allowing me to dismount. I search for an alternative way to get down. Lazarus turns his long neck so he can see me.

'I'm trying to work out how to get off without sliding down you because… well, you know why.' I shrug my shoulders.

He snorts and a puff of smoke shoots out his mouth.

'I need an extension ladder or I could wait until a gargoyle comes out to help me.'

He rumbles a low irritated noise and shakes his body like a wet dog.

I grip with my legs so I don't fall off, getting the message he'd prefer I slid down. 'All right, you grumpy lizard! Don't go getting all hot and sexy for me when I slide down.'

I throw my leg over his neck and, as I slide down, he releases a loud lion-like roar. I burst out in laughter, my legs nearly giving way when I reach the ground.

I walk to his head. 'You are amusing, Lazarus.' I give his nose a long noisy kiss. 'Stay in this form as long as you need to. I'm going to help the angels cook dinner so I'll see you later. Thanks for the day. It's one I will never forget.'

The angels are busy in the kitchen when I walk in. They don't turn to acknowledge me and continue as if I hadn't entered the room.

'Hi, guys.'

'Evening, Jasmine. Did you enjoy your day with Lazarus?' asks Malachi in a soft tone.

'It was unbelievable! Flying high above the land with the wind in your face is something I will never forget.'

'So you have decided to go?' Gabby asks, pulling a slab of meat from the refrigerator.

'Yes, I am leaving at the end of the week.' My tone loses its momentum.

'You're in love, my sweet soul, so why don't you stay?' Gabby asks, handing me several vegetables and a sharp knife.

'Because I love them both.'

'No, you don't. You love one and share a bond with the other. You don't want to hurt someone because your soul has felt that hurt before and it's still trying to heal. Jasmine, you must be honest with yourself first, and then you will be honest with them,' Malachi says, placing a chopping board in front of me.

'You need to make a decision because every day, every hour

and every minute you are here they are both falling more and more in love with you,' says Gabby.

I slam the knife through the vegetables, trying to block their sensible words from my ears. I will end up hurting the two men I care about. I need to leave sooner rather than later.

I decide to leave first thing in the morning, just after Drake and his family turn to stone. And somehow, I will try to avoid Lazarus' eagle eye and curtail his senses.

'I won't be the beast that rips people's hearts out. I have made my mind up to leave, even though I now know I have a lifelong bond with Drake and my heart beats for Lazarus,' I whisper.

'We know,' says Malachi in a calm, knowing tone.

'You mustn't tell anyone.'

'We can't as it will alter the future. We are not here to determine your life's journey, just to guide you and to help you to stay positive,' says Gabby. 'Remember, there's negative energy everywhere. Be careful who you trust and rely on your soul. It will sense who is good and who is not.'

'I will always remember that I am my grandfather's grand-daughter and that will forever keep me positive.'

'Definitely, cuz!' says Raven, walking in behind me. 'How was the scenic flight?' She nudges me in the side and I force a smile to my lips.

I spin around and encase her in my arms. 'I love you, I love you, I love you!' My eyes quickly fill with tears.

'And I love you. What's up, Jazzle?' She tries to loosen my tight bear hug.

'Nothing.' I wipe away the tears rolling down my face with a quick hand. 'I just don't tell you enough that I love you.'

'Keep that love going around,' says Jarius, walking into the kitchen in human form. He wraps his arms around both Raven and me, pulling us in tightly.

'You idiot, Jarius,' murmurs Lolana, shaking her head and rolling her eyes as she walks past.

'Evening, all.' Drake smiles, with Lysander close on his heels.

'Evening,' I say, collecting myself and turning to finish slicing the vegetables.

'What am I missing?' Lazarus says; the last to enter.

'Jazzy is telling us how much she loves us,' jokes Jarius.

I punch him softly in the arm and he jokingly rubs it as if I had hurt him.

'Is that so?' Lazarus questions.

'No, I wasn't saying I loved everyone.' I shake my head, then reconsider my position. 'Actually, I'd like to say thank you to all of you for caring for me and for making me feel like I am part of the family. So yes, I do love you all.' I force back the tears that are sitting just below the surface.

I take a quick breath to control my heartbeat but Lazarus is already narrowing his eyes at me.

'Sounds like a goodbye speech,' he says.

'Not at all. It's a good opportunity to say thank you when everyone is in the same room.' I calm the blood pumping through my heart.

'Well, too many cooks spoil the broth,' interjects Gabby.

'I think that's Gabby's polite way to ask you all to leave until dinner is ready,' I say.

'Ah, you love me crowding your style, Gabby,' Jarius jokes, lifting her up in his strong arms and spinning her around.

'Put me down. You're squashing my golden wings.' She giggles.

'Come on everyone, let them be or we won't get fed,' Lysander's sensible voice commands.

They file out, with Lazarus being the last to leave. He moves to whisper in my ear, 'You crossed your heart you'd say goodbye.' He lifts my hand and kisses my index finger, the same one that crossed my heart.

I smile and nod. He leaves with a sceptical smile on his face.

'That *was* your goodbye,' whispers Malachi.

'Shh.'

'He can only hear what I want him to hear.' He smiles.

I nod yes and cry while cutting the vegetables.

Dinner is loud and full of conversation and laughter. I smile and listen to each and every person, taking in the sound of their voices and heartbeat so I can lock it away in my treasured memories.

I retire to my room early, with Drake slipping by to tuck me into bed. He lies down beside me and I snuggle into his side, falling asleep in the arms of my protector.

Chapter Ten

I WAKE WITH my thoughts returning from a disturbing nightmare. I quickly run to the window to see what part of the day it is.

'It's dawn, human,' Xandria's tiny voice says.

I jump in fright. 'What are you doing here?'

'Attor wanted to see if you were still coming to see him in a few days,' she says, fluttering over.

'I'm leaving now to see him. Can you bring Blue Boy to the forest in the next hour?'

'Xandria is very clever and efficient. Blue Boy is already grazing near the forest. His saddle is under the same tree where Xandria first met you.' She lands on the bedside table, throwing her small hands on her tiny hips.

'Thank you and goodbye,' I whisper.

'No need to whisper. Lazarus is out hunting. He can't hear us.'

'Perfect!' I'm quick to grab a pair of jeans and throw on a clean t-shirt. I slip on socks and shoes and am ready to leave in less than sixty seconds. 'You need to promise you won't tell anyone where I am.'

'You can never trust fairies.' She giggles.

I run into the bathroom, grab a glass cup and race back towards Xandria. I surprise her and capture her in the glass, placing it upside-down on the bedside table.

'I'm so sorry, Xandria. I hope you will forgive me one day, but it was either this or I pluck your wings from your back.'

She squeaks but I can't hear her and move quickly to

the door. I open it quietly and listen for any movement in the house. I walk down the stairs and head for the back entrance. I gently open the door, step outside then pull it closed behind me.

I inhale a deep, calming breath and grab hold of my magical rainbow-coloured crayon. I draw my silent dome then head towards the creek, which is in the opposite direction to where the gargoyles are looking.

After walking for over an hour I reach the forest and find my saddle and bridle but no sign of Blue Boy. For a split second, I wonder how a small creature like Xandria could saddle and unsaddle my horse, as most days I have trouble throwing the saddle onto his high back.

I whistle, then panic when I notice my rainbow dome has disappeared. I grab my magical crayon and wave it above my head. I yell out for Blue Boy and hear his snicker. I call again and see him emerge from the trees. I release a loud sigh as he canters over.

'Hello, Blue.' I frantically pat his stunning white coat. He nuzzles me and searches my hands for treats. 'Sorry, boy. Nothing today.'

I saddle and bridle him and head across the vast plain towards Nogard Hollow. I pray I won't regret going there. The only comfort I have is that my powers are growing stronger and that I might be able to disarm them or at the least escape if things get out of hand.

Approaching Nogard Hollow has Blue Boy pricking his ears and lifting his head high. I panic at the thought of Attor and Falcon in dragon form when I arrive, as they can both easily burn me without warning.

I see Corbin standing out the front of the house. He walks down the grass-covered driveway towards me and Blue Boy. He stops and waves me over towards the corrals.

I kick Blue on and pray Corbin hasn't been turned by the other two beasts.

I reach him and immediately dismount, waving my magical crayon above our heads. He frowns and questions me with his narrowing eyebrows.

'Corbin, you are in danger. Attor has plans to snuff you out. Lolana is waiting for you at Elyograg Castle. You will be safe with the gargoyles and very welcome.'

His eyes show disbelief. He is about to open his mouth to speak but Falcon flies out the door, thankfully, in human form. 'Jasmine, how nice of you to return our favourite meal—horse.'

'Drop dead, leather boots.'

'All in good time and not before you do, princess.' He smirks.

I turn my back on Falcon and mime the words to Corbin, 'Go—trust me.' I walk towards Falcon and he turns and heads into the house. I follow, curious as to what he and his father need from me.

'Welcome home, Jasmine,' Attor broadcasts loudly.

'What do you want?'

'I admire a woman who gets straight to the point.' He flashes a false smile.

'Good for you. Now answer me!'

'Watch your tongue, sorceress, or I will gladly pull it out of your disrespectful mouth,' spits Falcon.

'What did my cousin ever see in you, you pathetic excuse for a man!'

'Not a man, princess—a dragon. Even though you may think Lazarus is all man, he is more dragon than you will want,' says Falcon, tapping his nose. 'I can smell him all over you. How romantic!'

I listen to his heartbeat and it beats a calm rhythm, as does Attor's. Corbin walks in and stands beside me. I glance up at him and frown at his decision to stay.

'I'm sure you didn't ask me to come all this way to find out how my love life is going.' I fold my arms across my chest.

'Of course not. Please come and sit down. I want our reunion to be a pleasant one.' Attor holds his hand out, gesturing for me to sit in one of the lounge chairs.

'I'd prefer to stand. I'm not expecting my visit to be a long one.'

Suddenly my feet are off the ground and I am being placed roughly into the lounge chair. I look up and Corbin is glowering down at me.

'Corbin?'

'Sit down and shut up, sorceress,' he snaps.

I've misjudged him and for a split second, I feel sorry for Lolana, who will be heartbroken by his treachery. I sit slumped in the chair and decide that, if I am in this alone, I will go down fighting. I sit tall and roll my petite shoulders back.

'Relax, Jasmine, dear. No one wants to hurt you... on purpose,' says Attor.

'Can you please tell me what you want so I can pack my horse and leave all this behind.'

'Must be a lovers' quarrel,' sniggers Falcon.

'Oh, do me a favour and tie a knot in your forked tongue, lizard.' I spin around in my seat so I have full eye contact with him.

'Enough flirting, you two,' Attor says. 'I will "get straight to the point" as you've politely requested. You will join me and my son in the fight against the gargoyles.'

'Don't you mean you, your son and *Corbin*?'

'One more smart mouth remark and I will leave you alone with Falcon for an hour and he can show you how to be respectful.'

Attor shoots up out of his chair and in a stride, is standing in front of me, glaring down. With anger fuelling me, I stand so we are face to face, except for me being a little... well, a lot shorter.

'Number one, Falcon is not my type so there's no need to leave us alone. Number two, you must have puffed a few too many to think I'd join you in harming anyone.'

'You, my dear blue-eyed girl, have more evil in you than you know. Your spiteful tongue is your undoing.' He lowers his head so he is an inch away from mine. 'You will do exactly as I ask or Raven will be the first to die because of your disloyalty towards me.'

'They will protect her.' I curve my back so I'm leaning away from him.

'Maybe they will but who is protecting you? She will hear your pain when I unleash Falcon onto you and she will come to save her beloved cousin.'

'Falcon won't kill Raven.' I dramatically fall backwards into the chair.

'You got the wrong dragon, princess. I will take great pleasure in snapping that witch's neck,' says Falcon through gritted teeth.

'So what is it going to be, Jasmine?' Attor asks, placing his hands on either side of the lounge chair. 'Live here with us or die knowing I will rip out your sweet cousin's heart when she comes for you?'

'I need time to think your proposition over. I've never thought about killing anyone and I don't know if I could do it,' I say, trying to play for time. I quickly echo to Raven and pray the denseness of the trees doesn't interfere. *Raven I'm in trouble but you must not come to help me. They will kill you on sight,* I echo, hoping that our telepathic path is clear.

Interrupting my echoing, Attor stands tall in front of me, trying to intimidate me which, unfortunately, works.

'Rubbish, girl. You wouldn't think twice about killing me after what I did to your grandfather.'

Raven pops into my head. *I hear you. Are you with the dragons?*

'*Yes and they want me to join them in eradicating the gar-goyles,*' I echo back.

'*We heard you were heading there, Xandria pushed the glass off the side table and alerted us of your ridiculous plan. Can you hold on until dusk so the gargoyles have full strength?*' she echoes loud and clear.

'*Yes and I'm sorry,*' I echo back.

'Why are your eyes flickering, girl? If you are conjuring up a spell I will rip out your heart quicker than you can lift your hand,' yells Attor.

'I'm doing nothing except realising that I have no choice but to join you. Under one condition though—Raven is in no way to be harmed and when they are all dead, we can both leave here alive and unscathed.'

'You have my word.' Attor smiles, clearly proud that he thinks he has changed my mind. Falcon sighs in the background. 'I made a promise, Falcon. Raven is to leave here alive and you will stand by my word,' he snarls.

'And I leave alive as well, leather boots,' I say, poking my tongue out at Falcon.

'That doesn't mean he can't rough you both up, Blue Eyes, so I'd be quiet if I were you,' adds Attor.

'I need time to practice using my powers or I will be no use to anyone.'

'We plan on hitting them on the weekend but since you're here we will hit them tomorrow during the day. So that gives you one day to practice,' says Attor.

'Can I practice on Falcon?' I snigger, happy that I've got the time I need.

'Bring it on, witch. Grab your broom,' snarls Falcon, moving closer to me in one swift stride.

'I will and I know exactly where to stick it!'

'Enough! Corbin, take Blue Eyes to her room. If she

needs to practice, she can use you. I'm sure you can handle a mere sorceress.'

Corbin is at my side in a split second and has my arm in his firm grip. 'Ouch, Corbin, you are hurting me.'

'Shut up, witch!' he snaps.

'Don't rough her up too much, we need her clear-headed for tomorrow.' Falcon laughs. 'Plus that's my job.'

Corbin drags me by the arm into the bedroom with my feet struggling to keep up. He flings open the door and throws me against the bed. 'Practice, witch!'

He points to his ears then places one finger over his lips as if to keep me quiet. I nod, understanding his actions.

'Whatever, lizard!' He slams the door and I motion for him to come closer. I wave my invisible silencing crayon in the air. 'It's okay to talk but we don't have long before they figure out what I've done. You need to leave before the fighting starts.'

'I won't leave you here with them. Falcon is steaming and will rip your heart out at any second.'

'He won't go against his father; he is too scared of him. Please go and be with Lolana. She loves you and the gargoyles will accept you as they have Lazarus.'

'You trust in me and I won't let you down.'

'Sheesh, you stubborn dragon, you need to go or you will die. I'm begging you to go and warn them of the attack coming.'

'Don't they know you're here?'

'I snuck away without telling them. Please, Corbin. They will all die, including Lolana,' I lie, wanting him away from here.

'I will fly over there and warn them, then I will return to protect you as much as I can.'

'Thank you. Go now, please,' I stand up and kiss his cheek. He smiles shyly and leaves the room.

I echo back to Raven. *Corbin is on his way. He is no threat*

*to anyone. They are looking at attacking the castle at first light,
which gives the gargoyles tonight to make plans. I will protect
myself, as should you. Killing you is their priority.'*

'Come back with Corbin.'

*'That will bring the dragons to the gargoyles in daylight when
they are at their weakest. I won't risk their lives for mine.'*

*'Don't be a hero, Jazzle. That is what gargoyles do—protect
you. Plus, we have Lazarus on our side.'*

*'I need to pretend that I'm working on spells or they will get
suspicious. I love you.'*

'I love you.'

I move several items into the middle of the room. I raise
my hand, and using the energy within me, I throw objects
around the room. I continue to do so until the room looks like
a hurricane has hit it. It exhausts me and I clear the bed of
debris and fall to sleep.

'Witch!' I hear Falcon spit.

'What, snake?' I murmur, from under the pillow I have
over my head.

'You should be practising. Where is Corbin?'

I push the pillow off my head and quickly get to my feet.
Falcon has his eyes shut and is holding his nose high in the air.
He is trying to sense Corbin. I throw the pillow at him and he
jumps, opening his eyes which are dark with anger.

'I need a bigger space to practice moving larger objects.
And I told Corbin to nick off and water my horse after he fed
himself because if he eats my horse I will eat him.'

'And I'm supposed to believe he was scared of your little
threat?' Falcon sniffs, trying to draw on Corbin's scent.

I close my eyes and concentrate, lifting every object in the
room, then shoot them off into different directions. I flick my
eyes open. Furniture, cups, plates and books zoom around the
bedroom. A large atlas hits Falcon on the side of his head and

he takes one large stride so he's standing in front of me with his hand wrapped tightly around my neck. His hot breath is pouring across my face as he squeezes, hindering my breaths.

'Let her go, Falcon. You can play with her when we get what we need,' says Attor.

He drops his hand and I fall to the floor, gasping and grateful for a lung full of air. 'You said I can walk away after I help you.'

'You have already given me what we want, Blue Eyes. I presume the gargoyles will come here tonight to protect you. It has been my plan all along to destroy them tonight and I knew you would somehow contact them to do so. So thank you.'

'I haven't contacted anyone so it will be a party for one tonight, Attor.'

'Learn how to lie better, Jasmine. I thought Lazarus would have taught you how to control that heartbeat. It is a delicious sound when you're anxious and angry.' He laughs, then turns to Falcon. 'Drop her in the cave, and when I say drop her I don't want any bones broken. Not yet.'

'Oh, that will be my pleasure,' snarls Falcon.

He grabs my arm, digging his fingers into me, dragging me towards the large doors, to the entrance of the cold dark cave. I echo to Raven to tell her of their plan.

'Raven! Attor is expecting the gargoyles tonight. I am being thrown down the cave and won't hear you.'

'I hear you and we are working on a plan. Corbin is here and Lazarus has returned from feeding. He has steam coming out his ears and is as mad as hell you went there alone. I'm having trouble keeping him from coming over there.'

'No! He will be killed! Please tell him I am sorry,' I echo as Falcon holds me over the edge of the cave wall. *'I don't know if I will survive this. I love you, I love all of you. Goodbye.'*

Falcon laughs. 'You don't know how much I'd love to drop you from here.'

'Your father said not to break any of my bones. If you drop me, I can guarantee you I will die.'

'Not so tough now are you, Jasmine? Did Corbin join the gargoyles?'

'I don't know, I swear! I asked him to water my horse, that's all.' I tremble. 'Please don't put me down there, I promise not to say another word until it's asked for.'

'It's a bit late to be switching sides, witch. I will carry you down but you best control that heartbeat or I may go against my father's wishes and eat you.' He leans in so he is snarling through my hair and close to my ear.

'You're not as evil as you make out, Falcon. Raven would never have loved the devil.'

His eyes flick to mine, wide and full of anger... or is it hope?

'You will never understand what she and I had. Never!'

He steps back and releases my arm. A familiar heat radiates from his body and the red dusty swirl of particles that help create him appear. He is in the midst of changing form; not dragon and not human.

I spin around and run for the double doors. I race through them and head for the front door.

Falcon releases a deafening roar and I hear footsteps coming towards me. I dive behind a set of long draping curtains, covering myself with my magic crayon. I pray neither of the beasts had time to catch my scent. I take soft but deep calming breaths, pulling my legs tightly into my arms, shrinking myself as much as I can. I try not to jump in fear when Falcon's loud dragon roar rattles the glass.

'How can you lose her?' spits Attor. 'She won't have gone far and when we catch her, I will deal with her myself since she is too much for you to handle.'

Falcon roars again.

'No, stay in dragon form, son. The gargoyles will arrive soon and we need to be ready. And remember, kill Lazarus first. The gargoyles will hesitate and won't attack us. It's not in their nature to fight. Leave Lysander for me and you can have the pleasure of ripping out Drake's heart and golden soul.'

Falcon rumbles low and deep.

'I would prefer Raven dead, son, but it is up to you if you want her alive for a while.'

I sit hidden behind the curtain and wait until I can't hear anything. The silence is deafening but I haven't heard either of the beasts move from the lounge room. I'm too scared to peek around the curtain and take my concentration away from listening so I can contact Raven.

I sit motionless, like the creatures in stone sleep. Even my eyes are dry from not blinking. It has been fifteen minutes since I last heard the dragons. It's time to make my escape but as I'm about to move I hear someone breathe.

'She isn't inside. Search outside and I'll check to see if she has taken her horse. If she has, it will leave the biggest bread-crumb trail,' says Attor.

I wait until I hear the sound of Falcon's dragon form as it moves away and the light feet of Attor heading in my direction. The front door opens and slams shut beside me, with Attor's feet skipping down the front stairs.

I release a breath I didn't know I was holding, panting to gain it back again. With shaky legs, I stand up and peek out the window above me. I see Falcon stomping around searching the tree line close by.

Attor is near the corrals with his nose high in the air. He must be trying to sense me or are the others on their way as dusk is approaching?

I concentrate and try to contact Raven, but as I'm about

to close my eyes, I see Lazarus flying high above the forest several miles away. The trees beneath him buckle over then flick up straight again. Why are the trees bending?

Answering my unspoken question, I see five gargoyles spring off the top and glide alongside Lazarus.

I stand with my mouth open in awe of their beauty but it's short-lived when I see Attor change form. He is enormous and as soon as he is totally transformed, he releases the most horrifying roar I have ever heard. It rattles the glass window in front of me and I duck in case it breaks.

Crawling on my hands and knees, I head towards the door and gently pull on the handle, opening it slightly. I peek out. Falcon and Attor are side by side, throwing flames and screeching their roars towards my rescue party.

I slip out and head to the side of the house so I can see the oncoming creatures. Falcon spots me and shoots a warning flame, setting the grass in front of me on fire. The only way around the flame is to run through it.

I glance over to the two beasts and Falcon has one eye directed at me. I keep my eyes locked on his, waiting for the opportunity to race through without him firing again.

Lazarus and the gargoyles land with a graceful but earth-shattering thud. I see the angels and Raven back near the tree line a safe distance away. There is no hope in hell I can run that distance and survive. I need to get to Blue Boy and gallop across this large battlefield.

Lazarus is first to approach, directing his billowing flame at the two beasts. The gargoyles flank him. Then I spot Corbin flying overhead. I wave my arms and Corbin spots me, roaring loudly enough to attract Lazarus' attention.

He sees me and I lower my waving arms. Drake moves beside Lazarus and growls a fearful sound, staring over at me. Taking a large breath and holding it, I run through the hot flames. In a blink, I'm through to the other side with a few singed hairs but unharmed.

Before I have time to decide what to do, I see Corbin diving towards me and I pray his claws, which are stretched out at me, have been filed recently. He's a hundred metres away and closing. I brace myself, ready to be lifted into the air.

But Corbin's flight is interrupted by a vicious jolt to the side, given by Falcon's large head. He hits the ground with an earth-quaking tremble and rolls heavily into a pile.

Before I can gasp in horror, I'm picked up in one of the dragon's mouths. The heat is intense and smells like barbeque chicken. Its sharp teeth dig into my sides and I feel at least one is piercing my leg. I hope the thickness of my jeans will hinder any further wounds.

I lift my head to see who has me and nearly wet my pants when I see Falcon's green eye glaring at me. He takes me over to where Attor is and drops me unceremoniously onto the grassy ground.

I scramble to my feet and take in the surroundings. The two beasts have me as bait in front of them, which stops Lazarus from throwing flame in this direction. No one moves but loud rumbling noises are growled back and forth.

Drawing my attention away is a cold, wet sensation on my legs. Falcon has punctured me several times in both my legs. My jeans are soaking up the blood.

I turn to face Falcon. 'You did this on purpose! You want them to see me injured so they'll attack first. Well, guess what, butt breath? I'm here to spoil your party.'

Falcon ignores me, keeping his focus on the others. I walk backwards, away from him and his father. I open my arms wide, pointing them to the large gum trees either side of me, and imagine pulling them out by the roots, like pulling a carrot out of the ground by its hairy top.

I skip backwards and stop when I'm a good distance away from them. Attor takes a step forward and roars, with his flame shooting straight for me. I keep my arms straight and cross them quickly past my chest.

The trees fly towards the beasts, hitting Attor hard on his neck, making him stagger sideways and drop to his knees. The other tree collides with Falcon's head, knocking him down flat. He moves one of his legs but is too groggy to stand.

That was too easy! I can beat these beasts by myself. I turn and run towards my protectors, with the noise level hitting higher than deafening. I look up to see Lazarus leaping over the top of me, his large belly filling the sky, before thumping to the ground. Corbin regains his balance and stands over Falcon in a fierce stance. Attor is quick to regain his composure and is in attack mode when Lazarus approaches him.

'No! Lazarus, come back. I can handle this. Please come back,' I yell, but he continues to circle Attor with fire and smoke exuding from his mouth.

I am about to run back when Drake growls from behind me.

'I have this, Drake. Trust me.'

I run under Lazarus' frantically swishing tail. I duck several times to avoid being knocked out by it. He roars and I know it's directed at me but I keep my eyes fixed on the killing machine in front of me—Attor!

He swings his tail and I drop to the ground only to see it hit Lazarus in the wing, tearing a gaping hole. He screams and I roll out of his way as he staggers towards me.

He regains his stance and charges at Attor with his wide razor-sharp mouth open, latching onto the dragon's neck. Attor squawks in pain and flings him to the side, then gives him a vicious whip with his tail. Lazarus pulls and tucks in his wings but is struck on his back.

'Jasmine, get out of the way,' I hear Drake yell. I roll over to see him standing too close to the fight.

I jump up. 'What the hell are you doing? Get back now!'

I spin around to see Attor moving like lightning towards me. I freeze, my mind too slow to act. But in slow motion, I see Drake standing in front of me holding my upper arms with his large gargoyle hands, looking down at me.

His body jolts as if someone has hit him in the back with a cricket bat. He gasps as if in shock then his eyes drop to his chest.

My eyes follow and I can see the tip of a dragon's sphere protruding out of it. The tip is only one inch away from mine. Blood trickles from the tip and runs down Drake's broad chest and stomach.

'No! No, no, no!' Please no, not you, Drake. Please not you,' I cry.

He jerks back as the sphere is withdrawn. He drops to his knees and I see the steely eyes of Attor beaming at me. 'I will kill you!' I shout.

My body trembles. I scream a low gutsy screech as I draw up through my legs, through my body, the earth's energy. With anger fuelling me, I draw deeper from the earth and under the devil himself. My chest is rising and falling at an incredible rate as the earthly currents race towards my soul.

I dig deeper, draw harder and mix it with all the anger I have built up over the years—my grandfather, my best friend, my ex-boyfriend and now Drake.

Opening my hands, I feel then see the large swirling anorics in them. The balls are heavier than normal and they are black in colour.

I flick a glance at Drake, gasping on the cold ground. I open my mouth wide and lock my eyes on the beast they call Attor.

An ear-splitting noise leaves my throat when I launch the

black anorics directly at him. He's knocked to the ground and I run like the devil is at my heels, stopping when my feet are against his leathery skin.

As I lift my hand above my head and imagine a long black sword in it, it appears. I thrust it into his chest where I hope his sinful heart is beating. Blood spurts out of his mouth and his body convulses, his tail swishing wildly.

I push harder, twisting the black sword. I abruptly draw it out, only to plunge it back in. Attor screams, spurting blood over my face. He moves his front feet, trying to stand, but fails.

I withdraw the sword for the second time, hearing his breath gurgle with blood. The sound excites me. I feel a burst of adrenaline spike in my veins, giving me the power to continue. I muster up all the strength I have and, using my body's weight, thrust it back into his evil heart. He coughs several times, his head dropping to the ground. He pants short sharp breaths, each one labouring until there are no more. His deadly tail is last to crash to the ground before lying motionless.

Falcon roars a painful sound and takes off, flying towards the place where I had arrived all those months ago. I stagger backwards, allowing Lazarus to stab him with his sphere tail. It slices him open. Lazarus slowly withdraws it only to plunge it back into his heart with force. It's the final and fatal blow, leaving Attor lifeless.

I race back to Drake and fall to my knees, the pain in my legs forgotten. I lift his head to rest on my lap.

'It's okay, Drake. I killed Attor. Everything will be fine now. We can go home now,' I cry, wiping the blood away that is trickling from his mouth and ears.

'I love you… Jazz,' he forces out through a straining breath. 'We will meet again soon.'

'No, no, no! You can't leave me. You're not meant to die, Drake. Please, someone help me! Angels do your bloody job!'

But the angels stand still. I sob, loud and out of control. 'Drake, I love you, please stay with me, fight hard to stay with me. We are bonded for life.'

'That's all I wanted to hear.' He forces a smile.

'That I love you. I do, I do!' My tears fall onto his blood-stained face. 'Why are you all standing around? Do something!'

A hand cups my shoulder. I blink my eyes several times to focus through my tears to see Raven standing beside me. 'Help me, Raven, I'm begging you. He's not meant to die! Not here, not now and not because of me!'

'He's going, Jazz. It's time to say goodbye,' whispers Raven.

I scan his handsome face and he smiles at me. 'You're strong, Drake! You're a bloody gargoyle! Nothing can break you.'

'He has pierced my heart.' He coughs.

'Change form and heal. Please, Drake.'

'My lungs have irreparable damage.'

'No, you're wrong. Change and heal. I will protect you.' I flick my head up and glare at the angels. 'Malachi, Gabby, you're supposed to be his protector. Do something!'

'They are protecting me, Jazz.' He smiles. 'My heart and lungs are filling with blood.'

'Don't leave me. You promised you'd protect me and you'd never leave me again. You can't do that if you're dead!'

'I will continue to protect you as I have promised, but it may be in a different form.'

'No, Drake. I want this form or your gargoyle form. Don't you dare leave me. A promise is a promise.'

He coughs and blood spurts from his mouth. I can hear the gurgle in his chest as his heart slows and his lungs flood with blood.

'It's time, Jasmine,' says Gabby. 'Say goodbye.'

'I love you, Drake.' I force the words past the emotional lump in my throat.

'I… love… you.' He slowly closes his eyes. I listen for his heartbeat but hear nothing but the slow beats of the creatures standing around me.

'Nooooo!' I scream at the top of my lungs. I throw my head back and stare at the sky above us. 'Why?'

I drop my head so my forehead is resting on his. My tears fall fast onto his face, pooling around his eyes. I kiss his forehead while crying uncontrollably. I'm unable to speak or move.

A warm hand touches my shoulder, but I shrug it off. I don't want sympathy from anyone.

His body vibrates and glows a throbbing blue colour. I stare at his face and he looks peaceful. Within a few long seconds, his body turns to thick ash, with his golden soul left lying in front of my knees. I stare in disbelief. This golden glow is the soul of my beloved friend.

I tentatively reach out and touch it. I pick it up and listen to hear his voice again. Nothing. 'I can't hear him.'

'It will take a few days, but he will find his voice,' Raven says.

'Can I take Drake's soul?' says Gabby, smiling at me. 'I need to take him home as there is a baby on the way and his soul may be required.'

I lift it up, keeping my eyes locked on to it. 'I'm so sorry, Drake.'

With gentle hands, Gabby places it into a square-shaped box. Malachi is at her side and together they walk off towards Elyograg Castle.

I fall to the ground and cry until it hurts to breathe. Raven is sitting cross-legged beside me, running her soft fingers over my forehead.

Night has fallen and I shiver due to the wet blood soaking my clothes. Lazarus joins Raven in human form and helps sit me upright.

The gargoyles sit around me with their heads held low.

Corbin is still in dragon form, standing alert, staring in the direction in which Falcon went.

'Everyone I care for dies,' I say, breaking the silence.

'Drake's death wasn't your fault,' says Lazarus.

'You're cold, Jazzle. I want to get you home and cleaned up.' Raven's voice is soft as if I was a volcano about to erupt.

'It's no longer my home.'

Lazarus picks me up in his arms, cradling my head on his large bicep. 'It is for now, Jasmine.'

He hands me over to Lysander, who, in gargoyle form, carries me back to the castle. For a split second, I wonder why Lazarus doesn't carry me, but my mind soon turns blank.

Raven runs a bath while I stand silent and dazed. She strips me of my bloody clothes and directs me into it. She sponges my hair and, with gentle strokes, washes my wounds.

I sit like a child. My tears have dried only because I'm dehydrated from crying. My mind is blank and my voice lost. I am numb to any pain and my heartbeat is silent. I am an empty shell.

Chapter Eleven

A STINGING PAIN wakes me from a peaceful dream I don't deserve to have. Malachi is painting a brown liquid over my leg wounds. With little care for my wounds, I force myself to sit up; I need to see what damage Falcon's teeth have done.

I fall back, unimpressed. I wish a leg was missing, or both of them. Drake lost his life and all I have to show for it is a dozen dragon teeth marks.

'Good morning, Jasmine,' hums Malachi's sweet voice. I give an uncouth sniff and then, in an instant, I am flooded with guilt for being so rude to such a beautiful angel.

'Morning, Malachi. Thanks for patching me up. The quicker I'm healed the quicker I can leave.'

'Good morning, cuz,' says Raven.

'What's so flippin' good about it?'

'There are plenty of things. Number one is that you're alive.' She wipes back my hair from my face, giving me a sympathetic smile.

'Care factor—zero!'

'Will you excuse us, Malachi?' she asks.

'Certainly.' He nods and smiles before leaving.

'Wake up to yourself, Jasmine!' she says. 'Everyone mourns Drake's death, but they also celebrate that he will be reincarnated very soon. Everyone else is alive and Attor is dead, thanks to you.'

'I still have to kill Falcon. And I need to skin Attor and drape his leather hide over me so when I kill Falcon he can smell the death of his father.'

'Stop those hateful feelings. You're drawing on hate. Your

anorics were black so you must have been drawing up negative energies. This is what Grandfather feared. He continually begged us to stay focused on the positive energies.'

'I remember and I won't draw on them again. I promise, Raven.' I blink several times, trying to summon up the courage to tell her my decision. 'I am leaving to start a new life, away from here and the elite creatures.'

'That's a shame for two reasons.'

'Why?'

'Firstly, Lazarus is as madly in love with you as you are with him and secondly, I am five months pregnant with Lysander's child.' Her hands drop to her stomach where she rolls her hands over an obvious protruding mound. How did I not notice this before?

'You're having a baby?'

'Yes, and we are using Drake's soul to help it mature.'

'How does that work?'

'Do you mean "the birds and the bees" and how Mummy and Daddy make babies?'

'No, silly. I've worked that part out by myself. I mean how does it work with you being a human and Lysander a gargoyle?'

'I carry the child like any normal human, we think.' She grimaces.

'You think? Are you in danger of having a rock inside you?'

'No Jazzle, the angels have seen the birth going according to plan.'

'How do you know it's a boy? You can't put Drake's soul into a girl, he'd kill you.'

'The angels predict it's a boy and Drake asked me to consider using his golden soul if something happened to him. I didn't hesitate to say yes as I couldn't have asked for a better one.' Her voice quivers.

'Please don't cry or I will join you.' I pull her in for a

comforting hug. 'I'm sorry I won't be here to support you. I'd love to hear him call me Aunty Jazzy. It has a nice ring to it.'

'Before you go, I can erase your memory or store it into your dreams?'

'No, thank you. I love Drake and he threw his life away for me. I need this pain in my life, as raw as it is. There is never a day that goes by that I don't think of Grandfather and now I will remember Drake.'

'I will miss you and I'm reluctant to let you go because I worried that you've tapped into the black sorcery.'

'Trust me as I trust you.' I smile, trying to reassure her.

'Where does Lazarus stand?'

'I love Drake and I am *in* love with Lazarus, but I need to leave him here with his kind. I am a magnet for people dying.'

'Don't I have a say in this?' Lazarus says, standing in the doorway.

'I'll leave you to it. Don't leave without seeing me.' Raven kisses my cheek before leaving.

'Hey,' I say shyly.

'Have you forgotten I can hear every word you say?' He smiles warmly before walking over to me.

'I'm numb at the moment and blocking you out is the last thing on my mind.'

'You need to stop blaming yourself for Drake's death. Gargoyles are protectors and he has given the ultimate sacrifice. He would do it over and over again, as would any of them. I admire them for their internal strength.' He sits beside me and glances down at my legs. 'Does it hurt?'

'A little but I'm sucking it up. I want to leave as soon as I can.' I drop my head to look at my twiddling fingers.

He lifts my face up with his single index finger. 'Why are you running away?'

'I have lost two people I love on this land. I can't lose you.

Falcon is still out there and no doubt getting his relatives to back him. He will want revenge for his father's death and I am the target. If I am here, I will put everyone in danger. I refuse to be the reason someone else dies.' I brush his hand away from my face so I don't have to look at his handsome green eyes.

'You love me, Jazz. That has to mean something.'

'It does. It means I want to keep you alive.'

He laughs. 'I can keep myself alive. Falcon doesn't scare me.'

'He scared me when his hands were tight around my throat. He will enjoy taking my life.' My hands automatically shoot to my neck, triggering the pain when I roll over the fresh bruises.

'I will protect you.'

'I can protect myself!'

'I know you can. I saw it with my own eyes.'

'Not you as well? I can control my powers without the help of all you do-gooders,' I snap.

'Why am I suddenly your enemy?'

'I'm sorry. I'm full of guilt and sorrow. I do love you, Lazarus, but this thing we have will never lead to us being more than friends. I need to leave and I wish you would accept that.' I smile and reach for his hand to hold it in mine.

'I'll come with you. We can work it out together.' He moves closer so our faces are inches away.

I lift my hands to encase his fine-looking face and draw it towards me. I kiss his lips and pull away to search his eyes. I don't want him to think he can change my mind and convince me to stay, but at this very moment, I need to be loved by him.

He grabs my head in a rough, manly manner and pulls me to his lips. I return his hot, hard kiss and drop my hands to his arms.

He flinches and I stop kissing him. 'You're hurt?'

'I will mend in time.'

'Show me.'

He stands and removes his t-shirt with a grimace. He turns his back and there's a two-foot gash and a smaller one, just under his arm.

I stand slowly, feeling my own pain as I do. I trace his slashed back gingerly.

Standing behind him, I slide my hands around his waist and pull my forearms up so I am holding his chest, one hand each holding a pectoral muscle. My bare stomach is against his bare back, skin to skin.

He holds his hands over mine and I snuggle my face into his injured back, leaving a trail of soft kisses over it. He lifts one of my hands to his mouth and blows warm air on each finger before kissing them. I love feeling his heated breath.

'With all my self-pity, I forgot that you were also hurt yesterday. Thank you for protecting me, Lazarus.'

In a slow careful movement, he spins me around so his emerald green eyes are staring down at me. 'I'd move heaven and earth for you. I love you.' He tips my face up to his so he can kiss me.

'I love you.'

He pulls me in, holding me just a little too tightly, but I stay quiet. He needs me as much as I need him. Our saddened hearts pump in unison, increasing in speed and in a rhythm neither of us wants to control.

He steps back and walks over to close and lock the bedroom door. In the blink of an eye, he is standing in front of me. I will never get used to the speed this man has. I chuckle and he smiles a cheeky grin.

He scoops me up and carries me over to the bed, lying me down before joining me. His warm body is welcoming and I automatically relax into him. He moves over the top of me but is gentle and doesn't put his weight on me.

Every movement is slow and calculated. He's being cautious of my injuries and probably his own. I open my legs and he slides both of his between mine. I cringe when his legs slide against my puncture wounds. He stills and I smile.

'I'm fine,' I whisper before I draw a silencing spell over us. 'Tell me to stop if you don't want me to go any further.'

'You're the one who said no, not me, remember?'

'Trust me, I've been kicking myself ever since.' His grin is cheeky.

He leans in and I wait for him to kiss my lips but instead, he kisses me next to my ear then laces my neck with soft, wet kisses. I muffle a groan while he continues to kiss my neck and my chest.

With a flick, my bra releases and he cups my breast with his warm, large hand. I groan, revelling in his touch as he continues to kiss my chest, releasing his own low vibrating appreciation, which accelerates my heartbeat.

Our underwear is quick to be discarded. I listen to our hearts and they beat out of control.

'Our hearts,' I whisper.

'Oh baby, I can hear every pumping beat and it's delicious.' He sniggers, nipping me with his teeth.

He moves back to look into my blazing eyes. His have darkened to a malty green. He hesitates before kissing me; he is locking my image into his memory, as I am his.

Our kiss is passionate, with a hint of desperation, as his warm hands roll over my body. My hands are quick to explore his every curve, his every muscle, as they contract under my fingers.

I want and need to be his at this very moment. I'll worry about my broken heart when I leave.

Lazarus' body warmth radiates through mine, collecting his positive energy and drawing it into my soul. As our kiss deepens, the heat from his body intensifies.

As our naked bodies meld into one, there's a spiritual connection to him I have never felt before. I feel the electricity build up between us and I try to smother it, but it only ignites further.

My internal bubbling is like a volcano about to erupt. My body feels as light as a feather, lifting high off the bed, heading for the paradise called heaven.

Lazarus holds me firmly in his overheated arms, encasing me with his strong toned body. He trembles and whispers his love for me with a lustful voice. Together, as one, we slowly float back down.

'I am so in love with you, Jazz.'

'And I am in love with you. But I'm still leaving.'

He silences me with a kiss. 'Shh, don't say it, not now.'

He rolls onto his back and draws me into his chest. I snuggle in tight and am happy that I'm a perfect fit. It's as if his body was a mould made to accept mine.

I kiss his chest and trace his yin-yang tattoo with my finger. 'Your skin is so soft,' I say, feeling his whole chest with my fingers.

'Don't go thinking about making me into a handbag. I heard what you said to Raven about skinning Attor. I actually feared you for a moment.' He chuckles, and it rumbles through his body.

'No handbag, but I need a new jacket.'

'Now I'm worried, as I know how you like to accessorise.'

'So now I'm the scary one.' I jump on top of him and straddle his waist. I pin his arms beside his head, pretending to hold him down but I know he could flick me off without blinking.

He's amused by my flimsy female attempt to restrain him and his eyes flicker with excitement. 'What are you going to do with me now? Should I be scared?'

'That depends, dragon, as I'm ready for round two.'

'Bring it on, witch!'

The next few days are full, with everyone trying to convince me to stay. The more they show me how much they care for me, the more I fall in love with them, making my departure more urgent.

It's me Falcon will return and hunt for. The hate he has for me is evident in the scars I have laced over my body. If my scent is gone from Elyograg Castle, he might leave them alone and continue his hunt for me. I won't be the reason for someone else's death.

Lazarus is practically attached to my side, never wanting to spend a minute away from me. He is a loveable guy and the gargoyles have accepted him into their home as they have Corbin.

Corbin has brought his horses and Blue Boy over from Nogard Hollow so he can care for them.

Lolana and Corbin have revealed their love for each other and, to her surprise, everyone was suspicious about her weekly disappearances and had expected something like this to happen. They are supportive, much to Corbin's relief.

I spend the afternoon packing my truck and checking my float, ready for an early morning departure. Lazarus leans against the truck and, when I put a bag into the back then turn to pick up another, he pulls it out, placing it back on the ground. Needless to say, it takes a long time to pack.

Our last dinner sees the angels setting up a huge banquet of food, more than the normal one they set. They lay out plates with colourful placemats and serviettes. There are wildflowers elegantly placed along the length of the table and wine, which I have never seen any of them drink before.

'The table is stunning, guys.' I smile at the two angels.

'We want your last memory of us to be special, and we hope it will entice you to return,' says Malachi.

'You're not one I will easily forget, Malachi,' I say.

'Ahem,' Lazarus grunts, patting his chest with his two fingers. He is letting me know he could hear my heart, which must have skipped a beat. It's hard when Malachi is a God-given delight to look at.

'I am standing right here, Jasmine.' He raises one eyebrow.

'Look, Lazarus, there's a rainbow of flowers down the centre to the table' I point excitedly to it.

'I'll take your word for it, babe.'

'Oh, I forgot you're colourblind.'

'I may be colourblind, but I see you in full HD colour.' He moves to stand behind me and wraps his arms around my waist.

I lean my head back into his taut chest. He kisses the side of my temple and his heat runs through my body. He places his lips next to my ear and breathes warmly down my neck. Oh, boy! He knows how to gain my full attention.

'Your delicious heartbeat is giving you away, babe.'

I listen to his heart and it's singing the same loud tune. 'As does yours,' I murmur, wiggling my shoulders into his chest.

He growls and my heart skips a beat. He chuckles low in his throat.

'Okay, dragon, you win.'

'Wow, guys. This table is amazing,' says Lysander, entering with the others close behind. 'We should say goodbye more often if this is the send-off.'

'Thank you, Gabby and Malachi.' I keep my heartbeat calm and my eyes off Malachi. Lazarus pinches my bottom; he knows I kept it calm on purpose.

Everyone sits, with Corbin and Jarius poking and punching each other until Gabby places her gentle hand on their shoulders. It makes me laugh at how she can, with one soft touch, stop two boisterous guys play-fighting.

I glance slowly around the table at the faces I'm happy to call my family. Lysander and Raven are both glowing with the added excitement of their child, less than four months away. Corbin and Jarius' friendship is becoming solid, like brothers, with Lolana comfortably slipping under Corbin's wing.

Demona, Gabby and Malachi are extraordinarily strong people with the gentlest of souls. It shows you don't have to be a bully to be strong-willed and strong in mind.

And then there's Lazarus, who is studying me as I glance around the long table. He places his hand on my leg and squeezes it gently.

Yes, I am a lucky girl to be loved by these amazing people and leaving here will guarantee they stay protected.

My heart sinks when I picture Drake lying on the cold ground with his head in my lap. An elusive tear runs down my cheek.

Lazarus leans sideways, collecting the tear with his warm lips. 'You look deep in thought, Jazz. Are you changing your mind about leaving?' His tone is curious.

'Quite the opposite. I'm looking at my reasons for leaving.'

Glasses are filled with wine and passed around. I haven't had an alcoholic drink since I found out my boyfriend was hooking up with my best friend, Kelly.

'Cheers, everyone,' says Lysander, standing and holding his glass in the air. 'To Jasmine. May she have safe travels and may they lead her back home here one day.'

'Cheers to Jasmine!' everyone yells, clinking their glasses together.

I take a sip and it's divine. I watch the angels pretend to sip the wine then put their glasses down, both pushing them away, replacing them with a glasses of water. Raven does the same and I presume it's because of the baby.

'I've never seen any alcohol on the dinner table or anywhere in the castle,' I say.

'Alcohol is not a good mix with creatures of our nature. We need to keep our bodies and blood pure,' explains Lysander. 'We can have a glass or two on the odd occasion, but it alters our perception, as it does humans.'

'Can you imagine a drunken dragon?' Jarius laughs. 'Everything would be on fire and smashed to pieces.'

Everyone joins in the laughter. 'Or worse, a gargoyle on steroids,' he jokes, puffing his chest and contracting his large biceps, looking like an ape. The thought of an over-muscled gargoyle appears before my eyes, making me giggle uncontrollably.

The laughter lightens my mood and the conversation is taken away from me and my departure.

'Here, babe, drink my glass of wine. With your heart ricocheting around in your chest cavity I may not be able to control myself.' Lazarus winks.

'It's our last night together. Who wants control?' I whisper, hearing his heart thud hard. I smile and he rolls his eyes, taking a deep calming breath.

After over-eating and unfortunately, over-drinking, I help the angels clear the table. They shoo me away to spend time with Lazarus while they wash the dishes.

I walk into the dining room and everyone has politely left, leaving Lazarus sitting at the table alone. I walk over to him and he pushes his chair out so I can sit on his knee.

I drape my arms around his broad neck and he slides his warm arm around my waist. He looks into my eyes and, for several long minutes, our eyes lock—blue on green. I will miss these moments.

'Let's forget tomorrow is coming and enjoy tonight,' I whisper.

'If that is what you want.' Lazarus tries to smile. I can hear his sad heartbeat and quickly lean forward to encourage it to pump faster, kissing his pouting lips.

'I know what I want.' I smile, releasing my grip from around his neck and trailing my hands over his fine chest.

'A dragon's gotta do what a dragon's gotta do.'

'Please do.' I raise my eyebrows. He jumps up, collecting me in his strong arms and heads out of the dining room. We are at the base of the staircase and he will need to carry me up several flights to get to my bedroom.

'I can walk up,' I say.

He displays a white-toothed Aussie grin. In several long strides, we reach my bedroom door. He kicks it open and I giggle like a young schoolgirl.

There is not one human male that could ever come close to the excitement a dragon gives me; to what Lazarus gives me. He closes the door then lets my body slide slowly down his. His fingers tug at the base of my t-shirt and I nod for him to remove it. When he pulls it off, he is less than an inch away from me, his warm breath heating my face.

His kiss is soft, as if he's frightened I'll break. I reach for the hem of his t-shirt and, without asking, I lift it up his stomach, over his chest and head. My eyes follow it as if I am unwrapping a birthday present and boy, what a present!

His taut six-pack stomach is bronze and hard, as are his two large pectoral muscles. My eyes trail along his solid arms; his biceps contract as he pulls me into his embrace and kisses me.

His eyes open with a question I can't change my answer to. He closes them and pulls me against him.

My body responds the only way it knows how. My blood pumps an adrenaline rush through my system, forcing me to kiss him with added passion. His hands roll over my body, but my mind stays in limbo, halting at his amazing mouth.

He lifts me with ease and carries me towards the bed. He lays me down and I sink into the soft feather doona. I realise that he has masterfully removed my clothes and his own.

He stands before me, running his eyes over my body, his fleuron green eyes darkening with lust.

I admire the man, the creature, standing lovingly in front of me. I need him now, more than I ever have.

Keeping our eyes locked, I reach up and cup his warm hand. He smiles and I melt like butter in a sizzling frying pan. He is one good-looking man, not to mention a strikingly handsome dragon.

'Have you finished your appraisal?' I grin.

'Have you?'

'Oh, I did that months ago,' I say, and he chuckles. 'But I must let you know I'm a very impatient woman.' My tone is heated as I pat the bed beside my bare hip.

'Is that so, babe?' He stays dead still.

'Lazarus! Come and kiss me before I explode!'

He pounces on top of me and in an instant; I am lost in his hot, heated kiss.

I WAKE EARLY, wanting to leave before anyone tries to change my mind. After the night I spent with Lazarus, it would be easy to persuade me to stay.

I meet Raven at the top of the stairs as I lug my bag from my room. At the bottom stands all my family, who are looking up at me, wide-eyed. Except for Lazarus; he is nowhere to be seen.

I walk down the stairs with Raven lecturing me on how to be safe on the roads and not to engage in conversation with strangers who seem odd or negative. I stop at the bottom of the stairs and, in turn, kiss and hug each one of them goodbye.

Raven's hugs are so tight my arms go numb. 'I love you, Raven,' I whisper, rubbing her protruding belly. 'Give this young man a kiss for me.'

'You can always return and kiss him yourself.'

'I'm protecting everyone here by leaving, especially your unborn son. You do understand my reasons for leaving?'

'I understand but we are all ready to fight to protect the clan and you.'

'If I'm not here there will be no reason for Falcon to come, as you are no threat to him.'

'It doesn't always work that way.'

'I refuse to fight or use my powers again. I've seen what happens when negative powers are used and now, I've tapped into mine. Grandfather died before me, leaving me with horrific nightmares. Now I have Drake's death haunting me.'

'It's not too late to erase it from your memory. It tore my heart, hearing you cry at night.' She kisses my cheek before pulling my pendant out from behind my t-shirt. 'At least keep this around your neck.'

'No more spells. It's time for me to grow up.' I flip my pendant back behind my t-shirt. 'I'll always wear this. I used to pretend it was your heart sitting next to mine.'

Raven hugs me before turning to run into Lysander's open arms. He kisses the top of her head and nods at me as if to say he will take care of her.

I express my gratitude to the others and head for my truck, wondering where Lazarus is. I collect Blue Boy from the paddock and open the back of the float, and he calmly walks in.

I turn and Lazarus is leaning against the driver's door, swinging the keys from his index finger. I smile, forcing back the lump forming in my throat.

'I'm off,' I say, walking towards him.

'That's if I give you the keys.' He grins.

'I will miss you.' I drop my forehead onto his chest so I am looking at the ground. If I look into his eyes, I know I will lose it.

He tilts my head up with his gentle fingers. 'I love you, Jasmine. How can I change your mind?'

'I can't stay. Please understand.'

'I understand we're love and should be together. Your reasons for leaving aren't good enough. There must be something you're not telling me.'

'Others will come in search for me. I need to disappear. I refuse to let any of you get hurt because of me.' An airy sob escapes.

'Let me come with you. I can protect you, Jazz.'

'Like Drake did? I'd kill myself if anything happened to you.' I sniff in my tears.

I hold the palm of my hand open, asking for the truck keys. With reluctance, he drops them into it.

I close my hand and look up into his loving eyes, mine filling with tears. I stand onto my tippy-toes and kiss his lips before jumping into the truck. I slam the door shut and turn on the ignition.

'I love you, Lazarus,' I say, before putting the truck in gear and moving away.

I drive as fast as I can without jolting Blue Boy around in the float. In my rear vision mirror, I see Lazarus spin a whirl of red particles and change into dragon form. I hear his loud, painful roar and I try my hardest not to cry, knowing he will hear me.

But the floodgates open and I bellow like I did when Drake died in my arms. I fight my tears so I can see the path in front of me and pray I don't hit a pothole and puncture a tyre five minutes into my departure.

I don't know where I am heading. All I know is that if I stay here, I will jeopardise the lives of the ones I love, even though my heart feels like it's being wrenched out of my chest. I love Lazarus and I doubt there will be anyone who will take his place. I will never have that connection to any other man, nor will I make love to another man the way we did.

My guardian angel, the wedge-tailed eagle, who I haven't seen in a while, is flying in front of me. Maybe it's a sign and I should follow it as it's never given me a reason to distrust it. I know it's connected to me in some magical way but I'm yet to work it out. But its sudden appearance tells me I'm doing the right thing by leaving.

I flick my eyes to the truck's side mirror. The reflection is one I will lock away in my heart forever. There are dragons billowing orange fireballs, with several gargoyles scaling the castle walls, heading to the roof. Raven is still encased in Lysander's arms, staring in my direction, with the angels waving me goodbye.

My heart thuds when I spot Lazarus, his large webbed wings open wide, hovering above them all, billowing a flame that would encase the castle. His heart is broken.

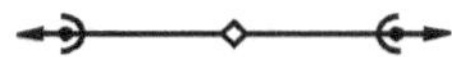